TROUBLE ON THE TRAIL

Marlowe waited for his chance, and it came when Clay turned to go through the doorway. Marlowe charged. Like a wounded buffalo bull, he stormed through the door after Clay. Into the open courtyard he exploded, intent upon crushing the life from the tall young man. With no show of excitement, Clay turned to meet the attack. When Marlowe's massive hands were inches from his face, Clay deftly stepped to one side and, using his rifle as a spear, plunged the barrel deep into Marlowe's belly. Marlowe, bent double by the blow, wheezed like a winded mule as the breath was knocked out of him. Spurred on by this added insult, he recovered quickly enough to spring at Clay once again. This time, Clay easily avoided the wildly swinging fists, and brought the barrel of his rifle across the side of Marlowe's face with sufficient force to lay him out cold on the hard-baked clay of the courtyard.

SAVAGE CRY

Charles G. West

A SIGNET BOOK

SIGNET
Published by New American Library, a division of
Penguin Putnam Inc., 375 Hudson Street,
New York, New York 10014, U.S.A.
Penguin Books Ltd, 80 Strand,
London WC2R 0RL, England
Penguin Books Australia Ltd, Ringwood,
Victoria, Australia
Penguin Books Canada Ltd, 10 Alcorn Avenue,
Toronto, Ontario, Canada M4V 3B2
Penguin Books (N.Z.) Ltd, 182–190 Wairau Road,
Auckland 10, New Zealand

Penguin Books Ltd, Registered Offices:
Harmondsworth, Middlesex, England

First published by Signet, an imprint of New American Library,
a division of Penguin Putnam Inc.

First Printing, September 2002
10 9 8 7 6 5 4 3 2 1

FOR RONDA

Chapter 1

People change. This was not a thought that often occupied Martha Vinings's mind at this particular time in the day. But it was a thought that had certainly come back to haunt her time and again since her marriage to Robert Vinings. Being of practical mind, she did not waste time lamenting the fact that the Robert who had wooed her so fervently and sincerely in Virginia—with promises of undying love and devotion—could become the dispassionate plodder who, pragmatic in his devotion to his mining claim, had seemingly lost all traces of the desire he had at first expressed. Maybe he was not to be blamed. The work was hard, and there were few pleasures offered in the rugged, unforgiving land that taunted and teased the many hopeful souls who sought to find their fortunes in her streams and washes. Few were the fortunate ones who struck it rich. For the majority, it was an endless succession of grueling toil over a ten-foot sluice box that offered little more than a pinch of the precious metal.

She straightened up to give her aching back a few moments' rest. As often happened, she caught the watchful eye of Robert's brother Charley, gazing intently in her direction. The faint trace of a smile turned up one side of his mouth, forming an expression that suggested thoughts inappropriate for a brother-in-law. Martha looked quickly away. She glanced across the sluice box at her husband, who never seemed to take notice of his brother's lecherous glances in her direction.

She thought now of the glowing enthusiasm Robert had possessed for the grand adventure he had planned for their honeymoon. At the time, anxious to escape the turmoil of the crowded farmhouse of her father—and the difficult times after the Union army had laid most farms in the county to waste—she joyfully accepted Robert's proposal of marriage. He had seemed so sure of himself, and of his plan to create a new life in the West, that she finally bought into his enthusiasm—in spite of her father's misgivings.

It had been a heartrending experience to leave her mother and father, perhaps never to see them again. But she knew that it would be easier for her father to have one less mouth to feed during the hardships that were to come. Her three younger brothers would be more useful than she would in helping her father make a new start. She would miss them all terribly, especially her brother Clay, who had been away from the family since joining the Army of Northern Virginia in December of 1862 at Fredericksburg. Clay, older by a year, was her favorite. They had seen Clay only once since he marched off to war—and that was a week before the last battle of Fredericksburg when the Yankee forces captured Marye's Heights and took possession of the town. She had prayed every night for his safe return, but there had been no word from him, even after Lee's surrender at Appomattox. When after a year there was still no word, her father assumed he was dead. But Martha could never bring herself to accept that fact—not Clay, not the one person in the family who always looked after her and never teased her. He always had time to listen to her fears as well as her dreams. No, Clay was a special person—too special to be killed by a Yankee bullet. She would not think of him as dead, preferring to keep a picture of his handsome, suntanned face tucked away in the recesses of her mind. He was just away temporarily.

It had seemed like such a romantic adventure when Robert told her of his dream: to make the long trek across the country, and gather up their share of the fortunes rumored to line every stream in the new land. They would fill their wagon with gold, then buy a farm in the Oregon territory. How wonderful it had all sounded then, to leave the pain and the shame of the tragic war behind; she and her husband creating a new life for themselves in the land of golden promise. At times she wondered if she had been more in love with the adventure than with Robert. There had been no mention that Charley was to accompany them. But, she supposed, as hard as the work had proven to be, it might have been almost impossible without Charley's help.

I guess lecherous looks won't hurt me, she told herself. Looking across the long wooden trough they called a Long-Tom, she stole a glance at her husband, working steadily to feed the sluice with the rocky soil of the streambank. And for a brief moment, she wished he would occasionally look at her the same way Charley did. It might make her life a little more bearable if there was still at least a faint spark of the passion he had professed when he had proposed to her.

Maybe Charley might decide to move on to the Montana gold fields—he had hinted that he might—since it was already obvious that their little claim would not yield the fortune they had hoped for. But she knew Robert would discourage any notion Charley might have of leaving. To properly work a Long-Tom required three or four men along the sides to keep the soil washing down toward the riddle. It was hard work for two men. For her part, Martha stood with her hoe and shovel, working the rocky dirt back and forth in the iron riddle as it dropped into the riffle box beyond. Robert's dream of riches threatened to break the backs of all three of them. It would be impossible to work his claim without Charley's help.

"Sun's gittin' low," Robert suddenly announced, breaking a silence that had filled most of the afternoon.

Charley paused to rest on his shovel, his lewd grin in place once again as he watched Martha prop the hoe against a large boulder behind her. Robert's simple statement was her signal to go back to the cabin and prepare supper while he and Charley worked on until almost dark.

"You're gonna have to go hunting pretty soon," Martha said as she rinsed her hands in the rushing water. "We don't have but a little of the salt pork left."

"I know," Robert replied. He straightened up and stretched his back, reaching his arms high up over his head. "I just hate to quit working now that we're starting to see a little color." He glanced at Charley then reluctantly admitted, "I reckon we've got to eat, though."

"I could use a day off," Charley said. "My dad-blamed back is killin' me."

"I reckon it wouldn't hurt to take half a day off," Robert reluctantly conceded. "Me and you could light out early in the morning, maybe find us a deer, and have him dressed down before noon."

Charley laughed. "I swear, brother, you sure are one to work a man to death."

"You got to git it while the gittin's good," Robert returned. "I don't intend to linger in this country no longer than I have to, what with the Injuns and such."

Charley grunted contemptuously. "Shoot, we ain't seen the first sign of Injuns anywhere near this valley."

"If we're lucky, we won't," Robert said. "Come on, let's empty that riffle box."

Martha made her way through the large rocks skirting the stream and started up the hill toward the cabin. As she climbed the steep slope, she was careful to hold her skirt tightly around her ankles, knowing that Charley was watching closely for any glimpse of leg. Why, she wondered, did Robert never instruct his younger brother to mind his manners when it came to her. Maybe it escaped his notice—maybe he just didn't care—she was too tired to worry over it now.

At the foot of the slope, Charley leaned on his shovel handle, watching his sister-in-law until she disappeared from view. Reluctantly turning his attention once again to his work, he glanced up to find his brother watching him intently. Not at all ashamed to be caught ogling his brother's wife, Charley just shook his head and grinned.

"Come on and help me empty these rocks," Robert said, hoping to avoid talking about what he knew was on Charley's mind. It didn't work.

"Hell, brother, it ain't hurtin' nothin' to look," Charley said. "Besides, the way she walks up that hill, wrigglin' her little behind, she's wantin' you to look at her."

Robert paused, shaking his head slowly, weary of his younger brother's undisguised lust for his wife. "No such a thing," he finally said. "She don't wriggle her behind, and you know it. Martha never has thoughts like that. She's the most decent woman I've ever known." He fixed Charley with a stern scowl. "I ought to give you a good whuppin' for saying such a thing."

Charley's grin was immediately replaced by a pouty frown. "I reckon you know that would be the hardest day's work you ever tried to do." The frown faded after only a second, replaced by the almost constant grin. "Dammit, Robert, I've got needs same as you— hell, more'n you, I reckon. Martha's a healthy young woman. She's got needs, too—and you ain't doing her no good."

"Damn you, Charley, you better watch your mouth!"

Charley brushed the warning aside. The time when he feared his older brother had long since passed. "Hell, Robert, don't you think I can hear everything that goes on behind that blanket? You ain't givin' her nothin' a'tall. It's a damn waste is what it is, and that's a fact."

Calmed by a weariness deep within, Robert didn't say anything for a few moments. When he spoke, his words were slow and measured. "Charley, I know what you got on your mind, and it's a sin. I don't wanna hear no more talk about it."

"A sin?" Charley exploded. "There ain't no sins out here in this country! I'll tell you what's a sin: It's a sin to waste a good woman when she ain't being seen to proper. Besides, it's all in the family." He turned to pleading. "Dammit, Robert, I'm your brother. It'd be different if there was any other women around here. If it was the other way around, I'd do it for you. Hell, look at them Mormons we saw back at Fort Laramie. They've got the right idea about it—and it ain't a sin to them."

Robert desperately wished that the problem didn't exist, that it would just go away. But there was Charley, standing before him, looking at him like a starving calf. He had no desire to share his wife with any man, even his brother. The very thought of it made him queasy inside. What Charley said was true, there had been no real passion between him and his wife for some time now. But that didn't change things. She was still his wife. Knowing Martha as he did, he knew she would be appalled by the suggestion—even if he gave it his blessing.

"You could ask her," Charley prodded. "She might want to."

"Hell no," Robert quickly responded. "I didn't say *I* was willing. Besides, Martha don't hold to sinning."

Charley began to plead again. "I'm just asking to be with her once in a while. I wouldn't expect it all the time, just once in a while to keep from going crazy out here. You know I respect the fact that she's your wife. It'd be different if we was back in Virginia. Things are different out here." He paused while he watched his brother intensely, searching for some sign of weakening. "Ask her, Robert. Just see what she says about it. Will you?"

Bone-tired and brain-weary, Robert wasn't sure whether he should kill his brother for suggesting such a thing or talk to his wife as Charley pleaded. *If I was half the man I should be, I'd kill him for lusting after my wife.* Finally beaten down by Charley's persistence, and knowing that he desperately needed his brother's help working the claim, he said that he might talk to Martha about it—but warned that Martha's say would be the final word on the matter.

Peering into the iron pot to make sure no uninvited pests had found their way into the beans while they were soaking, Martha set it over the fire and stirred up the coals. All the cooking was done in the stone fireplace Robert and Charley had built. She often wished she could have brought a stove to cook on, but they had to pack everything they owned on three mules, and there was no room for a stove.

"Damn!" she muttered to herself, as she brushed a couple of small white worms from the slab of salt pork she was about to slice. She regularly found worms in the pork, and weevils in the flour, but it still disgusted her. During moments such as these, she tried to discipline herself not to think of her home in Virginia, the home she had been so anxious to escape. Her tiny corner, partitioned off from her four brothers by a blanket, seemed luxurious to her now. She paused for a moment, staring at the slab of salt pork, her mind's eye recalling a time that now seemed long ago. She pictured a serious young man in Confederate gray, home on convalescent leave while his wound healed.

Robert had wooed her relentlessly, and she now admitted to herself that she had allowed her emotions to be fueled by romantic thoughts of a gallant young soldier, wounded in battle. She longed so for the passion that would sweep her heart away, that she willed him to be the prince of her dreams. She was in love with love itself. Suddenly she focused on the cold impersonal slab of meat in her hand and the intruding little white worm that wiggled rudely before her eyes. Here was her reality. Her reverie shattered like her romantic schoolgirl dreams, and she flicked the offending worm from the pork and brought her mind back to the mundane business of preparing supper. It was childish fantasy to think dreams came true. There was nothing to do but make the best of what life offered. Maybe things would change.

The evening meal was eaten in almost total silence. There seemed to be a heavy air hanging over them that Martha could not help but notice. It was as if the two men had been in an argument, yet there was no apparent sign of animosity between them. She decided that the cause was most likely simple fatigue. "You two are awfully quiet tonight," she finally commented, not really interested in the cause.

"I reckon," Robert replied, never looking up from his plate.

After supper was finished, Martha cleared away the dirty plates while Robert pushed his stool back, stood up, and went to fetch his pipe. Charley remained seated at the rough little table for a few minutes longer, watching Martha as she washed their plates. She could feel his eyes on her back as she swished the tin plates around in the bucket of dishwater. She was relieved to hear him rise and announce that he was going to walk down to the stream to get some fresh air. Charley gave a meaningful glance to Robert as he walked out the door.

Unable to make up his mind whether or not to relate his discussion with Charley, Robert stood by the rough stone fireplace, thoughtfully filling his pipe. He tamped the tobacco down carefully, delaying the ultimate decision as long as possible. All the while, his eyes never left his wife as she finished cleaning up after the meal. He stepped forward when she picked up the wooden bucket and started toward the door. "Here," he said, "let me empty that for you."

"Thank you," she said, letting him take it from her, mildly surprised that he seemed anxious to help her. It was unusual that he even noticed what she was doing.

After throwing the dirty water out, Robert set the empty bucket by the door, and said, "Just leave it there. In a little bit, I'll walk down to the stream and fill it for you."

"Why, thank you," she said again, amazed by his

strange attitude this evening. He had not shown such consideration for her since leaving Virginia. And now he was standing around awkwardly, as if working up the nerve to tell her something. Could it be, she wondered, that he might be entertaining romantic thoughts? It had been a long time since they had made love. Was it just a coincidence that Charley decided to leave them alone in the cabin? She unconsciously smoothed her hair back. Turning to face him, she looked into his eyes, waiting for him to speak.

"Uh, Martha . . ." he stammered, groping for the proper way to approach the subject.

"Yes, Robert," she replied expectantly, still marveling at her husband's shyness and puzzled by his obvious reluctance to speak his mind. *Has it been so long that he's become too bashful to express his desires?* It struck her that she was pleased by the change in his manner. In the past, he had not squandered any thought toward her pleasure, being wholly occupied with his own needs. If he had changed, then she welcomed it. His next statement caused her to question the very foundation of their marriage.

"I guess it's been kinda hard on Charley, living out in this wilderness with the two of us—him having no woman of his own. That can be awful grinding on a man." He hesitated, but since he had gone this far, he was determined to spit it out. "Well, what I'm trying to say . . . what Charley's trying to say . . . is that it would ease his troubles if he could spend some time with you."

Puzzled by his statement, Martha shook her head in confusion. "Spend some time with me?" she echoed. "Why would he . . . ?" She didn't finish the question because it suddenly dawned on her what her husband was proposing. She gasped. "Robert! What are you saying?" she cried, scarcely believing her ears.

"I know it don't sound right. It ain't me that's wantin' it. Charley just wanted to know what you thought of it." Bewildered at this point, Robert shook his head as if trying to clear it of confusing thoughts. "I don't know . . . Things are just different out here."

Her initial shock having given way to cool anger, Martha fixed an accusing eye upon her husband. "You want me to play the whore for your little brother?" she demanded, her tone heavy with the contempt she now felt for both of the brothers. She waited for him to answer. When he did not, she looked away in disgust, no longer wishing to gaze upon him. "Well, things are not different out here as far as I'm concerned. You'll have to kill me first. You can tell your little brother to keep his dirty thoughts to himself from now on." She looked back at Robert, the flame of anger flashing in her eyes. "And while you're at it, you can tell him to keep his eyes to himself, too. I'm tired of catching him gaping at me every time I turn around. You both disgust me."

It was not necessary for Charley to ask Robert about the success of his proposition to Martha. When the younger brother returned from "taking the night air," the frigid atmosphere inside the cabin more than conveyed the message. Both Robert and Martha pointedly avoided his eye as he drew a stool up to the fireplace and sat down. "The nights are gettin' a mite cooler already," he offered, seeking to break the heavy air that filled the cabin. His comment was met with a stony silence. The three of them sat without speaking for several moments more until Martha, still without a word, left the two brothers before the fireplace and retired behind the blanketed partition.

"We'll go huntin' in the morning. Bring us in some fresh meat," Robert called after her. When she had

disappeared behind the blanket that formed their bed-
room, he glanced at Charley. Frowning, he shook his
head—a silent signal that Charley had already
surmised.

Disappointed, but far from discouraged, Charley
just nodded in reply. *She might not be willing right
now,* he thought, *but we'll see when the right opportunity comes along.* In his mind, he was already planning
that opportunity. If he were to beg off tomorrow, and
stay here while Robert went off hunting, she might
not feel so high and mighty. Living right there in the
tiny cabin with his brother and his wife, he knew
whether or not Robert was taking care of Martha's
special needs—and he was well aware of the lack of
intimacy between them. Martha was ripe for the taking. Charley liked his chances.

"You know, brother," Charley broke the silence,
laying the groundwork for his plan. "I'm feeling kinda
poorly. I don't know what it is, but my insides are
aching. I think I better turn in." For added effect, he
uttered a slight groan as he went over to his straw
pallet in the corner of the cabin. "I hope I'll feel better in the mornin'."

Robert did not respond. Instead, he simply stared
at his brother for a long moment before returning his
gaze to the glowing coals in the stone fireplace, hating
himself for what he had proposed. *Bad business,* he
thought, *this whole crazy thing with Charley.* He
wished that he had possessed the courage to undertake this venture into the Black Hills without Charley.
The work was too hard for one man alone. He needed
Charley's help. That was a fact, but hidden deep inside
his soul he knew he needed Charley more to help
allay his fear of this untamed territory. Now Martha
was all het up about his unnatural proposal, and she
would no doubt be mad at him for several days. He

had known ahead of time how Martha would respond to such an idea. He shouldn't have asked, but Charley was so damned persistent. *Well, what's done is done. Maybe she'll get over it.* "Reckon I'll go to bed myself," he muttered. "I'm tired."

It was a good hour before daylight when Robert roused himself from his blankets. He took one look at his sleeping wife, rolled up in her blankets with her back to him, before he went to the fireplace to stir up the dying coals. When he had coaxed the glowing embers into a fresh flame, he added some wood from the stack by the fireplace and stood watching it for a few moments to make sure it caught. Satisfied, he glanced over in the corner where his brother was still deep in slumber. "Charley," he called softly. When there was no response, he walked over and nudged him with his toe. "Charley," he repeated, this time a good bit louder.

"What is it?" a muffled voice finally answered from under his blanket.

"Get up. We've got to get movin' if we're gonna get us a deer this mornin'. I'm thinkin' we'll more'n likely run up on one on the other side of the ridge where they've been eatin' in those berry bushes." When Charley failed to move, Robert gave him a little harder nudge with his toe. "Come on, Charley. It'll be daylight before long. I wanna be back here before noon." He lowered his voice again. "We'll let Martha sleep a while longer." Recalling his wife's anger from the night before, he decided it best not to disturb her. Maybe when they returned to the cabin with a fresh carcass of venison, she would forget about the unholy proposition that had sent her to her pallet early, showing him her back all night.

With a show of great effort, Charley finally responded to his brother's cajoling. Raising up on one elbow, he looked up at Robert with a painful expression. "I'm a'feared you're gonna have to go without me. I'm feelin' poorly this morning. I'd best stay here and try to get over it."

On the other side of the blanket that divided the interior of the tiny cabin, her eyes wide open, Martha lay still and listened. She could guess what brother Charley's ailment was, and she was determined that there would be no cure for it in this cabin. She was spared the trouble of setting the young man straight because her husband also had a fair notion of the cause of his brother's illness.

"You might as well haul your lazy bones outta them blankets," Robert commanded. "I ain't going without you. Besides, you can be sick up on that ridge. You're goin' with me."

"Damn, Robert, you don't need me to go hold your hand. I'm not foolin'. I'm sick. I need to stay here and look after things."

Robert was not to be denied. There was no doubt in his mind what Charley was up to. And while he probably would not have opposed it the night before, if Martha had been willing, he now resented his brother's designs on his wife—and he was thoroughly ashamed of his lack of backbone for considering it. He was determined now, and in a low voice close to Charley's ear, he told him in no uncertain terms, "I know what you've got on your mind, and I'm tellin' you it ain't gonna happen." With that, he jerked the blanket back and growled, "Now get your pants on—we're goin' huntin'." The woman on the other side of the blanket relaxed.

Martha pretended to be asleep until she could no longer hear Robert and Charley saddling the horses in the corral. She continued to lay still long after the sound of the horses' slow plodding hooves had faded into the early echoes of the new day. Certain she was alone, she then got up and dressed. After a brief look at the fire to make sure it needed no attention, she picked up the wooden bucket and walked down to the creek.

The morning air was brisk as the first long golden fingers of sunlight touched the tips of the pines. There would not be many more days before she would have to fill the bucket at night for her breakfast water. The thought was not a pleasant one. She had hoped they would be gone from this isolated valley before the first signs of winter came calling. She could not bear the thought of another winter spent with her somber husband and his leering brother. She harbored a genuine fear that, if they didn't get out of the valley before the winter snows closed them in, the long monotonous days and nights might lead to trouble between the two brothers—and she might be caught in the middle.

A sudden wave of melancholia swept over her as she kneeled beside the water, watching her bucket fill. Virginia seemed so long ago and so far away. Was it possible that no more than a year and a half had passed since they had set out from the lush hills of Virginia after bidding her tearful parents good-bye? How cheerful and attentive Robert had been during those first few weeks. How soon the hardships of the trail and the ruggedness of the lofty mountains had tempered him, revealing a side of him that Martha did not know. "Well, missy," she said as she lifted the bucket from the water, "you've changed as well, and this won't be the only mistake you make in your life." She took a few steps up the bank before stopping to add, "But it might be the biggest one."

Making her way back up the hill, she stopped to enjoy the first warm rays of the sun upon her face, pausing a moment to listen to the flutelike voice of a meadowlark beyond the trees to her left. Moments later, it was answered by another on the far side of a low line of boulders on her right. She realized that it had been a long time since she had even noticed the singing of the birds. When Robert and Charley were first building the cabin—when she had first seen the savage beauty of this rugged mountain country—she would often pick the tiny blue-and-yellow wildflowers that grew beside the stream. She had marveled at the crystal clearness of the bubbling stream as it hurried down through the rocks to join the creek that bisected the narrow valley, teeming with all description of wildlife—from the tiny water ouzel that dived into the rushing stream, picking food from the rocky bottom, to the occasional glimpse of an elk crossing over to the meadow on the opposite side of the ridge, the little valley could seem a virtual paradise.

Thinking of these things, Martha was sad that she had lost her appreciation for the wondrous canvas that mother nature had painted. The daily toil of trying to extract their fortune from the rocky soil had dulled her senses—and now this latest, boldest, problem with her brother-in-law. *I mustn't lose sight of the beautiful things in life, else I'll soon be nothing more than a bitter old woman.* Then, farther up the hill, she heard the clear notes of the meadowlark's song again. It seemed to be following her progress as she carried the bucket of water toward the cabin. At first charmed by the throaty call, she smiled. Seconds later her smile suddenly froze. A slight movement in the pine boughs to her left caused her heart to pound in her chest, and she sensed that she was being watched.

Don't panic, she warned herself. *It's probably just a raccoon or a porcupine.* It occurred to her then that Charley might have sneaked back to the cabin, and the thought angered her. She hurried her step, determined not to show any sign of fear. If it were Charley, she was confident she could deal with that impudent scoundrel. She would set him straight, no doubt about it. Moments later, she would have been glad to discover Charley skulking after her. What she saw almost caused her to scream.

Glancing to her right, she was suddenly terrified to see several moving figures among the boulders, paralleling her path up the hill. Her heart, pounding away at her chest moments before, was now threatening to burst from her breast. A rustle of boughs caused her to jerk her head back to the left, and she heard her breath escape sharply, for there, no longer hidden in the thick pine forest, three Indian warriors filed through the trees, pacing her.

Unable to control her panic any longer, she dropped her bucket and started running, desperate to reach the cabin and the rifle she knew was there. She had no thought that the Indians could possibly be friendly, thinking only to reach the safety of the tiny log cabin. Her sudden flight seemed to have no effect on the warriors pacing her. They calmly continued to flank her path as she ran for the cabin, unconcerned with her obvious panic, and paying no attention to the wooden water bucket now tumbling and bouncing wildly down the slope.

The fact that the savages did not set upon her at once gave Martha a minuscule portion of hope, and she pushed herself to the limits of her will to escape, straining to make her legs move faster. At last, the open door of the cabin was no more than a few yards away, as her legs—pushed far beyond their capability to support her—turned to lead. With one last desperate surge of willpower, she reached the doorway, almost collapsing on the dirt floor. Catching herself on her hands and knees, she forced herself to get up again. Staggering to her feet, she came face-to-face with a terrifying apparition that stopped her cold, holding her suspended in a paralyzing fear.

He stood, calmly watching the terrified woman, an expression approaching boredom on his fearsome face. He was taller than the Indians she had seen at Fort Laramie the summer before. Naked from the waist up, he wore no paint on his massive torso. The two rawhide bands on his biceps were the only ornaments, other than the two eagle feathers that hung from his long dark hair. Though not in war paint, his face suggested a promise of unbridled fury, with eyes dark and penetrating, set behind flintlike cheekbones.

As she stood shivering in fear, he seemed to be looking her over, evaluating his find, his face still expressionless, only his eyes moving slightly. When he made no move toward her, she gradually began to recover from the initial shock that had staggered her, and thoughts of survival returned. Seeing Robert's extra rifle standing propped against a corner of the fireplace, she made a sudden lunge toward it. He made no move to stop her, merely turning to watch, studying her motions. With some measure of confidence restored, now that the rifle was in her hands, Martha aimed the weapon at the intruder and found her voice. "Get out!" she screamed, doing her best to inject some authority in her quaking voice.

Without changing the expression of curiosity he wore, he made no response to her shouted command. Looking directly into her eyes, he brought his hand up before him, and slowly opened his fingers to show her the cartridges he held. Panic-stricken once more, she started to bolt toward the door, only to discover other warriors blocking her escape. Trapped, she

backed slowly into the corner by the fireplace, pointing the empty rifle at the frightful savage still patiently
studying her every move. All the while, he had not
moved from his original position in the middle of the
cabin, but after a few moments, he at last made a
small show of animation. Taking his eyes from her, he
glanced around the interior of the cabin, taking some
interest in the things he saw there: the table and
stools, the clock on the mantel, the pots and skillet.
Then he brought his gaze back to the trembling
woman in the corner, holding it there until one of the
warriors standing in the doorway spoke to him.

"The tracks around this place show there were two
men," Wolf Paw said. "There were more horses, but
now there is only one and three mules. Should we
wait for the men to come back?"

"No," the tall warrior replied. "We'll burn this coyotes' nest and be on our way. We have been far away
from the village for too long. It isn't wise to stay here
in the land of our enemies, the Sioux. We are few in
number, and the smoke may be seen." He glanced
back at Martha, huddled wide-eyed in the corner.
"The woman interests me. I will take her. You and
the others take what you will." He moved deliberately
toward Martha, who did her best to show a willful
defiance. Forcefully, but without haste, the warrior
reached out and took the rifle by the barrel. Martha
held onto it in a stubborn attempt to resist. The warrior did not try to wrest it from her grasp. Instead, he
merely held it firmly in his hand while his eyes
searched deeply into hers. Realizing the strength in
those piercing black eyes, Martha released the rifle.
With a faint nod of approval, the warrior turned and
handed the rifle to Wolf Paw. Then he held out his
hand to Martha.

"Please let me go," she pleaded, pressing her body against the log wall. "Just take what you want and leave."

If the fearsome warrior understood her words, he gave no indication, but he continued to motion for her to come forward. Fearing that her life was very soon to end, she nevertheless took a tentative step toward his outstretched hand. Something in his manner told her that to resist was useless. He took her wrist in his hand and led her toward the doorway. His touch was like fire. She could feel the powerful tendons in his fingers and the muscles in his arm. And while his hands obviously held the power to crush her, she was surprised by the gentle touch upon her wrist.

Bumped roughly by some of the warriors pushing impatiently past her as she was led outside, she fought to contain her panic. Behind her, she could already hear sounds of dishes crashing against the walls and furniture being tossed aside as her and her husband's possessions were being picked over. All this was mixed in with the excited chatter of the warriors as they talked among themselves. Forgetting her fear for the moment, she angrily pulled back in an attempt to free her wrist when a half-naked savage held up the silver picture frame that held her only photograph of her parents. The powerful hand that imprisoned her arm clamped down so suddenly that she thought her bones would be crushed. She cried out in pain, and just as suddenly, the pressure was reduced as the silent warrior continued to lead her away from the cabin.

Out beside the tiny corral, Martha watched in horror as some of the warriors drew their knives and slaughtered the mules. Almost overcome with the dread of what her fate was to be at the hands of these savages, she sank down at the feet of her captor, the hopelessness of her situation smothering her like a heavy cloak. The tall warrior, obviously the leader of this pack of raiders, stood watching the plundering, seemingly disinterested in participating himself. He barely glanced down at the terrified woman at his feet as she watched her home being destroyed.

Then a short stocky warrior came up to them, leading her horse, the gentle dapple gray that Robert had purchased for her in Fort Laramie and that had carried her across the wide prairie to these mountains. She felt a sob catch deep down in her throat at the sight of her horse in the hands of these savages. She feared that the gray was to meet with the same fate as the mules, and finding it unbearable to watch them slaughter the mare, she turned her face away.

The tall warrior reached down, took her by the chin, and turned her head back to face him. Looking into her eyes, he spoke words that she could not understand. When it was plain that she did not know what he asked, he patiently tried again. This time with sign and gestures, until she understood that he was asking if this was her horse. She slowly nodded. Satisfied, he then spoke briefly with the stocky warrior, who grunted in reply and led the horse away.

Though it had seemed much longer to the frightened woman kneeling in the dirt of the corral, the raiding party had actually been there no more than half an hour when the cabin was set ablaze. Finished with their savage business there, the warriors, numbering twenty, gathered up their horses and loaded them with the spoils of their raid. Still with no hint of what the Indians had in store for her, Martha grew more and more frightened by the moment. Most of the warriors paid little attention to her as they swaggered back and forth, comparing their loot, occasionally laughing at one another when they modeled Robert's or Charley's clothing. Their tall leader exhibited no interest in any of the white men's apparel, smiling only slightly when one of his party pranced about with Martha's bonnet upon his head.

Black clouds of smoke billowed from the doorway and windows of the cabin as the fire began to consume the inside of what had been her home for more than a year. Gripped by fear, her eyes searched the ridge beyond the cabin for some sign of her husband. Her only hope for salvation was for his return. At once her despair was deepened with the realization that there were too many warriors. Robert and Charley were fortunate to be away, otherwise they would most likely be dead. This realization was immediately followed by one that was bound to be as certain: If she were taken away by these savages, she was as good as dead. She would never see her husband or anyone again. The finality of this thought caused her to strengthen her resolve to somehow escape. If at all possible, she must make a run for her life, or she might never be heard from again. The opportunity came sooner than she expected.

Turning his attention to the business of getting his braves organized and underway, the tall warrior walked over toward the burning cabin to talk with the others, leaving Martha unguarded. Looking around, she realized that the burning cabin had claimed everyone's attention. *I may never get another chance,* she thought, *I've got to do it!* Forcing herself to move very carefully, she rose to her feet. Knees trembling, she slowly backed away until she felt the corner post of the corral at her back. Not one of the Indians happened to look her way, so she quickly moved behind the corner post, her heart threatening to pound through her chest. Still there was no outcry from the band of warriors. Encouraged by their lack of vigilance, she stole swiftly along the side of the corral, doing her best to stay low, praying the slender rails would hide her escape. Once she reached the back corner of the corral, she paused for a moment to steal one more look back toward the noisy celebration around the burning cabin. Still unnoticed by the raiders, she steeled herself to run for her life. Pushing away from the corner post, she started running as fast as she could across the meadow in a desperate attempt to reach the forest beyond.

"Black Elk!" one of the warriors cried out. The tall war chief turned to see Wolf Paw pointing toward the meadow beyond the corral. "The woman!"

Black Elk did not respond for a moment. Watching the fleeing woman running for her life, he did not feel any urgency to pursue. After a moment, he calmly said, "She cannot get far." He strode leisurely over to his pony and leaped gracefully upon its back. "She runs in the same direction we are going, anyway."

No more than fifty yards from the thick forest of white spruce, Martha tried to push her exhausted limbs harder. Gasping desperately for breath, her heart pounding in her throat, she began to stagger uncontrollably. *Got to get to the trees!* she pleaded. *Just a few yards more!* Then the pounding of her heart rapidly became louder and louder, and she uttered a cry of despair when she realized that it was the sound of horses' hooves pounding the meadow grass behind her. She knew she was doomed. Still she tried to will her body to move faster.

Five yards from the trees, she suddenly felt the heavy breath of the Indian pony as the weight of the animal pressed against her side. Jostled by the prancing white stallion, she would have been knocked to the ground had it not been for the powerful hand that grasped a handful of her long auburn hair. Breathless and exhausted, she cried out in pain as she was forcefully brought to a stop.

Without releasing her hair, Black Elk threw one leg over his pony's back and dropped to the ground beside her. "Don't run," he said, speaking in his native tongue. His face remained devoid of expression, so she had no notion what he was saying. But his next actions conveyed his feelings. Still holding her by her hair, he administered several sharp strokes across her back with a short rawhide quirt he carried. She screamed out in anger and outrage. The pain was considerable, but not as stinging as the shock of the beating. Never before had she been whipped like that, not even as a child. Her natural reaction was to fight back, and she beat her fists against his chest. Surprised, his face registered the first sign of emotion she had seen, although it was no more than a raising of his eyebrows and a slight widening of his dark eyes. Standing firmly before her, he did not try to stop her from pounding his chest, waiting patiently until she had exhausted herself. Then, as if disciplining a child, he whipped her again—this time a little harder. "Don't run," he repeated softly.

Releasing her hair, he watched her drop to the ground. He stood over her for a few moments while she cried, her head sagging in humiliation and pain. After a little while, he took a length of rawhide rope and tied her wrists together. Taking her by both hands, he pulled her to her feet and roughly lifted her up on the horse she had ridden from Laramie.

"We go now, we have wasted enough time," he said, with no hint of anger in his voice. Leaping upon his white war pony, he nudged the stallion with his heels, heading up through the trees at a slow walk, leading the woman captive behind him.

Chapter 2

Clay Culver reined his horse to a stop on a low bluff bunched with tall poplars and sturdy water oaks that cast a solid cool shade upon the narrow river crossing. He slid down from the handsome chestnut's back to stretch his legs a bit while he looked across the shallow ford, filling his eyes with a scene he had lain awake many a night trying to envision during the past few months. The modest farmhouse on the other side of the little Rapidan River looked smaller now than he had remembered. Maybe, he allowed, it was because the little peach tree his father had planted by the back porch had grown as high as the eaves of the roof. It was barely reaching the kitchen windowsill when he had marched off to war.

Wrapping the reins loosely around a dogwood branch, he walked down through the trees to the edge of the water, where he paused to scan the valley from east to west and back again. There was still a little evidence of the war's destruction here, but it appeared that his family had been lucky. Although there were some fence posts missing along the high ridge that ran down to the river, at least the house was still standing, as well as the barn. Evidently the Union army had crossed the river farther down toward Fredericksburg.

The missing fence posts were more than likely used to build fires for Union patrols foraging for food. No doubt his father and brothers had been working hard to reclaim fields gone fallow during the conflict. His pa was a good farmer, a hard-working man—Clay was not surprised that the place was looking prosperous once more.

He wasn't sure why he hesitated on the riverbank. Maybe it was to permit his mind to realize that he was really home. When he had lain in the hospital bed, with the yellow-green fluid oozing from his battered shoulder, he had rehearsed this scene over and over in his mind, the moment when he finally saw his home again. He told himself that he would let loose with a raucous Rebel yell, and charge across the ford, hell-bent for leather, galloping up to the house to a joyous reunion with his family. Why then, now that the moment had finally come, was he overcome with a sense of sadness and reluctance? He recognized the fact that the war had changed him, and it lay heavy upon his mind. Maybe he had seen too many months of endless marches with shortages of food and ammunition—and too many insignificant little meadows and churchyards strewn with the bodies of men he had marched alongside merely hours before. He had been knocked from his horse by a burning hot shard of shrapnel and left to lie bleeding and unattended at the bottom of a deep ravine for hours before help arrived. Then, after the doctors patched him up, he was ordered to report to an infantry unit, instead of his old cavalry regiment. He was told that he might as well be in the infantry. There were no extra horses to replace the one shot out from under him.

Before he even realized it, his mind had slipped back to those days of profound sadness that had heralded the death throes of a once-proud army. After ten long months in the trenches at Petersburg, General Lee was forced to evacuate the town. Clay Culver remembered the night, April second, as clearly as if it were only yesterday—instead of over a year ago. He permitted his mind to recall the night, and soon he was reliving a time when he had ceased to be a boy.

"Sergeant Ivers said to pack up your kit. We're pulling out of here tonight."

Clay looked up to see his friend Wes Fanning striding toward him. "Pulling out where?" Clay asked. They had been occupying the trenches for so long, he was not going to respond quickly until he was sure of the orders. Only the generals knew the whole picture of their situation, but the lowliest of soldiers knew that the Union forces had the Army of Northern Virginia virtually surrounded. There had been some talk among the rank and file about a spring offensive to break through Grant's armies and push them back. But the poor condition of the horses, and the lack of rations to feed the men were signs enough for Clay that they were in no condition to launch any kind of offensive. "Pulling out where?" Clay repeated.

"Sergeant Ivers said the captain told him we'd be marching to Amelia Court House to get rations and hook up with the boys from Richmond. That's all I know."

No one was sorry to leave the squalid conditions that had been their lot for the better part of a year. In fact, there was an air of excitement about being out of the trenches and back in the field. It didn't last long, however. The poor condition of the troops turned the optimistic mood to hunger and fatigue after the first day's march. To make matters worse, when they reached Amelia Court House, the promised rations were not there. The troops from Richmond had not arrived, having been delayed by flooded roads and poor traveling conditions. With Grant's Union armies following close behind, it was imperative to keep the army on the move in hopes of joining with General Johnston's Army of Tennessee near the Roanoke River. General Lee waited for his troops from Richmond for an extra day. While they waited, he sent wagons out to scour the countryside in search of food, but there was little to be had. It had been three days since Clay had eaten anything beyond a little parched corn he and Wes had hoarded from the last of the supplies at Petersburg.

On the march again the following day, the ragged troops left Amelia Court House with Union troops close behind. The day's delay had cost them, however. With only a few miles covered, they encountered Union troops firmly entrenched squarely across their line of march. In no condition to fight, Lee ordered a change in direction to the west in hopes of marching around the ambush, and maybe to supply his troops at Farmville. It was the worst time in young Clay Culver's life. He was tired and hungry, hungry enough to eat anything that even resembled food. Gone were the romantic illusions of glory he had sought when he had left his father's farm near Fredericksburg.

Like his friend Wes, and so many other young men, Clay had lost his enthusiasm and eagerness to fight after his first major skirmish as a foot soldier. Advancing toward a suspected Union position on a thickly forested hillside, he got his second close look at man's fragile mortality. Caught in the open while crossing a small road at the foot of the hill, Clay's regiment was suddenly cut down by a blistering barrage from the trees above them. Men on either side of him cried out in pain, dropping in their tracks as they tried to scramble for cover behind a shallow bank. Clay had bur-

rowed as far as he could into the scant protection the
bank offered, and laid there for three hours while the
rattle of cannon and the hiss of miniballs pinned the
regiment down until reinforcements arrived.

Now, on this rather ordinary day in early April,
there was no energy available to waste on thoughts of
victory. Weary and hungry, most of Clay's comrades
in arms harbored thoughts only of survival. Still there
were some, Sergeant Ivers among them, who urged
the men to maintain their spirit. "Supplies are waiting
in Farmville," he promised. "We'll play a different
tune for them Yankees then. General Lee's always got
something up his sleeve."

Clay did his best to maintain his faith in the Confederate army's ability to regroup and take the fight once
again to Grant's troops. But with more and more men
breaking ranks in desperate attempts to find food
while others simply dropped beside the road, unable
to take another step, there were soon great gaps in
the line of march. Taking advantage of these gaping
holes in the Confederate line, Union cavalry dashed
in upon the Confederate wagons, destroying a great
number of them and killing hundreds of Clay's
comrades.

Clay and Wes, their luck still holding, found themselves among the weary troops that staggered into
Farmville on the seventh of April. As Sergeant Ivers
had promised, desperately needed rations awaited
them. But Union forces were so close behind that
Confederate cavalry had to make a stand in the streets
of Farmville while the rest of their army escaped. With
no chance for rest, the ragged troops continued to
march westward, their only hope to reach Appomattox
Station before Grant's forces cut them off. It was not
to be.

Appomattox was where it all ended, that chilly

April morning near the little town of Appomattox Court House. Of all the many days of fighting—the long exhausting marches, the frequent nights with nothing to eat, the magnificent charges, the demoralizing retreats—that one day at Appomattox stood out as a day he would relive over and over in his mind.

The approaching dawn had seemed to herald a morning of dark defeat. Bleak and chilly, the first light of day had spread reluctantly upon the Confederate battle line, stretched out on the western side of the village. Before them, the Union forces were amassed, well positioned with earthworks and long lines of cannon. But in those early hours, few men on either side were stirring. Clay thought of his friend, Wesley Fanning, and his ability to sleep in the most perilous conditions. He and Wes had fought side-by-side for over a year—ever since Clay returned from the hospital and found himself assigned to an infantry regiment commanded by General John B. Gordon. On that morning, even Wes was tossing fitfully in his blanket, trying to stay warm. Soft murmurings along the line of soldiers on each side of him confirmed the uneasy wakefulness of his comrades in arms.

Shortly after first light, some of the boys on his left pulled some fence rails over behind the line and built a fire. Clay, staying low to keep from tempting a Yankee sniper, moved closer to catch some of the fire's warmth. It seemed that the Union army must have been waiting for Clay to rouse himself. For he had no sooner joined those around the fire when the Yankee cannons roared out the initial barrage. Like angry dragons belching fire and thunder, they turned his section of the line into a heaving mass of smoking earth, sending all of the men scrambling back to their positions. Almost immediately, the Confederate cannons behind him opened fire, signaling the attack. Clay and

Wes exchanged glances, a silent promise that they would see each other again at the end of this day. Then joining in the fierce Rebel yell that had started back down the line, they left the cover of the fence row, and charged toward the waiting Union rifles.

Wes Fanning advanced no more than thirty yards before he broke the unspoken promise just made moments before. Clay heard a soft exclamation, as if Wes had merely stubbed his toe—or cut his finger. When he turned to look at his friend, Wes collapsed heavily, a miniball having split his face apart. Clay would never forget the look of astonishment in Wes's eyes. His mind registered the horror of it, but there was no time to ponder the loss of his friend. Finding himself in a storm of flying lead, he forced himself to charge forward, his rifle before him. He went forward mindlessly, for the simple reason that the men on either side of him went forward. In the heat of the cannons' thunder and the whining miniballs, all reasonable thoughts were abandoned—charging onward through the hailstorm of death, not even aware of his own maniacal yell until the whole world was suddenly plunged into darkness.

The Confederate attack had been thrown back. Still the fighting went on for two hours before General Gordon sent word to General Lee that he could hold no longer. The final hour of the Confederacy was at hand when Lee was forced to send a flag of truce to General Sheridan's headquarters. It was over. Clay remembered very little of the events that took place on that day, or the days that followed. Lee's surrender to Grant in the McLean house near Appomattox Court House, the disarming of the troops, were all merely blurs in Clay's memory as he lay unconscious in a makeshift hospital on the edge of the village.

*   *   *

Now, months after the surrender, Clay found himself a survivor, back from the dead—healed physically, but still permanently scarred inside as he stood gazing upon his home. When that Union cannon exploded almost point-blank before him, hurling him into total darkness, it was no less than a miracle that he had managed to emerge from death's waiting embrace. For months, not knowing who he was, or where he came from, he lay bedridden, tended by a kind Virginia family, who were more than willing to give comfort to one of the South's fighting men. Their name was Loudon, and they had lost a son, John, in the long siege of Petersburg. Clay supposed they saw something of their son in him, prompting them to take him from the ghastly hospital where he had been left to die.

Gradually Clay's lost identity began to return, and he started to recover. The day came when he was ready to leave. Saying a tearful farewell to the family that had cared for him, Clay set out for Fredericksburg on foot. The clothes on his back—shirt, trousers, and shoes, once belonging to John Loudon—were now his only earthly possessions. His situation might have left a lesser man with no sense of purpose. More than a few men were broken in spirit after being cast into the cauldron of bloody combat. Clay Culver emerged from the horrors of war knowing he possessed a steel inside him that would never admit defeat.

· Although starting out on foot in borrowed clothes, Clay was not one to suffer a beggar's lot, no matter how dire the situation. He immediately kept an eye out for an opportunity to improve his status. Feeling that his impoverished circumstances were caused by the Union army, he naturally felt that the Yankees should provide restitution for his losses. He found what he was looking for eight miles northwest of Appomattox when he happened upon a Union cavalry detachment camped on the banks of the Appomattox River.

Keeping out of sight, he made his way around the camp until he found a place to hide close to a temporary rope corral where the entire detachment's horses were collected. Seating himself comfortably behind a screen of laurel, he then patiently waited out the afternoon for the sun to set, utilizing the time to select the horse he planned to *borrow* when it was dark enough. A spirited chestnut with blond mane and tail caught his eye at once. It no doubt belonged to one of the officers, since it appeared well groomed and a bit spunkier than the others. *You're a fine-looking animal,* Clay thought as he watched the horse tossing its head and pawing the ground as if ready to fly from the picket line where it was tied. *I'm gonna liberate you from your Yankee jailers tonight.*

The afternoon passed easily enough for Clay. He was tired from walking that morning, so he was content to lay back in the laurel, taking his leisure, watching the Union camp. He wondered what their mission was, this far away from any town or army headquarters. Possibly, they were still scouring the countryside in search of pockets of Confederate resistance, even these long months after the surrender. Whatever their task, there seemed to be a generally carefree air about the bivouac, with most of the men gathered in small groups around campfires. As darkness approached, and the glow of the campfires became brighter, the cheerful voices of the soldiers seemed to become louder as they floated to Clay on the cool evening breeze. Off to one side of the camp, a young soldier with a soft tenor voice began to sing a melancholy tune that Clay had heard before but couldn't name.

Soon several other voices joined in, one in a fine harmony. It was a peaceful evening with little to remind one of the horrible war so recently ended.

Feeling almost too comfortable to rouse himself to his task, Clay finally decided it was dark enough to discharge the chestnut from the Union army. The notion that he was acting the part of a horse thief never entered his mind. The war may have been over, but his was still a soldier's mind, and this was certainly an enemy camp bivouacked by the river. In addition, the Yankees had killed his horse. They should rightfully be required to replace it.

Leaving the cover of the laurel, he made his way along the riverbank, being careful to keep a sharp eye for pickets or sentries. *They haven't even posted sentries,* he realized when he had stolen to within twenty-five yards of the rope corral holding the horses. *They sure as hell ain't worried about being attacked.* The light from the campfires traced a patchwork of shadows that flickered upon the tree trunks, faintly lighting his path as he carefully made his way along the bank. When he reached the small clearing where the horses were picketed, he paused to listen to the voices drifting up to him from the water's edge. Hearing nothing to indicate any concern from that quarter, he proceeded to the rope and made his way down it, counting horses as he went. *One, two, three, fourth from the end.* The Union mounts whinnied softly as he gave each horse he passed a gentle pat on the neck.

When he came to the chestnut, the horse jerked its head back as if to pull away from him. But Clay had always had a way with horses, and in a few short moments, he was gently rubbing the chestnut's muzzle. Just as he untied the reins from the picket line, he heard a voice behind him.

"What the hell are you doing?"

Clay froze, but just for a brief moment. "What the hell does it look like?" he shot back.

There was a vacant moment while an obviously confused horse soldier strained to identify Clay in the darkness under the trees. "Is that you, Townsend?"

"Who'd you think it was?" Clay asked, keeping the horse's head between him and the Union soldier.

"Well, what are you doing with the lieutenant's horse? Sergeant Warren told me to rub the lieutenant's horse down."

"Told me, too—musta forgot," Clay said, his voice halfway muffled by his hand over his mouth in an effort to disguise it. He started rubbing the horse's withers and back, pretending to busy himself with the job. He was hoping that it was too dark for the soldier to make out exactly what he was doing.

The Union soldier stood dumbfounded for a long moment before deciding that the sergeant's absentmindedness was his good fortune. "Well, ain't no use in both of us standing out here. I reckon you got the job. I'm going back to the fire."

"Don't blame you," Clay mumbled.

He couldn't help but grin when the Yankee soldier ambled off toward the glowing campfires, but he didn't waste time crowing over the success of his bluff. He could envision the soldier's surprise if he should happen to chance upon Townsend back in the camp. Taking the chestnut by the bridle, he backed it away from the picket line, and walking as fast as he could in the darkness, led the animal up away from the river. Behind him, no cry of alarm rang out as the Union cavalry detachment took their leisure, content in the knowledge that extreme vigilance was no longer essential. *That's right boys,* he thought, *just lay back and enjoy your supper. By the time the lieutenant finds out he's now on foot, I'll be long gone.*

He was forced to smile again now as he thought back on that night, and he reached down to stroke the chestnut's neck. He was a fine judge of horseflesh, even if he did say so himself. The chestnut had taken to his new owner from the first time Clay crawled up on his back. Maybe it was partly because Clay had not thrown a saddle on him, and Red—as Clay had named him—appreciated the feeling of freedom. Looking back on that night later, from the safety of his father's farm, Clay would wish he had taken the time to look for a saddle. But at that moment, he had felt no comfort in tarrying.

Young Stephen Culver walked the mule down the path from the upper cornfield. He ambled along behind the animal, which was still in harness, dragging the singletree bumping along in the dust. Before he turned the corner of the barn, he would pick it up and carry it; it annoyed his pa to see the singletree bouncing over the ground. Stephen had put in a good day's work, plowing a two-acre piece he and his older brother John had cleared. He had stayed with it until late in the afternoon, an hour or so after John and his pa had called it a day. It would be ready for planting tomorrow. Little James, the youngest, could help with that.

Stephen was justly proud of the job he and his two brothers had done, bringing the farm back to where it was almost as productive as it had been before the war. If they had a good spring, with not too much rain, they should have a prosperous year. And Stephen took special pride in knowing that it was largely due to his being able to take much of the responsibility, since his pa was laid up with rheumatism for long spells at a time.

Approaching the back corner of the barn now, Stephen reached down and plucked the bouncing single-tree from the ground without slowing the mule. As he rounded the corner, his eye caught sight of a lone rider, making his way slowly up from the edge of the river. "Ho, Henry," Stephen called out to the mule, then stood there for a few moments, trying to identify the visitor. In the late afternoon sun, he found it difficult to make out the stranger's features at first. He rode a fine-looking horse, but at that distance, it appeared the man rode bareback. So it could hardly be one of those new officials, coming over from Fredericksburg to inspect the farm again. *Another hungry wretch, looking for a handout, I expect.* They had seen more than a few since the end of the war. *This one sure has got himself a fancy horse.* Stephen glanced toward the house to see if any of the others had spied the visitor. There was no one on the porch. He looked back at the stranger, who was now approaching the front gate. Suddenly, Stephen's heart leaped into his throat and he was convinced he was seeing a ghost.

Standing dumbfounded, staring at a vision he expected to dissipate into thin air at any second, Stephen dropped Henry's reins and rubbed his eyes. When he looked again, he realized that it was not a ghost he was seeing—it was his brother Clay, returned from the dead. No longer frozen in his tracks, he started running toward the gate, yelling at the top of his lungs. "Clay! Clay!" Then yelling back at the house, "Pa! Mama! It's Clay!"

Grinning from ear to ear, Clay slipped down from his horse to greet his brother, almost being bowled over by the collision as the two hugged and slapped each other on the back. "I swear, John, I hardly recognized you," Clay said, when he stepped back to look at his brother at arm's length.

"I ain't John. I'm Stephen," he replied laughing. "I reckon I've growed up some since you've been gone."

"Stephen!" Clay exclaimed, shaking his head in disbelief. "Well, I'll be damned. I reckon you have at that."

He turned to see the rest of the family running from the house to greet him—John and James leading—with his father and mother hurrying along behind, all four faces shining with joy. The boys almost knocked him down again in their enthusiasm. His mother and father stood beaming, impatiently waiting for the rowdy reunion of their four sons to subside. Then John and Stephen, suddenly aware of their parents' waiting, stepped back, pulling young James away as well.

For a moment, Rachael Culver stood quietly smiling, looking into the eyes of her eldest, searching his face as if to assure herself that he was real. "Praise the Lord," she whispered, and tears began to well up in her eyes as she stepped forward to hug her son. Clay took her in his arms and tenderly embraced her. His father waited until she stepped back again to look at Clay once more.

"They told us you were dead," Raymond Culver said. "Said you were killed at Appomattox."

"Well, I wasn't," Clay replied, smiling, "but there was a time there when I wasn't sure."

His mother, still holding him by the hand while she filled her eyes with the pleasure of her lost son returned, shook her head slowly. "You're awful thin, son." Clay only smiled in response.

"You're riding a mighty fine-looking horse," Stephen commented. "Did the army give him to you?"

"How 'bout putting him in the corral for me," Clay said, as his mother led him toward the house, "and I'll tell you about that horse later."

"While you're at it," John reminded his younger

brother, "you'd best unharness that mule, too—unless you're planning to leave him like that all night."

"I mighta been," Stephen answered with more than a hint of resentment. "Save me the trouble of hitching him up in the morning." He took the chestnut's reins and led him away toward the corral while the rest of the family walked Clay to the house.

Amid the joyous reunion, Clay suddenly realized someone was missing. "Where's Martha?" he asked.

An awkward moment of silence followed his question, and he knew immediately that something was wrong. "Where's Martha?" he repeated.

John and James hung their heads, seeming to suddenly find the ground calling their attention. His mother gazed directly into his eyes, but reluctant to answer, sadly shook her head and left the chore to his father. "We don't know where your sister is," Raymond Culver said.

Clay was at once alarmed. Martha had always been special to him. The two had been as close as any siblings could be. "What do you mean? Is she gone?" He didn't like the sadness he now read in his mother's eyes.

"A lot's happened around here since you went off to war, son," his father said. "Come on up on the porch and set down, and I'll tell you about your sister."

To begin with, the news of Martha's wedding to Robert Vinings was somewhat of a shock to Clay. Martha had often sought Clay's advice on many different things, and once she had asked his opinion of Robert. Robert had started calling on Martha a few months before Clay left to join General Lee's Army of Northern Virginia. At the time, Clay had little opinion of the cobbler's eldest son. He really didn't know the man. On the few occasions he had been exposed to Robert, he seemed to be a somewhat sober, even plodding, man. Clay was more familiar with Robert's younger brother Charley, and that was by reputation only. Charley was well known in the taverns in town and was reputed to get into a scrape once in a while. Clay didn't fancy having Charley for a brother-in-law, if Martha was thinking in such terms. She had been quick to assure him that, although Robert was obviously set on wooing her, she was not sure her feelings for him were of such strength that she would entertain thoughts of marriage. Robert was planning to enlist in the army, anyway, she told Clay, and she had no plans to wed with anyone about to march off to war.

The news of Martha's wedding was indeed a great surprise to Clay. Robert had evidently turned out to be a much more ardent suitor when he returned from the army. He had been wounded and said he had been discharged, even though the wound was evidently not a serious one. As if his sister's wedding was not astonishing enough, he could scarcely believe his ears when his father then told him that Robert and Martha— along with Charley—had packed up and left for the goldfields in Dakota territory.

"I tried to talk them out of it," Raymond Culver explained. "But there wasn't nothing I could say to change their minds. They were going, and that was that."

Clay was mystified. "Who put that notion in their heads? What on earth does Robert Vinings know about placer mining?"

"He don't know a damn thing," John answered for his father.

"Watch your language, son," Raymond Culver quickly reprimanded.

"And Charley don't know much about anything but drinking and fighting," John added.

"John's right. Robert didn't know anything about mining for gold, but he figured he could learn. So off they went. Robert's pa fixed 'em up with a team of mules and a wagon. I give 'em as much in the way of supplies as I could—and they took off for Fort Laramie."

"Dakota territory," Clay repeated to himself. "I thought that was Indian territory." Looking around at the faces of his family, and seeing nothing but looks of dismay, he shook his head solemnly. "That sounds mighty foolhardy to me." To himself, he was thinking, *I should have been here to talk some sense into her.*

He must have displayed an accusing expression, for his father quickly jumped to his own defense. "I tried to talk to them, but it wasn't no use. They were two grown people, married and free-willed—nothing I could do to stop 'em."

"I guess not," Clay allowed, still of the opinion that he could have somehow influenced his sister, had he been there. He thought about what his father had just told him for a few moments longer before concluding, "So that's why you don't know exactly where Martha is now." Reading more than concern in their faces, he had a sudden feeling that there was more to it than that. "Martha is all right, isn't she?"

Raymond Culver glanced briefly at his wife before sighing sadly. "No, son, she ain't all right. We got a letter from Robert last month saying your sister was took by wild Indians. They burned the cabin they was living in and run off with Martha."

Like a blow from a hammer, the news struck Clay right between the eyes. *Martha abducted! She may even be dead!* At once, he felt a staggering sense of guilt for not being there to protect her. He had always watched over his sister, from the time they were little more than toddlers. He had taught her how to swim, showed her how to catch a fish. It didn't matter that a rational mind would tell him that he could not possibly have protected his sister when he was half a continent away. He felt responsible for her. Even the news that she had married didn't change that.

Recovering from the initial shock of his father's words, Clay searched Raymond Culver's eyes, hopefully looking for some sign that there was more to the story, something more encouraging. When there seemed to be nothing more from anyone, he questioned his father. "Where was Robert when the Indians attacked? And Charley? Why weren't they killed? Didn't they try to stop them?"

Raymond simply shook his head, choked with the emotion of having to relive the tragedy. When it was apparent that his father was too wrought with sorrow to continue, John answered. "All we know, Clay, is what was in Robert's letter. According to him, both him and Charley were away from the cabin, deer hunting. They didn't know anything about the raid until they came back and found their cabin burned down . . . and Martha gone." He paused and shot a quick glance at his mother before adding, "They said there wasn't no sign of blood or nothing, so they were pretty sure the Injuns just carried her off."

"What the hell did Robert do about it? Didn't they go after her?" Without knowing if he had reason to or not, Clay was already angry with Robert and Charley for permitting Martha to be stolen.

John shrugged. "All the letter said was that they had tried to track 'em, but they couldn't catch 'em."

Clay sat there in silence for a few minutes. He tried not to picture his sister in captivity, straining to push thoughts of rape and torture aside in order to clear his mind for rational thought. When he had ridden across the Rapidan less than an hour earlier, he was unsure what his immediate plans would be now that he was home again. His mind had been so occupied with the simple objective of returning to his home that he had spent very little thought on anything beyond that. Now there was no longer any uncertainty. He was heading west. If Martha was still alive, he would find her. He would not assign any blame, but unlike the rest of his family, Clay could not be content to rely on the likes of Robert and Charley Vinings.

Chapter 3

With the buildings of Fort Laramie now in sight, Clay dismounted and led Red down a low bank to drink from the river. While he stood watching him slake his thirst, he pondered the trail he had taken over the past few weeks. His visit with his family in Virginia had been a short one, staying only long enough to outfit himself for the task he felt compelled to take on. There was a deep sadness in his mother's eyes when she watched her son—only recently returned from the ravages of war—riding off once more, maybe this time for good. It pained him to cause her more concern, but in his mind, there was no choice in the matter.

John and Stephen both wanted to go with him, but they were needed at home to run the farm. His father couldn't make it without them. And Clay could plainly see that they could get along just fine without his help. Besides, little James was already beginning to do a man's work. In fact, when he thought hard on the matter, Clay decided that he might be one too many trying to make a living from his father's farm.

Red raised his muzzle from the water, and turned his head back toward his new master. "Had enough, boy?" Clay asked. The big horse shook his head from side to side, throwing a spray of tiny droplets of water as he did. Clay led him back up the bank and stepped up in the saddle his father had given him. He reached down to pat the stock of the shiny new Winchester-66 rifle riding in the saddle boot. He had already developed a habit of keeping a close eye on the weapon. There were not many of them available. He wouldn't have one himself were it not for the fact that his uncle worked for the manufacturer. One of the first of the new rifles manufactured by Oliver Winchester—and the first model bearing his name—it was a marvelous weapon in Clay's mind. With a magazine holding sixteen cartridges, the rifle could be fired as rapidly as a man could cock it and pull the trigger. Clay felt he could hold off an entire company of cavalry with the repeating rifle. And, unlike the Henry that preceded it, the Winchester was fitted with a wooden forestock that protected a man's hand from an overheated barrel. The side ammunition port made it a good deal easier to reload, but the feature that pleased Clay the most was the accuracy of his new weapon. He had acquired quite a reputation for himself as a marksman when he was in the army, so he appreciated Mr. Winchester's dedication to accuracy. While he might grudgingly admit that the army's single-shot Springfield could be a shade better at long range, it was no match for his Winchester under most conditions.

In one sense, he felt a measure of guilt for accepting the rifle. It had been a peace offering from his father's brother—an attempt to make amends for his decision to remain in New Haven when the war broke out. But his father and his brothers insisted that he should receive something for donating his share of the farm to his brothers. And they wanted to contribute something of their own toward the mission to rescue Martha. All things considered, he found himself suitably outfitted for the task he had set for himself. Since he was the one going in search of their sister, the whole family had wanted to do their share as well, contributing all they could. Clay figured giving up his share of the farm to his brothers was fair—he never had any strong urges toward farming, anyway.

A natural feeling of uneasiness about riding into a Union army post descended upon him as he passed the outbuildings, and headed toward a building with a flagpole before it. The war had been over for a year, but it was not easy to rid himself of the sense that he was riding into an enemy camp. Blue bellies, as he had come to know them, were everywhere as he made his way at a slow walk up to the headquarters building. He had no earthly idea where to go in search of his sister, but he knew that Robert Vinings's letter had been sent from Laramie. So that looked to be the natural place to start.

As he stepped down from the saddle, he heard a voice behind him. "That's a right fine-lookin' horse you got there, mister."

Clay's hand automatically clamped around the butt of the Winchester, pulling it out of the saddle sling as he dismounted. Turning toward the voice, he found a young private smiling at him. Realizing at once that the soldier's remark had been nothing more than a casual compliment, he rested his rifle in the crook of his elbow and returned the greeting. "Thanks. He's a pretty stout horse, all right." He remembered to give a silent thanks to the lieutenant who had originally owned him—glad that the horse had been the personal property of the officer, and consequently, had no army brand. "Is this where I can find the commanding officer?"

"Usually," the private replied. "But he ain't here now. He's out at the peace talks." When Clay's blank expression told the soldier that he didn't know what the young man was talking about, the private explained. "There's a big powwow going on with a bunch of the Injuns. He's over to that. Sergeant McCoy is inside. More'n likely he can tell you most anything you need to know."

"Thanks," Clay replied, and stepped up on the porch.

Sergeant Lionel McCoy was polite—friendly, even—but there wasn't much help he could offer. The two men Clay inquired about, Robert and Charley Vinings, had been to see the colonel some time back. They had asked for help in finding Martha, but the colonel could offer very little assistance. Due to the fact that their cabin was over four days' ride from Laramie, and there was little chance in overtaking a war party after so much time had passed, the colonel could see no wisdom in mounting a patrol to ride that distance. Since they had been camped in Sioux country—and weren't supposed to be there, he reminded them—the best he could offer was to inquire about the woman during the peace talks. McCoy told Clay that many bands of Sioux had gathered to talk of peace with the army. The colonel had asked about a white woman captive, but none of the chiefs had any knowledge of one in any of their villages. Beyond that, there was very little the army could do.

"What about the two men?" Clay asked. "Do you know where they are now?"

"I'm sorry, mister. I'd like to help you, but I don't know what their plans were when they left here. One of 'em was pretty hot about it, as I recall. I reckon he expected the colonel to send about a dozen patrols out lookin' for the lady. The colonel tried to explain that it would be a useless waste. We don't have the manpower to go chasing all over creation lookin' for one woman." Realizing that his tone might be reflecting a sense of indifference on the part of the army, Sergeant McCoy added, "You might check with O.C. Owens at the sutler's store. I saw them hangin' around there before they left."

"Much obliged," Clay said, and took his leave.

O.C. Owens, a wiry man in his early sixties, barely glanced up from the counter when the tall young man walked into his store. O.C. had spent most of his life trapping and trading among the Indians before failing eyesight and frazzled nerves reduced him to clerking in the sutler's store. And he had seen enough young greenhorns, fresh off the pilgrims' trail, to recognize one without close inspection. "Mornin' to you, sir," he offered politely as Clay made his way through an array of blankets and trinkets—meant for Indian trade—as well as stacks of canned goods and boxes of dried apples to supplement the soldiers' fare. "What can I do for you?"

"Mornin'," Clay returned. "Are you Mr. Owens?"

"I am."

"I'm hoping you can help me. I'm looking for two fellows from Virginia. Sergeant McCoy said you might be able to help me. He said they were hanging around here for a while." O.C.'s eyebrows lifted slightly, and his face took on a cautious look—a look that Clay would learn to expect in this part of the country when a stranger came asking questions about anybody. Clay went on, "One of 'em's my brother-in-law. My sister was stolen by some Indians, and I'm trying to find them."

O.C. hesitated a few seconds while he appraised the straightforward young man. Finding no deceit in the young man's eyes, he said, "They was here, all right. Did some tradin' with me. Vinings was the name, if I recall." When Clay nodded, O.C. continued. "So the lady that got stole was your sister . . ."

"That's right," Clay replied, anxious to know if the man could give him any help. If Owens couldn't, he wouldn't know where to start looking for Martha.

"And you come all the way out here from Virginia to try to find your sister," O.C. went on.

"That's right," Clay said in a matter-of-fact tone. "If she's still alive, I aim to find her."

There was something in the young man's bearing that told O.C. this was no idle boast. He probably meant what he said. He might find her, but most likely he'd die trying. "You know much about the territory north and west of here?" He asked it knowing that Clay had probably never set foot west of the Missouri before.

"No," Clay confirmed. "But Robert and Charley have been out here for over a year. I was hoping I could catch up with them, if I just had some idea where they're searching for my sister."

O.C. said nothing for a few moments while he took a long hard look at the young man across the counter from him, deciding what he was going to say. Finally he told Clay what he knew to be true. "Young feller, I don't know how good you know your brother-in-law, but them two boys ain't got no intentions of lookin' fer your sister. They found out the army ain't gonna go lookin' fer her, and they wasn't too interested in ridin' into Injun territory and takin' a chance on losing their own hair." He watched Clay closely for his reaction, but he saw no shock in the young man's eyes, just a stone-cold glint, and a noticeable set of his jaw. "They had a little gold dust they traded for a new outfit, and joined up with a party from St. Louis headed fer the gold fields up in Montana territory."

Clay said nothing for a long moment while he thought over what O.C. had just told him. He could not really say he was surprised that Robert and Charley Vinings lacked the intestinal fortitude to venture into hostile country. *But, dammit, Martha was Robert's wife!* It was hard to understand a man like this. Clay could feel the anger rising in his spleen, and the thought of Robert and Charley riding off to look for gold while Martha was suffering who-knows-what, was incentive enough to find the two cowards if he had to ride all over Indian territory to do it. But first, he reminded himself, he had to find Martha.

"You'll be going back to Virginia, then?"

Clay glanced up from his thoughts to look O.C. straight in the eye. "No," he answered softly. "I'm not going back to Virginia. I came out here to find my sister, and I expect that's what I'll do."

"That camp them fellers had was up in the Black Hills, if they was tellin' the truth about it. The Sioux is mighty particular about white men messin' around in that part of the country. Tell you the truth, it's a dad-blamed miracle that them two boys got outta there with their scalps." He paused to gauge the effect of his words on Clay, then went on. "A man sure oughta know which way his stick floats if he's thinkin' 'bout ridin' into Injun country."

"I understand what you're trying to tell me, Mr. Owens—and I appreciate it. But Martha is my sister, and I reckon I'll just have to chance it. I can't just cross her off and forget about it. Like her husband did," he added.

O.C. shook his head slowly back and forth while studying the young man standing before him. There was something about this young fellow—a quiet confidence that made a man think he'd do to winter with—and would watch his partner's back in a fight.

Clay started to thank him for his help, but O.C. interrupted. "I tell you what, son. If you're determined to go get yourself kilt, I'll give you the best piece of advice I can give you. Ride on down the river about thirty miles to where Red Cloud's Sioux is camped. There'll be other chiefs there, too. But he's near the tent the soldiers set up for the talks. Tell one of the soldiers there that you want to talk to Badger. You find Badger, you tell him O.C. sent you. He might help you." O.C. paused, then, "Might not, too, but it's worth your while to try."

"Badger," Clay repeated. "Is he a soldier?"

"Nah, he scouts for the army when he feels like it. He's the only man I know that moves freely through all the Sioux camps, whether they're at war or not. Folks might think the famous Jim Bridger is the Injuns' friend, but the Sioux look at Badger as one of their own kind. And I reckon he is more Lakota than white. Anyway, you find Badger—tell him what you're planning to do."

Clay had little difficulty in finding the meeting site. There were hundreds of Indian campfires along the banks of the river. It seemed that in every direction he looked, there were groups of Sioux or Cheyenne warriors talking among themselves, and between the groups of lodges, young warriors rode back and forth on their ponies, proudly displaying the nimble-footed quickness of their mounts. Clay had never seen this many Indians gathered in one place before. They by far outnumbered the detachment of soldiers deployed near a large tent in the center of the meeting ground. The sides were rolled up on the tent to let the warm breeze through. Inside, Clay could see a small group of officers seated on camp chairs while, before them, maybe fifteen or more Indians sat on the ground. The thought struck him that the soldiers would be helpless to defend themselves against such numbers should the treaty talks turn nasty.

Feeling as if he were riding into a boiling stew of hostility, Clay continued forward. Looking neither right nor left, he made straight toward the large tent, his body erect in the saddle, ignoring the blatant stares of the warriors he passed. *Mr. Owens said these were peace talks,* he thought, as one after another warrior reined up to inspect the magnificent chestnut he rode. *If these savages are peaceful, I don't want to see them when they're on the warpath.*

Once through the ring of Sioux and Cheyenne warriors that surrounded the tent area, Clay nudged Red into a trot until he reached the detachment of mounted infantry that represented the army's strength. A group of several soldiers standing at ease before the tent watched him approach with obvious disinterest. When he pulled up before them and dismounted, one of them asked if he could help him.

"I'm looking for a man named Badger. I was told I could find him here."

The soldier, a man of perhaps forty or forty-five, with sergeant's stripes on his arm, scratched his chin as he searched his memory. "Badger? I don't know anybody by that name." He turned to his companions, and asked, "Any you boys know somebody named Badger?" When no one did, he turned back to Clay. "I'm sorry, mister," shaking his head apologetically. "Is he one of the peace commissioners?"

"I don't know," Clay replied, "I don't think so. O.C. Owens, over at the sutler's store, said I could find him here."

The sergeant shook his head. The name meant nothing to him. "Sorry I can't help you."

"Well, much obliged," Clay said, and turned

around, looking at the surrounding Indian camps as if hoping to discover some clue that might tell him where he should go from there. He was about to take his leave when the sergeant stopped him.

"Hold on a minute. Here's somebody who might know."

Clay turned to see a tall thin man with scraggly whiskers and deep-set eyes stepping out of the tent to stretch his legs for a bit. The expression on his face reflected pain from joints grown stiff with age, as he rolled his shoulders to loosen them. He seemed to pay no attention to the small group outside the tent entrance until the sergeant called to him. "Mr. Bridger, feller here's looking for somebody called Badger."

Bridger cocked his head to give Clay a looking over. After a long moment, during which he appeared to be considering whether he was even going to acknowledge the statement, he finally responded with a simple, "Is that a fact?"

"Yessir," Clay replied. "Badger—I don't know his first name. O.C. Owens said I might find him over here."

"I don't know that he's got a first name," Bridger said, "and I've knowed him for twenty years." He continued to look Clay over for a few moments more. Then deciding that Clay was most likely looking for Badger for peaceful reasons, he took a few steps away from the entrance and pointed toward a group of lodges close by the riverbank. "Them's Red Cloud's people. Find Little Hawk's lodge, and Badger will most likely be nearby."

"Much obliged," Clay said, turned and nodded to the sergeant, then stepped up into the saddle.

"That's a right fine-looking sorrel you've got there," the sergeant commented.

"Thanks," Clay replied, smiling. "The fellow I got

him from still wishes he hadn't let him go." Red
snorted in agreement, and leaped forward at the touch
of Clay's heels in his sides, showing off for the benefit
of those watching, as he pranced shamelessly away
from the tent.

Clay guided the big chestnut stallion toward the
group of lodges pointed out by Jim Bridger, aware of
the eyes that silently watched his progress. He knew
very little about the wild people who inhabited the
lands west of the Missouri, only tales occasionally
brought back east from mule skinners who made the
long trip hauling freight—and newspaper accountings
of Indian raids upon helpless settlers. So he felt an
uneasiness that made him want to keep his hand resting upon the stock of his Winchester as he guided his
horse around small groups of warriors talking around
their campfires. As he approached each group, the
talking stopped while every pair of eyes turned toward
him. Not sure if he should appear cordial or polite,
he just kept his eyes straight ahead while he passed.

There was a gathering of six men seated before a
tipi decorated with drawings of warriors on horses
chasing buffalo. One of them was a white man, and
Clay had no doubts that this was the man he sought.
Sitting Indian-style on the ground, eating from a bowl
carved from bone, was the man known simply as Badger. At first glance, one might mistake him for an
Indian. He was dressed much in the same fashion as
his companions—entirely in animal skins, except for
the weathered old campaign hat with the front and
back brim turned up. Upon closer inspection, one
would notice the stubble of a beard, more gray than
the black of his shoulder-length hair. Upon even closer
inspection, one would realize that the clear blue eyes
were not those of an Indian. And those eyes were

watching Clay closely as he rode up, although his face gave no indication of even a passing curiosity.

"Mr. Badger?" Clay inquired, stepping down from the saddle.

Badger's five Lakota companions, all silently staring at the lone white rider up to that point, now turned as one to watch Badger's response. "I'm Badger," was the simple reply.

If Clay had expected a more cordial greeting, he would be disappointed, for the crusty old scout held a cool reserve for strangers, especially white strangers. Already feeling the coolness of his reception, Clay stepped closer to the men, and said, "O.C. Owens said that you might be able to help me."

"That so?" Badger replied. "And who might you be?"

Badger listened, unblinking and expressionless, as Clay told him who he was and the mission he had taken upon himself to find the Indians who had stolen his sister. If Clay's story provoked any compassion from the rough scout, it was not obvious to the eye. Badger's first reaction to the account of Martha Vinings's abduction was that she and her husband weren't supposed to be there in the first place. It seemed simple logic to him that, if a man sneaked into a bear's cave to steal his food, "He might oughta expect to run into a bear." If this young fellow's sister and her husband were up in the Black Hills, then they probably got what they deserved. The longer Clay talked, however, the more Badger's coolness thawed, for he soon realized that Clay was not a settler, a gold miner, or a trader. His only reason for being there was, as the young man had stated, simply to find his sister. It couldn't hurt to at least show some hospitality.

"Set yourself down, young feller, and have something to eat."

Clay dropped Red's reins, and settled himself opposite Badger, nodding politely to the other faces seated around the fire. They nodded cordially in return, having seen Badger's friendly gesture. A solidly built middle-aged Indian woman came from the tipi and glanced briefly into the iron pot hanging over the fire. Satisfied that there was enough boiled meat to accomodate another visitor, she quickly moved away again—but not before giving the young white man a thorough looking over.

Badger handed Clay his bowl, and said, "Here, dip in there and get some of that meat." When Clay nodded but hesitated a moment, he added, "It's deer meat . . . it wouldn't be polite not to eat some, even if you ain't hungry." He smiled and Clay realized that Badger's Indian friends did not understand English.

"Thanks," Clay said, and dipped eagerly into the iron pot. He *was* hungry, but he had hesitated because of stories he had heard about some Indians' love for dog. And this gristled-looking mountain man looked as close to an Indian as a white man could.

Badger gave his guest a few minutes to eat some of the venison before talking again. "Now . . . Mr. Culver, was it? What was you lookin' for me for?"

"I was hoping you could help me find my sister," Clay answered. He felt that Badger had already assumed as much. "I don't have a lot of money to pay you, but my family scraped up a little, and I can pay you fifty Union dollars to help me look for her."

Badger didn't say anything right away while he studied Clay's face. When he did respond, it wasn't to encourage Clay's resolve. "You know, son, there's a heap of territory between the Black Hills and the divide. And there's a whole lot of different tribes and villages spread all over creation. I wouldn't be honest if I didn't tell you there ain't much hope in finding one white woman in all that country." Seeing the disappointment in Clay's face, he tried to console him somewhat. "Just because she was took don't mean she's being treated bad. Most Injuns treat captive women pretty decent."

"Can you guide me?" Clay asked simply.

"I'm sorry, son, but I'm fixing to head back to the Powder River country with my family." He gestured toward the tipi with his head. "I've been scouting for the army for the last six months, but they've laid me off for the time being. They said the army's cut 'em way back on expenses. They even cut Bridger back to five dollars a day." Seeing no weakening of the determination in Clay's eyes, he offered one favor. "About the best I can do for you is find out if any of the Sioux has got your sister. 'Course all the Sioux ain't here at these talks, but I can find out from the ones who are here. Most likely they'll know about some of the others."

Clay was silent for a few moments, obviously disappointed. Then he thanked Badger for his help. "I'm much obliged to you, Mr. Badger, but I reckon if I can't find somebody who knows the country, I'll just have to go by myself."

Badger shook his head slowly. "You seem like a nice enough young feller. You're just gonna get yourself kilt, especially now since these talks ain't goin' so good. There's already bad blood over so many white folks traipsing through Lakota hunting grounds. That's what these talks was all about. The army said they wanted to get the Injuns to quit attackin' wagon trains traveling across their lands on the way to the gold diggings north of the Yellowstone. Red Cloud told 'em that his warriors wouldn't be attackin' the dang settlers if they wasn't trespassin' into Lakota huntin' grounds. Now, come to find out, some colonel just showed up with a whole passel of soldiers, fixin' to build forts along the trail whether the Injuns agree to it or not. Well, that didn't set too pretty with Red Cloud. He's already said him and his folks is packin' up and goin' back home. There's gonna be trouble over this, and you don't wanna be caught in the middle of Lakota territory right now." He pushed his hat back while he scratched his head, and paused to see if his words had any effect on Clay. "Why, hell," he went on, "you wouldn't get ten miles from Fort Laramie before some buck bushwhacked you for that fancy horse you're ridin'."

"I appreciate your concern, Mr. Badger, and I thank you for the food, but I best be on my way." He got to his feet, and turned to leave. He was about to put a foot in the stirrup when he thought of something more. "Could I trouble you to point me toward the Black Hills?"

"You're still set on going alone?"

"I reckon I don't have much choice. I've got to find my sister."

Badger shook his head, exasperated. "You do beat all I've ever seen. How the hell are you gonna find somebody when you don't even know where *you* are?" Before Clay could answer, he went on. "Just hold on for a minute, and let me think." Ordinarily, Badger wouldn't care if a greenhorn wanted to commit suicide or not. But this Clay Culver showed a lot of quiet determination that he couldn't help but admire. It would be a shame to think of this young man lying cold somewhere out on the prairie while some buck rode off on his horse. *But, hell, I ain't got no time to wet-nurse no innocent young pup.* He thought about it a few moments longer while Clay stood there, puzzling over the old scout's hesitation. Then making up his mind, Badger said, "I can take you as far as the Powder, but you'll be on your own from there."

Clay could not hide the excitement Badger's change of heart brought. "Thank you, Mr. Badger," he said, beaming. "I really appreciate it. When will we be starting?"

"Tomorrow morning, sunup. Little Hawk—that's my wife's brother—anyway, Little Hawk's band is pullin' out of here tomorrow, and we'll be travelin' with them. So if you still think you want to go to the Powder River country, you'd best go on back and fetch your pack animal and your possibles, 'cause I ain't gonna waste time lookin' around for you come sunup."

"I don't have a packhorse. All my possibles are in that saddle pack," Clay replied.

Badger was amazed. "You mean you come all the way out here from Virginia with nothin' more'n you could carry on that horse?" Clay nodded. "Well, mister, you shore do travel light. I'll give you that." He shook his head, chuckling as he said, "You must not eat a helluva lot."

Clay shrugged. "I brought a little coffee and salt from home. I hunted for what I needed to eat. I'm a fair shot with a rifle." He didn't feel the necessity to tell the old scout that he had slept in the open for over two years when he was in the army—winter and summer—with nothing but a rubber sheet and a blanket. He had flint and steel, his new Winchester, and a Green River knife. As long as he didn't run Red to death, he had felt confident that he could make it all right. Sleeping and feeding himself had not been the problem that feeding Red had been. Like most army mounts, Red had been grain-fed. The little bit of grain Clay packed had lasted only eight days. After that,

Red had to learn to survive on nothing more than prairie grass.

"Well, boy, you've got grit a'plenty." Badger started to say more, then another thought struck him. "What was you gonna do if you found your sister? Throw her on that horse, too?"

"I reckon not. I reckon I planned to get another horse."

"Where was you gonna git it?"

"The same place I got this one," Clay replied, his face expressionless.

Badger's grizzled face cracked with a thin smile. He didn't have to ask where Clay had gotten the sorrel; he had a pretty good idea from the determined look in the young man's eyes. It was still too early to judge, but Badger had a feeling that he was going to like Clay Culver. "Well, Clay Culver, come on with me, and I'll show you where you can tie that fancy horse of your'n. You can sleep in my lodge tonight."

Badger got to his feet. Speaking in the Lakota tongue, he excused himself from his companions around the small campfire. Clay, of course, could not understand his words, but from the laughter of the five warriors, he guessed that he was the butt of the joke. He didn't care. Badger had agreed to take him to the Powder River country, and that was a start toward finding Martha.

"First thing," Badger said as Clay followed him toward a large tipi near the center of the camp, "we'd best go see Little Hawk."

Although there were many curious eyes that followed their progress as they made their way through the camp, Clay sensed few hostile stares. For the most part, there were simply looks of curiosity, no doubt wondering what business the white man had with their chief. Little Hawk, upon hearing Badger's greeting, came out of his lodge to meet them. Wearing only a breechclout and leggings, the chief stood tall and straight, almost as tall as Clay himself, and half a head taller than Badger. His chest and left shoulder were marked with old scars, wounds from many battles. Though his hair was generously streaked with gray, he still had the rigid bearing of a young warrior, and Clay sensed a quiet dignity about the man that immediately commanded his respect.

Badger and Little Hawk exchanged polite greetings before the old scout explained Clay's presence in the camp. Clay stood back and waited while they talked, glancing around him occasionally whenever members of the tribe paused to stare at him. He was beginning to feel a bit uneasy, and he couldn't help but recall some of the bloodcurdling tales he had heard back East about Indian atrocities. Still, Little Hawk looked friendly enough when he glanced past Badger and nodded at Clay.

"Little Hawk says you're welcome in his village," Badger finally said when he turned again toward Clay. He felt no need to tell his guest that he was welcome for two reasons only: He was vouched for by Badger, and he was not wearing a soldier's uniform. After the recently unsuccessful peace talks, Badger knew there was going to be war between the Lakota and the soldiers. Red Cloud had spoken for Little Hawk and many others when he angrily withdrew from the talks. The Lakota would protect their hunting grounds from any white men attempting to travel over the trail that Bozeman had blazed. There would be bloodshed if the wagons kept coming.

The situation was not an easy one for Badger himself, for he was forced to make a decision as well. He had worked for the army as a scout for many years, but his wife and her family were in Little Hawk's camp. Little Hawk was his friend. He could not draw the tommyhawk against his friend—his wife's brother. Nor could he in good conscience draw down on a soldier. Already, Badger's mind was beginning to ache with these troubling thoughts, and when the time came to choose, he hoped there would be some out for him. For the time being, he would return to his wife's village and think on it later. Badger had never bothered his mind by looking too far ahead into the future, preferring to deal with each new day as it dawned. *Hell, maybe Red Cloud and the other chiefs will forget about making war on the soldiers.* Even as he thought it, he knew better. It was coming, sure as water was wet and flowed downhill.

Turning back to Clay, he said, "Come on. You can pull your saddle off and throw it in my lodge. Then you can turn your horse out with the pony herd to graze." When he saw the young man arch an eyebrow in response, he chided, "Afraid somebody'll steal him? All Injuns are horse thieves, but they don't steal horses from their own people. Ain't nobody gonna steal your horse."

Clay didn't say anything for a few moments while he looked around him at the circle of lodges. "How come those horses are hobbled by the lodges instead of running loose with the others?"

"It ain't unusual for a man to keep his favorite war pony hobbled by his lodge, in case he might need him in a hurry," Badger answered patiently. "But there ain't much danger of gittin' attacked here at Laramie. Some warriors just do it, anyway—habit, I reckon. Hell, my horses are running with the rest of 'em."

In spite of Badger's assurance, Clay was reluctant to turn Red loose in the company of several hundred Indian ponies. The old scout appeared to be a straight-talking person, but Clay still harbored some inborn

sense of suspicion. He had heard some stories of the
tricks and treachery of some Indians, so he cautioned
himself to be wary. Granted, the stories he had heard
were second- and thirdhand. Still, it might not be wise
to discount them entirely. How could he be sure Badger was not the biggest scoundrel of all? Clay decided
he would never relax his guard that night, and he
stood watching the big chestnut for several long minutes before finally turning away to return to Badger's
tipi. Reluctant or not, he was forced to trust the crusty
old mountain man, for without his help he had no
chance of finding Martha. Red, on the other hand, did
not share his master's cautious intuition, and was soon
grazing happily in the midst of a sea of horses. Clay
watched for a moment longer before drawing his rifle
from the boot and throwing his saddle on his shoulder.
The shiny new rifle did not escape Badger's eye.

"I swear, that's one of them new Winchesters,
ain't it?"

"Yep," Clay replied and handed the weapon to the
old scout.

Badger took it eagerly and examined it closely,
bringing it to his shoulder and down again several
times, sighting on various targets around the encamp-
ment. "I heard about it, but I ain't ever seen one.
That's some rifle. Is it as accurate as it is pretty?"

"I can hit most anything I aim at," Clay replied
modestly, causing Badger to cock an eyebrow.

"I hope so," the old mountain man stated evenly
as he returned the weapon.

Supper that night consisted of some more boiled
meat, placed before him in the same bowl he had used
that afternoon. In addition, Badger's wife put meat
cakes of some kind between Clay and her husband.
Badger picked one up and began gnawing on it, indi-
cating to Clay that he should do the same. Clay had

learned not to be particular about what he ate when he was in the army, but he hesitated before taking a bite of these cakes, picking one up and turning it over and back, to examine it.

Badger seemed amused by his tenderfoot guest's cautious antics. "It's pemmican," he volunteered. "It's good. Take a bite."

Clay smiled, embarrassed that his caution had been that transparent. "What is it?" he asked.

"Pemmican," Badger repeated in a tone that indicated he thought even a greenhorn from back East should be familiar with the term. "This here's dried buffalo Gray Bird pounded up with some fat and marrow and wild cherries to give it a little flavoring. We won't have no more fresh meat till we get a chance to do some hunting tomorrow or the next day."

Satisfied then that he knew the ingredients, Clay bit off a piece of pemmican. To his surprise, it proved to be quite appetizing. He slowly chewed it, then bit off a larger chunk. Nodding his approval, he looked up at Gray Bird, who was watching him intently. She smiled broadly, then went back outside to tend the fire. Still nodding, Clay turned toward a grinning Badger. "I like pemmican," he said.

Clay awoke the next morning amid a whirlwind of activity as the women of Little Hawk's camp made preparations to leave. He opened his eyes to discover Badger standing over him.

"Better 'rouse your ass outta that blanket, son, or Gray Bird'll strike this tipi right on top of you."

Clay sat straight up, ashamed to be caught sleeping when it appeared everyone else was up and working. He took another look at Badger, a wide grin on the old scout's face, and sprang up from his bed as if his blanket was on fire. "Damn," he mumbled, "I don't know why I slept so late." Feeling the warm flush of embarrassment creeping up his neck, he remembered his intention of the night before to sleep with one eye open.

Gray Bird was already untying the rawhide straps that tethered the bottom of the tipi when Clay walked outside. She smiled at him and said something that he of course did not understand. He took it to be a "Good morning," since she did not look as if she expected a reply. At that particular moment, he was more concerned with what to do about a full bladder, when to worsen his situation, Badger offered him a cup of coffee. Clay looked around him nervously. There was no obvious place to relieve himself now that the rising sun eliminated all the convenient shadows of the night before. There was not even a tree within a hundred yards of the lodges. His concern must have been transparent, for Badger grinned and said, "You can go behind the tipi, but you'd best be about it before Gray Bird takes it down."

Clay glanced at the Indian woman, still busily loosening the ties around the bottom of the tipi. He wasn't any too comfortable with the thought of doing his business with Gray Bird moving like a busy beaver as she worked her way around the circumference of the lodge. But if he didn't get to it, there wouldn't even be a lodge to hide behind, so he didn't hesitate further. It didn't help his sense of modesty that Badger was so highly amused by his predicament.

Although there were other lodges around Gray Bird's, no one seemed to pay any attention to the embarrassed white man standing close behind the tipi, pleading with his sluggish organ to hurry. Just managing to finish as Gray Bird worked her way to the rear of the tipi, Clay strode quickly back to the fire where Badger was still holding the cup of coffee for him.

"I reckon I've got room to hold it now," Clay said,

making an effort to seem unperturbed. One look at Badger's beaming face told him that it was not convincing. *By God,* he told himself, *I'm damn sure not going to be the last one up anymore.*

By the time the sun had gained a reasonable foothold in the morning sky, the Lakota camp was loaded on packhorses and travois and ready to depart the banks of the North Platte. Clay could not help but be amazed by the efficiency of it. The women did all the work, while the men saw to their horses. Clay concerned himself with saddling Red and repacking his own meager supplies while Badger conferred with Little Hawk and other men of the village over the trail to be taken.

Clay no longer harbored cautious feelings as he moved about the camp, for there had been no signs of hostility from anyone. *Besides,* he figured, *if they planned to scalp me, they'd have most likely done it last night while I was sleeping like a baby.* Still, he remembered what Badger had said the night before— there would be war between the Sioux and the soldiers. Clay told himself that he would not be concerned with any such war, other than to steer clear of it. His main concern was to find Martha. That accomplished, he wouldn't mind catching up with Robert and Charley Vinings. He figured he had a score to settle with those two. As he looked around him in this seemingly peaceful camp, he could not imagine that he had any cause to fight these people. And he was still too fresh from Appomattox to feel any loyalty to Yankee soldiers. *If the Sioux and the Union army want to fight, let 'em. It ain't none of my affair.*

For the next few days, Clay rode beside Badger in the advanced scouting party, as Little Hawk's village traveled toward the Powder River valley. Behind them, the rest of the village stretched out for over a mile with the horse herd in the middle of the procession. They were followed by women, some riding, their lodges and possessions on travois, leaving deep scars on the prairie floor. Flanking scouts rode far out from the moving village, vigilant for signs of game or any enemy that might threaten the safety of the people. Children were all about the wide column, some riding ponies, some on foot, running in and out among the leisurely moving horses. Clay looked back on the procession behind him. For all the appearance of bustle and confusion, it was surprisingly efficient, and it certainly was a spectacle for a greenhorn's eye.

According to Badger, the trail they traveled was generally in the same direction as the disputed Bozeman Trail, which more and more white wagon trains were using. "This is what the Sioux is all het up about," he said. "This feller Bozeman cut a shortcut to the goldfields right smack through Sioux territory, and Red Cloud and the other chiefs aim to put a stop to it. And they didn't get it done peaceful back yonder at Fort Laramie, so they figure on gettin' it done another way."

"If it comes to war, as you say, whose side are you gonna take?"

Clay had asked the one question that had troubled Badger for more than a few days now. Unlike Clay, Badger felt a strong loyalty to the blue-coated troopers at Fort Laramie. They were just one army to him, he had never had to concern himself with north and south. He had served as scout on more patrols than he could remember, and many of the officers and enlisted men were his friends. Added to this was the fact that he was a white man—even though he had an Indian wife, a man couldn't go against his own kind. On the other hand, he couldn't see himself leading a cavalry patrol against Little Hawk. This was one of the reasons he was now going back to the Powder River country with his wife—he preferred to be away from the fort when Red Cloud announced an end to the peace talks by walking out. "I don't rightly know," he finally answered Clay. "I reckon I'm on both sides, so I guess I'll try to stay clear of it." He didn't say anything more on the subject, but he was giving a great deal of consideration to the notion of going back up in the mountains, trapping, until the fighting was over.

It didn't take long for Clay to become comfortable in his new living arrangements with Badger and Gray Bird. He even became accustomed to Gray Bird's unblinking gaze, which seemed always upon him—and which immediately transformed into a broad smile that made her eyes crinkle whenever he caught her staring. *The woman certainly knows how to take care of her husband,* he thought, watching her scurry around to anticipate Badger's every need. There was little wonder why the old scout chose this way of life.

On the second day out from Laramie, one of the outriders spotted a herd of antelope grazing near a small stream. A hunting party was organized to obtain some fresh meat for the camp, and Clay was invited to join them. Realizing that it was an opportunity to learn something from the skilled Sioux hunters, he stayed back, watching closely as they stalked the nervous beasts. When they had worked their way into range, however, Clay was then confident that he could hold his own from that point on. Unlimbering the Winchester, he brought two of the antelope down with two shots placed neatly behind the front legs. No one else got more than one animal. His marksmanship drew nods of approval from the other hunters, and he turned to see an admiring smile on Badger's face.

"That's some right fancy shootin'," Badger allowed.

He had been more than a little curious to see if Clay was a real rifleman, or just a greenhorn with a shiny new toy. "Yessir, that shore is a mighty slick-lookin' rifle. I was wonderin' if you could hit anything with it."

"I generally hit what I'm aiming at," was Clay's simple response. It was not a boast, merely an honest answer. He tossed the rifle to Badger since the old scout looked as if he wanted to examine it again.

After checking it over thoroughly, Badger admitted, "It's a sight fancier than my old Henry. That's a fact. But I reckon me and my rifle has got to know each other pretty well. We sorta take care of each other."

"I reckon any rifle's only as good as the man pulling the trigger," Clay replied when Badger returned the Winchester to his hand.

"I reckon," Badger agreed. The old scout was beginning to realize there was a good bit of steel under the calm exterior of his new young friend.

There was a big feast in the camp that night. Clay ate his fill of the fresh meat. It was a new experience for him; he had never eaten antelope before. Gray Bird scraped and cleaned the hides, rolling them up to be worked on later when they reached the Powder.

Lying beneath the open sky of the prairie, Clay felt a sense of peace and belonging that he had not experienced elsewhere. Looking around him at the people who had already befriended him, he wondered at the tales of the "savage redman" he had heard before. Far from the savage image they had been given by the white man in the East, these Lakota were a happy, fun-loving people, who enjoyed their families and were as one with the wild land they roamed. He decided then that he had much to learn about the nomadic natives of the Great Plains.

On the morning of the fourth day they entered the foothills, and Clay saw the first dark silhouettes of the tall mountains called the Black Hills. As he reined Red to a stop and sat gazing at the silent range to the northeast, Badger pulled up beside him.

"Paha Sapa—the Black Hills—if your brother-in-law knew for sure he was in the Black Hills, then somewhere in them mountains is where his cabin was."

"I expect that's where I'll start looking, then," Clay replied.

"It'll be a day or so before we git directly west of them mountains. Wait till we strike the Belle Fourche—that'll be time enough for you to head out. And don't go talkin' about going into the Black Hills. Some of these folks know a little white-man talk, and them mountains is sacred territory to the Lakota—big medicine. They don't look too kindly on any white man ridin' through there." He let it go at that, but he was thinking, if Clay went riding off into the hills by himself, not knowing anything about the country, it would likely be the last anybody would see of him. *Damn greenhorns, can't wait to git theirselves kilt,* he thought, but that wasn't what really bothered him. He had taken a liking to this determined young man, and that was what bothered his mind. He didn't enjoy the thought of Clay's scalp on some warrior's lance. And even though he was convinced that Clay would give a good account of himself in a fight, he knew his young friend didn't understand the way of survival in Indian territory. *Ain't no skin off my back,* he tried to tell himself.

When Little Hawk's band of Lakotas reached the Belle Fourche, there was a Sioux hunting party already camped there from a village near the Tongue River. They were led by a cousin of Little Hawk's wife named Black Crow. The camp was busy preparing for a hunt the following morning on a herd of buffalo they had been following since early that afternoon. Little Hawk decided to take advantage of the opportunity to add to the village's food supply. Since the neighboring Sioux hunting party was small, Black Crow welcomed Little Hawk's hunters.

According to Black Crow, the buffalo were grazing in a shallow valley a short distance to the east of the river, working their way slowly toward the north. His scouts had found a deep gulch ahead of the herd, a bit to the east, that would serve as a perfect trap. The problem had been that his hunters were few, and there were not enough of them to stampede the herd and turn them toward the gulch. For that reason, they had planned to simply ride into the herd on their ponies, killing as many as they could before the massive herd of buffalo moved through the valley. So it was that Black Crow looked upon Little Hawk's arrival as a definite sign of good fortune. Now there would be a sufficent number of hunters to drive the buffalo toward the gulch, where a great many of the mob would be forced over the edge of the open ravine by those in the rear.

This was a time of excitement for Clay, causing him to forget for a moment the single-minded purpose of his journey. He had never seen a buffalo, even at a distance, and he was anxious to join the hunt. Badger advised him that this was not going to be like any hunting he had done in the past. This was simply an exercise to store up their food cache with a great quantity of meat and hides.

"We're just gonna run 'em over the edge of a gulch so they'll break their necks." Seeing a look of slight disappointment in Clay's face, he added, "That rifle of your'n wouldn't hardly knock a bull down, anyway, without you place your shots right." He nodded toward a group of warriors readying their weapons. "Now those boys can take one down with nothin' but them bows, but they have to ride in close and place their arrows right behind the last rib for a lung shot."

Clay nodded soberly. He carefully considered every bit of information Badger offered, but he was confident that his Winchester could bring one of the great beasts down if a Sioux hunter could do it with an arrow.

"It wouldn't hurt to lay over here a couple of days, anyway," Badger continued. "We're gonna need a good supply of dried meat if we're goin' lookin' for your sister." He shot an appraising look in Clay's direction. "You might find a buffalo robe to be right handy, too, since you ain't got nothin' but that one blanket. You're gonna need a packhorse, too. Have you got anything to trade?"

"I've got that fifty dollars," Clay replied. He had not missed the fact that Badger had casually said "we" when he spoke of searching for Martha.

"Fifty dollars don't mean much to a Lakota warrior. I don't know if you noticed, but we ain't passed many stores out here on the prairie. Ain't you got nothin' else?"

Clay thought for a moment. "I've got an old army revolver in my saddlebag. It's not very accurate over twenty yards."

"Got any bullets for it?"

"A box."

"That'll do. Gitcha a horse good enough to carry a pack, anyway."

They started out for the buffalo before sunup the next morning, following Black Crow's hunters as they rode silently through the foothills. Even the ponies seemed to be aware of the nearness of the great herd, and they moved on muffled hooves through the gently waving prairie grass. Stopping at a point a quarter of a mile downwind, Black Crow divided the hunting party into three groups. Clay and Badger went with the riders who were to cross over the valley and drive the herd from the eastern side. Even at this distance, Clay could smell the great herd as they started milling around in the early morning light. Musky and strong, the scent carried on the morning breeze, filling his head with excitement for the hunt.

Although the plan was for a wholesale slaughter by driving the animals over the steep edge of a gulch, some of the younger warriors were anxious to make individual kills to show off their skill as hunters. Clay watched with interest as the young men stripped down to nothing more than breechclouts and their weapons. He noticed that each hunter tied a rope around his horse's neck and let it trail behind. When Clay asked the purpose of the trailing rope, Badger replied, "To grab a'holt of if he falls off'n his horse."

By the time Clay's party had made a wide circle to come up on the herd's eastern flank, the sun was just beginning to probe the darkened ravines with lengthening fingers of light. They were close to the congregation of milling beasts, so close that Clay could feel the trembling of the earth. Still he had not yet seen them. As they waited for Black Crow's signal, one of Little Hawk's warriors appeared on foot. He wore a wolfskin on his back with the head attached, and he came directly to Badger. While the two talked, there was a great deal of hand gestures and nodding heads, as the man in the wolfskin gave Badger the lay of the land and the most likely avenue of the chase.

When Badger translated the scout's instructions, Clay was curious as to why the man wore a wolfskin when he moved in so close to the buffalo. "Wasn't he afraid he might spook the buffalo with that getup on?"

Badger shook his head. "Nah. Buffalo ain't worried about a wolf or two sneakin' around the herd. They're used to seein' 'em, following along, hopin' to git a chance at a sick animal, or a calf away from the bunch." He was about to expound on the damage a buffalo could do to a wolf when he was interrupted by a loud, high-pitched war whoop from the far side of the valley. The drive was on!

An immediate explosion of noise erupted from the group of riders waiting in the narrow confines of the grassy draw as war whoops and gunfire launched the chase. Clay was caught up in the mob of galloping horses that drove hell-bent for leather out of the mouth of the draw and onto the valley floor. From behind the herd, and from the far side of the valley, the rest of the large hunting party galloped, filling the tiny valley with enough noise and pandemonium to cause confusion in the massive herd of buffalo. The leading bull, and those around him, broke into a run. But due to the size of the herd, the dark mass of shaggy beasts started slowly, with those animals in the rear barely trotting at first—some doing no more than shifting about nervously from side to side—until those just ahead of them began to run. Then like a bobbing sea of massive bodies, the entire herd moved toward the upper end of the valley, slowly gaining momentum until the rearmost were running as fast as the leaders.

Caught up in the excitement, Clay found himself yelling a loud Rebel yell at the top of his lungs, as he let Red have his head. The big sorrel needed no encouragement to race with the Indian ponies, and soon horse and rider were flying down into the valley at don't-give-a-damn speed with no thought toward caution. All around him, the Lakota hunters charged down upon the frantic sea of buffalo. Already, some of the young men were cutting individual buffalo out, as their swift, nimble-footed Indian ponies darted in and out of the moving mass of hair and muscle. One slip would mean sudden death, yet the young braves seemed bent on outdoing each other in their daring.

Clay continued to gallop alongside the herd, following Badger, whose feet were flailing the sides of his horse, beseeching the animal to run faster. By the time they had covered half of the valley, Clay could feel Red gradually losing ground to the smaller Indian ponies, but the big chestnut would not admit defeat, his hooves pounding on the valley floor as he strained with every muscle in his body. The big red horse had too much heart for his own good. For his horse's sake, Clay was relieved when the lead bulls were finally turned at the head of the valley and driven blindly toward the edge of a deep gulch.

The leading bulls, suddenly finding themselves at the edge of a sheer precipice, tried desperately to turn. But there was no way open to them, and like a colossal train wreck, the frantic bodies behind them piled up upon each other until the weight of the massive herd hurled those in front over the edge. The valley was filled with a crescendo of noise, a combination of gunfire, war whoops, and the bawling of the doomed buffalo. A great cloud of dust rolled up the length of the narrow valley, restricting Clay's vision so that the panic-stricken beasts appeared ghostlike as they bumped and stumbled their way onward.

It was not clear through the dusty chaos, but Clay guessed that as many as a hundred buffalo pitched over the steep edge of the gulch before the herd was able to turn itself, and charge toward the open end of the valley. He pulled Red up beside Badger's horse, and the two of them watched the herd until it disap-

peared into the hills. Then they joined the other hunters who were making their way around the steep sides
of the gulch in order to reach the carnage at the bottom. No sooner had the last stragglers of the mam-
moth herd disappeared when the women and children
of Little Hawk's village arrived, ready for the
butchering.

At the bottom of the gulch, Clay was astonished by
the pile of dead and crippled animals. The hunters
were already finishing off those that still bawled or
struggled to rise on broken limbs. It was a mass carnage the likes of which Clay had never before seen
and could not have imagined. He stood back and
watched as the men used their ponies to drag the huge
bodies clear of the pile. Once clear, the women set
upon them immediately, skinning and butchering. Everyone, even the children, took part, working with an
experienced efficiency. Clay, at first thinking this business of stampeding a herd over a cliff was wanton
waste, changed his mind when Badger told him that
almost every bit of each animal would be salvaged.
"Yessir," he expounded, "buffalo's a wondrous animal
to an Injun. The hides are used fer robes and lodge
coverings, the meat is cut in strips and dried, the bones
is used for tools, even the horns and hooves is used—
and he shits firewood. As long as there's buffalo, an
Injun don't need nothin' else. There won't be much
left when these women get through." Clay just shook
his head, amazed by the fever of activity in the
small canyon.

"There'll be a big feed tonight," Badger said.
"You'll git a chance to sample some real good eatin'.
You ever et buffalo hump? Or tongue?"

"Reckon not," Clay said, smiling, "but I'm anxious
to try it."

"Well, you'll git your chance tonight," Badger said, laughing as they walked over to a carcass that Gray Bird was busily butchering.

The scout's wife smiled up at her husband, cut off a bloody chunk, and held it out to him. Badger took the offering eagerly and ripped off a huge bite. His mouth stuffed full, he offered the remainder of the chunk to Clay.

"What is it?" Clay wanted to know.

"Liver," Badger said, extending his hand. "Eat it. It's still warm."

Clay backed away, shaking his head. "No, thanks. I don't eat the insides of any animal, especially if it's not cooked. You can have the guts—I'll eat the outside meat."

Badger laughed. "You don't know what you're missin'. Look at the young'uns workin' on that warm liver—same as candy to Injun young'uns."

"I don't like candy," Clay replied dryly. "There's a helluva lot to eat on a buffalo without having to eat the insides."

"It'll surprise you what a man will eat if he gits hungry enough," Badger said, his expression turning serious for a moment.

Badger's remark triggered a fleeting picture that flashed through Clay's mind of a starving regiment of Confederate soldiers—wearily slogging along roads rendered to rivers of mud by the spring rains—forced to retreat from the trenches at Petersburg in a desperate attempt to avoid Grant's columns. He remembered the utter desolation felt by the hungry troops when supplies promised to be at Amelia Court House were not there. Pushing on toward Appomattox, his belly pasted flat to his backbone, that was a time when he would have eaten raw liver—or a raw chicken—if he could have gotten his hands on one. No, he would not be surprised what a man would eat if he was hungry enough.

As Badger had promised, there was a huge feast that night, as well as the following nights until the last of the work had been done, the meat and hides all packed, and the camp ready to resume the trip to the Powder. Clay acquired a taste for the fat meat of the buffalo's hump immediately. He also found himself to be very comfortable amid the jovial and lighthearted people of Little Hawk's village—so much so that he experienced a sudden feeling of guilt when after two days, he realized that he had not thought about Martha since the hunt began. He promised himself that he would part with his new friends in the morning, and get his mind back on the business of finding his sister.

Although Clay awoke early the next morning, he found himself in an empty lodge. Badger and Gray Bird were already up and preparing to depart the Belle Fourche. Knowing from experience that Gray Bird would not delay the striking of her lodge for a sleepy white man, Clay wasted no time in getting his possibles together. Outside, he declined the offer of some boiled meat from Gray Bird, and seeing no sign of Badger, walked down to the water's edge where he had hobbled Red for the night.

"Don't sass me, Red," Clay warned when the big chestnut side-stepped away from the saddle. The protest was of only one step's duration, then Red stood quietly, accepting the saddle Clay threw on his back. "Probably miss the days after I first got you, when I didn't use a saddle. Don't you, boy?"

"That horse ever answer you back?"

Clay turned to see Badger riding along the riverbank, leading two packhorses. He laughed. "He

doesn't say anything when other folks are around."
He led Red up from the edge of the water to meet
Badger.

"This'un's your'n," Badger said, and handed Clay
the lead rope to a mouse-colored horse with a shaggy
mane. "I traded your pistol for her."

Clay paused to puzzle over the loaded horse.
"What's all that stuff on her back?"

Badger shook his head impatiently, as if bothered
by such an asinine question. "What does it look like?
It's dried meat and skins you're gonna need before
we're through. I swear, Clay, what was you planning
to do if we don't find that sister of your'n before
spring?"

"But I can't pay for those supplies," Clay protested.
"You said yourself, money's no good out here."

"You don't owe nothin' for the meat and skins.
They're your'n. Hell, you helped in the hunt, same as
ever'body else. You're entitled to a share of the
meat." Before Clay could express his appreciation,
Badger changed the subject. "Now, I found out somethin' from one of Black Crow's warriors that might
interest you. He told me him and a couple of his
friends come across a burnt-out cabin in a canyon
deep in the mountains over yonder. There was sign.
Looked to be Blackfoot to him. I'm thinkin' it's
more'n likely the place your sister got stole."

Clay's heart was beating against his chest. "When
did you find out?"

"Couple of days ago."

"Why didn't you tell me sooner?" Clay demanded,
irritated that Badger had seen fit to sit on the
information.

Unfazed by his young friend's agitation, Badger answered simply. "Right now, two days won't make that
much difference—the sign's pretty old—and our sup-

plies were pretty slim to go traipsin' off after a Black-foot raidin' party. We needed that hunt."

Partly angry that he hadn't been told before now, and at the same time overjoyed to know that the old scout was planning to help him find Martha, Clay didn't know what to say. Finally, he asked, "Does this mean you're going with me?"

Badger huffed as if reacting to a minor irritation. "Well, you sure as hell wouldn't git far on your own."

"I'm much obliged," Clay said, his grin a mile wide. His common sense told him that his chances of finding the band of Indians that kidnapped his sister were far greater with Badger's help. But his confidence in his ability to accomplish damn near anything he set out to do assured him that he would get a helluva lot further than Badger figured.

Chapter 4

Martha Vinings sat back on her heels, arching her back in an effort to stretch muscles grown stiff from the constant bending. While she stretched, she glanced about at the Indian women scattered around her on the hillside. They worked in groups of two or three, chatting cheerfully as they dug into the hard earth with tools made from bone or antlers, harvesting the wild camas bulbs that would later be buried under a fire and baked for several days. Only she worked alone. Pausing for a moment, she stretched her neck and shrugged her shoulders to relax the stiff muscles. Glancing back toward the other women, she caught Moon Shadow's eye. Black Elk's wife favored her with a slight smile.

Of all the women in Bloody Axe's village, it seemed ironic to Martha that Moon Shadow had been the only one to treat her with kindness. Over the weeks since her capture, the other women had progressed in their treatment of her from open hostility to general indifference. Moon Shadow alone had shown compassion for her from the beginning—this in spite of the fact that Black Elk had brought the white woman to live in her tipi.

There was no doubt concerning Martha's status—

she was a slave, and she was Black Elk's property, the same as his horses and weapons. In spite of this, Moon Shadow never demonstrated any sign of animosity toward her white slave, often interceding on Martha's behalf whenever some of the other women were bent upon abusing her. Even after the first day back in the village, when Martha attempted to escape again—only to suffer another taste of Black Elk's quirt on her back—it was Moon Shadow who rubbed grease into the welts, and spoke to her in compassionate tones. From the first day of her capture, Martha had resolved that she would resist enslavement, vowing to fight for her dignity—to the death if necessary. Moon Shadow's kindness had all but defused her determination to fight back. Before very long, their relationship leaned more toward friendship than one of slave and mistress.

In the tipi at night, Martha often stole glances at the Blackfoot warrior and his wife, and puzzled over the union of the two. Black Elk was a fierce warrior of such obvious strength that he stood out among all the other men of the village. And Moon Shadow was such a frail little woman, certainly not among the fairest of her sisters. In time, Martha learned that the marriage was arranged as a favor to Bloody Axe, Moon Shadow's father. Black Elk had shown no interest in taking a wife, but he did this for his chief. Watching the two of them now, Martha was touched by the tender regard the fierce warrior showed for his fragile wife. Moon Shadow confided in her that she wanted to give Black Elk a son, but she'd been unsuccessful in doing so. It grieved her to fail him, although he never complained. The other women were concerned for her. They said she was too weak to carry a baby. Martha couldn't help but feel deep compassion for Moon Shadow's plight.

Turning her attention back to the business of gathering camas bulbs, Martha thought about her life before being captured. It seemed a century ago instead of a matter of months. The first couple of weeks, she constantly thought of rescue. Now it seldom crossed her mind. There would be no rescue. For who would rescue her? Robert? She wasted no thought on that hope. She didn't fault Robert for his weakness. It was simply not in his nature to face a challenge such as would be required. No, she could not put her faith in her husband, nor his conniving brother for that matter. There was no one. Even if there were, how could they find her? They had traveled for four days to get to the Blackfoot village—she might as well be on the moon.

Rising to her feet, she picked up her basket, and looked around her, searching for another patch of the edible roots. Moon Shadow called to her, and pointed toward an area close to her. Martha smiled and nodded, then went to work beside Moon Shadow. "Ground hard," Moon Shadow offered in way of conversation.

"Ground hard," Martha repeated in agreement, using some of the few words she had learned. The thought of it amused her. What would her father think of his daughter if he could see her now? He would no doubt remind her that he had discouraged her from going west in the first place. Then her thoughts strayed to the cabin in the Black Hills. At the time, she had wondered what on earth they would eat when the last dried beans were consumed, and they were reduced to nothing but the wild meat Robert and Charley could kill. When all about them, the earth was filled with plants and roots of all kinds—camas, wild carrots, wild turnips, bitterroot, and others she did not know the names of. She had certainly come a long way from Virginia and the life she knew there. A word from Moon Shadow interrupted her thoughts.

"Black Elk," she uttered in a tone approaching reverence.

Martha looked up and followed Moon Shadow's gaze toward the ridge above them. He had stopped to watch his wife for a few moments, waiting for her to sense his presence. When she saw him, he signaled with one arm to call her attention to the antelope carcass draped across his horse. Moon Shadow beamed and waved to him, and he proceeded down the trail toward the village.

"Good," Moon Shadow said to Martha. "Black Elk has brought the antelope skin that I asked for. Now I will help you make a new dress to replace those rags you're wearing."

Seeing that Martha was unable to follow all of her words, she repeated them while using sign to help, pointing to Martha's worn and ragged clothes. Martha smiled and nodded her understanding. The two women picked up their baskets, and followed Black Elk down the trail to the village.

Separated from the Blackfoot village by some two hundred miles of rugged mountain country, Robert Vinings sat with his back propped against a small boulder overlooking a rushing stream that cut the center of German Gulch. Breaking off a piece of the pan bread he had baked over the coals of the fire, he wiped it across his tin plate, then around the edges, neatly mopping up every last drop of bean gravy until the plate was almost dry. Watching him, smirking silently, a look of disgust on his face, Robert's brother Charley suddenly threw the remains of his supper into the water, complaining, "When the hell are we gonna spend some of the dust we've got for some decent food?"

Robert jerked his head back, recoiling in surprise.

"What do you mean?" he asked. "What's wrong with the food?"

"It's the same old shit day after day—beans and pan bread, beans and pan bread."

Robert was genuinely puzzled by his brother's outburst. "What's wrong with that? It's nourishment." When Charley only shook his head, the look of disgust deepening, Robert asked, "What do you want? We could take a day off, and go hunting if you want."

"Hell, I don't wanna go huntin'." He stood up and stared at the offending tin plate in his hand. The impulse to throw it in the stream was strong, but he knew he wouldn't have anything to eat on if he did. So, instead, he reached down and gave it a halfhearted swish in the swiftly running water, then flung it back up the hill toward the tent, where it bounced noisily across the rocky ground. He cut his eyes at Robert, silently daring him to comment on his little fit of anger. *I might just throw your ass in the damn creek,* he thought. They had quarreled over this before. Robert didn't want to part with a single speck of gold dust, especially at the inflated prices asked for food in the towns; Charley was sick and tired of living like a beggar when they had panned a sizable poke from their claim. He was anxious to spend some of the gold and reap some benefit from their months of labor. There were saloons and bawdy houses in Virginia City—places where a young fellow could enjoy himself. What was the use of mining gold if you couldn't enjoy it?

"Now, Charley," Robert began. "You know we've talked about our plan to work until we get enough for both of us to have us some kind of business."

"I don't wanna hear about your plans no more. I don't know who gave you the right to plan for me, anyway. I'll make my own damn plans and do what I want with my share." He glared defiantly at his brother for a long moment, but he knew Robert would not rise to his bait. Robert never showed any violent emotion. And since Martha had been carried off by Indians, Robert had become more and more like an old woman—worrying about every little leaf that fell off a tree. It was getting on Charley's nerves. *I know what's eatin' at him. He's ashamed of himself for not going after those Injuns—not rescuing his sweet little darling. Damn fool! Well, ol' Charley's got better sense than to dangle his ass in front of a gang of redskins— not for no damn woman.*

Charley occasionally entertained thoughts of Martha, but not of the same guilt-ridden variety that hung over his brother's head. Regret was what came to mind when Charley spent any time thinking about his sister-in-law. *I should've just had my way with that bitch while I had the chance. Hell, Robert wouldn't have done anything about it. Well, I bet she'd druther take a roll in the hay with me now—since she's probably been rode by a dozen Injun bucks. I'd like to see how persnickety she's actin' right about now.*

Robert watched his brother as Charley stomped angrily up the hill toward their tent. *Going into our gold dust again*, he thought to himself. *He'll be riding into town to throw it away in the saloon.* Robert couldn't understand what had gotten into Charley in the past few weeks. He'd gotten sullen and moody, and he'd taken to riding into town to hang out with the loafers who were always looking for someone to buy them a drink. Robert tried to impress upon his younger brother the importance of working hard and saving their earnings in order to have a fortune to start a new life elsewhere. But Charley had started to run with a bad crowd in the mining towns, and there was really no way Robert could force him to be more frugal. They were seeing some color, but not in quantities so great that they could squander it.

It would have been more fortunate if they had gotten to the Montana goldfields sooner, in the early days of Alder Gulch. By the time they arrived, it was difficult to find a patch of creekbank that hadn't been turned over with a spade. Little towns had already sprung up—Virginia City, Junction, Adobetown, Summit, and others—all in a stretch of less than twenty miles. The two brothers had scant success panning for gold in Alder Creek or Stinking Water. It was here that Robert first began to worry about Charley because, when they had no success in their efforts to find the precious metal, Charley casually suggested that they might consider jumping someone else's claim, or even dry-gulching some defenseless miner. Robert found it hard to believe Charley could even consider such a thing. But Charley just shrugged it off, saying that it was a dog-eat-dog world in the goldfields—the strongest were justified in taking from the weak. Robert wondered then if he and his brother were going to eventually have to part company. When news of a new strike in German Gulch reached Virginia City, Robert was quick to suggest that they should pack up and go. The prospect of a more lucrative claim was enough to appease Charley's grumbling for a while. So they wasted no time in staking out a new claim.

They struck pay dirt right away, washing thirty dollars a day from the stream. The claim showed good color for over a month before the take dropped to around ten dollars a day. It wasn't long after that when Charley's enthusiam for the work waned once more, and soon Robert found that he was doing most of the work while Charley was doing most of the spending.

When Charley started hitting the saloons again,

Robert feared that he was going to run through all their savings. So he secretly started filling a separate poke with a portion of the dust every day, and hid it under a rock at the corner of the tent. Charley was none the wiser.

"I'm goin' to town to get me a drink," Charley announced upon emerging from the tent.

"I don't suppose it would do any good to ask you not to spend our gold to buy drinks for the riffraff that hangs around town," Robert said.

"No," Charley shot back. "I don't suppose it would. Half of that dust is mine, and what I do with my dust is my own damn business." His defiant stare was enough to cut short any further entreaty Robert might have felt like making. "Don't wait up for me," he smirked as he threw a saddle on his horse.

Robert stood watching his younger brother ride up the ridge once again to come home who-knew-when, all liquored up, usually belligerent, and not much good for work the next day. When Charley's horse disappeared from sight, Robert went back to the fire to stir up the coffeepot still heating on the coals. Pouring himself a cup of the bitter black brew, he settled down by the fire to watch the approaching darkness descend upon the gulch.

These were the times when Robert sadly reflected upon the path his life had taken. Sitting alone in the growing darkness, he could admit to himself that he lacked the courage to forge a life for himself in this untamed country. He was afraid. Thinking back over the years, he realized that he had been afraid all of his life. When the war came, he had avoided enlistment for as long as possible, joining up only because he had to in order to save face. His first battle had been a nightmare he would never be able to forget— filled with the screams of dying men and horses, amid a tempest of cannon flame, and the deadly rain of grapeshot that maimed indiscriminately. Terrified, he had lain in a muddy ditch, paralyzed by the horrifying sounds of death that hung over the battlefield in a hellish chorus. When the order to fall back was sounded, it was all he could do to force himself to leave the cover of the ditch, in mortal fear of the rifleshot that he was convinced was waiting for him. When it did indeed find him, it was a blessing. For he was hit in the left shoulder as he ran to the rear. After two days in the hospital, he was sent home to recuperate and enjoy a hero's welcome. He never reported back after recovering, telling everyone in Fredericksburg that he had been discharged. The tides of war had turned so badly for the Confederacy by then that he felt secure in his belief that there would be so much chaos in Lee's retreating forces that his desertion would never be noticed. Thousands of men had deserted on both sides. Was it such a terrible thing? For him, personally, there was no choice. He could not conquer the cold fear that gnawed away deep inside him. He could not go back to that hell.

Thinking back on it now, he was amazed that he had the courage to propose marriage to Martha Culver. She had shown a fondness for him before he left to join the army, but would not commit herself to a lasting relationship. Maybe it was the image of a wounded soldier returning home that swayed her affections. He wondered, *Would she have married me if she knew I had really deserted my regiment?*

There had been a short period of absolute bliss, when his every thought was filled with the wonder of his new bride. But soon the realization that the war was coming to an end, bringing with it the almost certain exposure of his military record, began to prey on his mind. Living with this on his conscience, Robert sought to escape the memory of his cowardice by leaving Virginia far behind and finding new beginnings in the West. Even then, he did not possess the courage to undertake the adventure alone. So he persuaded Charley to go with him and Martha in a search for gold. The thought of Martha immediately released the demons of guilt upon him again. He had hoped to hide his lack of fortitude from her, but he lived in constant fear the entire time they had worked the stream in the Black Hills. *I guess she knows by now.* Maybe she had already guessed that his lack of ardor might have stemmed from the burden of fear that was with him every waking hour.

His mind would be forever tortured by the knowledge that his first thought upon returning and finding Martha gone, and the cabin burned to the ground, was to be thankful he had been away when the Indians attacked. If only he'd possessed the courage to go after her. But the thought of being captured and tortured by wild savages still terrified him. Thinking about it now, he could not resist the impulse to peer around him—peering into the darkness—even though there were reportedly no hostile Indians anywhere close to German Gulch.

"Get a'hold of yourself," he scolded, still stealing furtive glances into the darkness. He knew he'd better busy himself before he started seeing shapes forming in the shadows. So he dumped the contents of his coffee cup, got up, and went around the tent to the back corner. Rolling a stone the size of a large watermelon over on its side, being careful not to make marks in the sand, he reached down to retrieve a large knotted rag under it. *You're gonna thank me someday for this, Charley,* he thought.

With the bundle in hand, he walked back to the fire

and beyond where several large stones ringed the base of a dwarf cedar. As he had done at the corner of the tent, he carefully rolled the smallest of the stones aside and pulled a buckskin pouch from the hole beneath it. He kneeled there for a moment, hefting the pouch, feeling its weight. This was the sum total of his and Charley's toil, a pouch that held a sizable fortune. He only wished that Charley was as concerned about providing for their future as he was. The thought caused him to shake his head sorrowfully.

Untying the knotted corners of the rag, he exposed the little mound of gold dust it held. Taking care not to spill any, he poured a small amount on top of the mound on the cloth. Then he returned the buckskin pouch to its hiding place, and resettled the stone. He reknotted the corners of the rag, and held it up to feel its weight. Satisfied, he retraced his steps to the back corner of the tent to return it to its hiding place.

"You sneakin' back-stabbin' bastard! So that's your game, is it?"

Robert, still on his knees, felt his heart stop for a moment. The sudden voice had so startled him that he couldn't find his own. Terrified at first, he relaxed a little when he recognized the voice as his brother's. "Charley," he stammered, "you scared the hell outta me. I thought you went to town."

"I bet you did," Charley shot back. "I thought I'd better hang around a while, and just see what kind of mischief you were up to behind my back. My own brother . . ."

"What?" Robert started, then: "Now, wait a minute, Charley, don't go getting the wrong idea."

"Oh, I ain't got the wrong idea. Nossir, not a'tall, you cheatin' skunk. I figured you were cheatin' me all along."

"Charley, I swear . . ." Before he could finish, Charley's boot caught him squarely in the back, sending him face forward in the dirt.

Rising to his hands and knees, Robert tried to crawl out from under his enraged brother's reach. Charley quickly bent down, and with both hands, lifted the huge rock that had hidden the cloth filled with gold dust. So intense was his anger that he raised the stone as high as he could manage, then slammed it down. There was a dull thud as the heavy rock smashed against the side of Robert's head.

Charley, still consumed by his own anger, stood over his fallen brother, waiting to administer more punishment. "I'll teach you to steal from me."

After a moment when Robert failed to move, Charley took a step backward, just then realizing that he might have killed his brother. "Get up, Robert," he commanded. But there was no response from the still body at his feet. He poked the body with his toe. No response. He stood staring down at Robert for a long time. Then he went to the fire and pulled a flaming brand from it. Going back to the body, he held it close to Robert's face to inspect the results of his uncontrolled fury. As the light from the flame flickered across Robert's face, Charley jerked back, recoiling in shock. Looking up at him, one eye bulging from its socket as a result of the crushed skull, his brother stared back at him. The one eye fixed on him, condemning grotesquely. Frightened, Charley nearly stumbled as he quickly backed away. "It's your own damn fault!" he cried out. "You shouldn'ta cheated me." Still not certain if his brother were alive or not, he waited, watching for any movement until it became obvious that Robert was never going to move again.

Charley went back by the fire and sat down to think over what had just taken place. It was not his fault, he reasoned. Robert was stealing from him, and he had been justified in hitting his brother with a rock. He didn't intend to kill him. It was an accident—and Robert deserved it for deceiving him.

He poured himself a cup from the coffeepot that was still heating on the edge of the fire. Frequently glancing at the still form several yards away in the darkness, he tried to decide what to do. The foremost thought that occurred to him was that now all the gold was his. He was considerably more wealthy now that he had Robert's share. The thing that was important, then, was to make sure he held onto it. He had to think about that.

This claim in German Gulch was not an isolated camp like the cabin they had built in the Black Hills. There were neighboring digs on both sides of his, almost in hollering distance. People might ask questions. The more Charley thought about it, the more he worried about someone getting nosy about Robert's disappearance. The earlier days of the vigilantes in Alder Gulch were over now, but they would still hang a man for murder. Charley decided the best thing to do was to go on into town, like he had originally planned, have a few drinks with the boys, let everybody see him in the saloon. Then he could come back and "discover" poor Robert, bushwhacked by some murdering bandit.

"I'll sing out loud enough for everybody up and down the creek to hear me," he said, feeling smug about his plan. "I'll even show 'em the empty rag where the gold was hid under that rock." Satisfied that things were at last to his liking, he started back into the trees where he had tied his horse. Glancing at the body of his brother as he passed, he said, "It's your own damn fault. Gold was wasted on you, anyway."

Chapter 5

Clay Culver stood for a moment, staring into the charred timbers of what had once been his sister's home. Scattered here and there among the cold lifeless ashes, he saw pieces of broken dishes and occasional scraps of scorched cloth—the only evidence that Martha had been there. Looking around him, he tried to imagine her in these rough surroundings. The sluice box at the foot of the hill, that had been tumbled and dragged from the stream, the tiny cabin, the two-rail corral left intact to guard the bleached bones of the mules—it was a far cry from even the modest house on the banks of the Rapidan in Virginia. There was a deep ache inside him as he thought of how terrifying it must have been for her. The image his mind recalled was of a young schoolgirl, instead of a grown-up young lady, for she was in her last year of schooling when he last saw her. He remembered what she had told him when he packed his few belongings and left to join the army. *Now, don't go trying to be a hero, Clay Culver. I'm depending on you to come back home— even if I have to go find you, and bring you back myself.*

Several yards away, near the corner of the cabin, Badger knelt, tracing a moccasin print in the ashes

with his finger. He had already scouted around the
entire clearing, searching the ground for any sign outside the obvious evidence of the attack. He had to
conclude that there was little to go on other than who
was responsible for the raid.

"They was Blackfoot all right," Badger said, getting
to his feet again. "They left their callin' card." He
picked up the two halves of a broken arrow and held
them up for Clay to see.

Clay walked over to examine the arrow. "You suppose Martha was wounded?"

Seeing the immediate concern in Clay's eyes, Badger hastened to reassure him. "Probably not. I doubt
if there was any shootin' a'tall—no need to, with nobody there but the woman."

"But what about this?" Clay questioned, holding up
the broken arrow.

"Like I said, that's just their callin' card. Probably
shot it in one of them posts there, just so the Sioux
would know they had been in their territory. I expect
one of Black Crow's boys pulled it out and broke it
in two."

Although somewhat reassuring, Badger's specula-
tion did not free Clay's mind from worrying about
Martha's treatment at the hands of the Blackfeet. He
could not rid his mind of the picture of his sister,
beaten and starving, toiling under the watchful eye of
some savage. For that reason, he was anxious to start
out in search of this band of Blackfeet, and was becoming impatient with Badger's apparent dawdling.
Finally, he prodded the scout. "I expect we're just
wasting time around here. We might as well get
started after them."

"That so?" Badger asked. "Which way you think
we oughta go?"

Clay shrugged. It seemed obvious to him. "That

way," he pointed. "The tracks lead off toward that ravine."

Badger nodded thoughtfully, as if giving Clay's suggestion deep consideration. "Well," he said, "them tracks'll lead you back to the Belle Fourche. Them's Black Crow's tracks."

"How do you know that?"

"'Cause they're fairly fresh," Badger answered, his tone patient as if counseling a child. "Besides, it's the right number of horses. There ain't much sign left from that party that burnt this cabin—been too long. I found a few tracks leading out past the corral there, leading yonder across that meadow. The grass is growed up since then, but I did find part of a small print next to the corner pole of the corral. My guess is it's a woman's. Your sister mighta made a run for it, tryin' to git to them woods yonder."

The thought of it made Clay's heart pound, and the urgency to go after them returned. Badger saw it in his face, so before Clay had a chance to say anything, the scout held up his hand to silence him. "Now, hold your horses, son. Let's take a little time to look the sign over real good and make sure we're on the right track." He didn't say it, but he also wanted to determine if the woman was truly captured, not killed trying to escape. He had a strong feeling that Martha was still a captive, but there was still the possibility that their search might end in the spruce trees on the other side of the grassy meadow.

Badger stood for a moment at the back corner of the corral, looking across the meadow, figuring that, if the woman were running, she would head for the nearest point of cover. This was the direction in which he started out, toward a point where some tall pines jutted out beyond the timber line. Clay followed along behind, leading the horses while Badger scanned the grass around him as he slowly walked toward the trees. He paused briefly when he discovered a lone hoofprint that had been deep enough to prevent its being washed away by the summer thunderstorms. He nodded as if to confirm his opinion, then continued toward the edge of the forest.

Before reaching the outer line of pines, Badger stopped when he came to a tiny spring, no more than a trickle of water bubbling up from deep in the mountainside. Kneeling low to the ground, he traced several deep scars, etched in the soft ground around the spring. "Well, she didn't make it to them trees. They caught her right here is what I'm thinkin'." He pointed to the deep prints left by a horse coming to a sliding stop. Leaving Clay to study this small bit of evidence, he proceeded to have a look in the trees beyond. "I reckon she ain't dead," he announced when he rejoined Clay.

"How do you know that?" Clay wanted to know.

"Ain't no bones. Even if wolves or coyotes got her, there'd be some bones scattered around. They'd a'been chewin' and pullin' on her carcass in every direction, fightin' over the best parts."

Clay winced, repulsed by Badger's graphic description. "All right!" he blurted. "I understand. Let's get on with it."

There wasn't much to go on. The only thing they could tell for sure was that the Blackfoot raiding party had left the meadow in a direction that was generally northwest. Badger could only guess that the party was heading for their home territory. When questioned by Clay, he explained his reasoning. "They was a small party—no more'n fifteen or twenty, I'd say—and they was a long way from home. I wouldn't expect them to hang around too long in Sioux territory with no more of 'em than that."

"Can you track them back to their village?"

Although it seemed a foolish question to him, Badger remained patient, allowing for Clay's inexperience. "I expect not. I doubt if a coyote could follow a trail this old. The only thing we can do is head for Blackfoot country and start lookin'. I know it's not much to go on, but it'll have to do, 'cause there ain't no tellin' where this band's village is by now. This late in the season, they're followin' the buffalo, layin' in supplies for the winter. They could be anywhere between the Yellowstone and the Milk this time of year."

This was not very encouraging news to Clay, and although his resolve was as strong as ever to find his sister, he was beginning to have serious doubts about the possibility of success. Badger was talking about searching a territory between here and the Bitterroot Mountains, from the Yellowstone up into the British possessions.

Badger sensed his young friend's dismay, and he tried to reassure him somewhat. "We'll work our way up to Fort Union. There's a friend of mine usually hangs around there, if he ain't been scalped by now. He's one of the few white men I know that can move among the Blackfeet without no trouble. Used to trap for the Hudson's Bay Company before the American Fur Company built Fort Union. They was the only ones could deal with them damn Blackfoot. Ol' Pete Dubois—damn Frenchman—if anybody knows where the different bands are camped, it'd be Pete. He might know about any white captives, too." He paused and nodded, thinking back on times past when he trapped for beaver along more rivers and streams than he could name. "We'll set out in the mornin' for Fort Union."

"I'm much obliged, Mr. Badger. I hope I can find a way to pay you for your services." Since traveling with Badger and Gray Bird from Fort Laramie, Clay had been touched by the obvious affection the old trapper's Lakota wife held for him. He wondered now if he might be asking too much of Badger to leave his family and friends. And yet, Badger certainly didn't strike Clay as the kind of man who would go anywhere, or do anything, he didn't want to. Still, he felt he had to say something, for it looked to be quite uncertain how long they would be away. "I feel I'm asking a helluva lot of you. I reckon I could go on to Fort Union by myself, and let you get back to your family."

"I reckon," Badger replied. "I could tell you where Fort Union is. That's easy enough. It's where the Yellowstone branches off from the Missouri. Problem is, how do you find the Yellowstone? There's a heap of country between here and the Yellowstone, and a heap of water to cross. And there ain't no signs tellin' you which river is which. You'd have to guess—Belle Fourche, Little Missouri, Powder, Tongue—you might pick the wrong one and find yourself tryin' to talk a passel of Injuns outta liftin' your scalp. I expect I'd better go with you."

That ended conversation on the matter, and Clay was satisfied that he had a guide. Badger could have told him the real reasons he had made up his mind to take him up into Yellowstone country. It was as much Badger's nature to yearn for faraway places as a bear's need to hibernate. He was content living with Little Hawk's people, but he could not stay in one place for very long before he longed to be on a lonely mountain trail, away from other people. Gray Bird understood her husband's needs, and knew that he would always return to her tipi when he had answered the call within him. It had been a while since Badger had shared a campfire with Pete Dubois, and part of the reason he was going to take this young fellow to Fort Union was to see if ol' Pete was still alive.

Badger had always considered himself to be a reliable judge of people. And this young Clay Culver seemed to him to be a straight-dealing man of worthwhile character. He had taken an almost instant liking to him. Clay didn't waste many words, saying only what needed to be said, and Badger liked that. They should travel well together. Aside from the natural urge to wander, there was a deeper, more serious reason that prompted Badger's willingness to go. By taking Clay to look for his sister, Badger would not be faced with taking sides if Red Cloud called on his people to fight the soldiers.

Early the following morning, Badger rode out across the meadow, leading his packhorse. Clay followed on Red, leading the mouse-colored mare. Behind them, the grim remains of his sister's cabin lay stark and black, like a cancer on the otherwise pristine slope of the hill.

Far to the northwest, the morning approached. Still and cool, a soft mist rose from the river and floated ghostlike several feet above the water. Already the Blackfoot village was alive and bustling, as the women scurried back and forth, carrying water from the river or gathering firewood to replenish that burned during the night. Thin streamers of smoke reached up from the smokeholes in the lodges to gather into a filmy haze above the village.

The sun had just begun to peek over the bluffs on the eastern side of the river, but already Moon Shadow and Martha had put the meat on to boil for Black Elk's morning meal. The men were going to hunt today, for buffalo had been spotted moving several miles away toward the south. It would be a busy day for all the people of the village, but especially for the women who would do most of the butchering, then pack the meat and hides on travois to bring back to camp.

This would be the second such hunt for Martha, and this time she would know what to expect. The first time had been a near-chaotic confusion of dead carcasses, swarmed over by laughing women and shouting children, as the butchering began. She had been at once overwhelmed and repulsed by the sight of so much blood as the animals were skinned and the meat cut into sections. Moon Shadow had rescued her, and in her patient way, showed her how to cut away the various portions of the carcass. Martha learned quickly. Before her capture, when a deer or antelope had been killed, Robert and Charley skinned and dressed it. She did very little of the actual butchering. With Moon Shadow's help, she became quite competent. And by the time the two of them were butchering the third buffalo that Black Elk had killed, Martha was holding her own. Now, on this day's hunt, she would do a major portion of the work, for she was much stronger than Moon Shadow.

These were strange times for Martha Vinings. For all her fears when she was captured, she was at first confused that she had not been tortured and raped. Other than a few light whippings for disobedience, she had been treated kindly, and at once befriended by Moon Shadow, whom she soon came to regard fondly. The dark-eyed fawn with the slight and fragile body seemed to delight in teaching Martha the basic things that every Blackfoot girl knew. She learned how to tan hides and make clothes from them, dry meat and prepare it for the winter caches, make pemmican, and a hundred other things. Before Martha was fully aware of it, she had begun to think in terms of the village, and thoughts of escape no longer filled her waking hours. Even the other women of the village had warmed to her presence among them, some even making friendly overtures. Still, she told herself from time to time that she must not forget where she came from, and that escape was her duty, and certainly the desirable thing. Even these thoughts troubled her. Why, she wondered, did she never long for Robert and pray to God that she should be reunited with him? She wondered if she should feel guilty for not trying to escape. There were opportunities, for Black Elk had discontinued tying her ankles at night soon after they had returned to the Blackfoot village. She had told herself that it would be foolish to run. She would be lost and probably wander farther and farther into hostile territory. Even if Black Elk did not track her down, what chance would she have of finding her way back to civilization? Although the thought lay dormant in the back of her mind, she would never admit to herself that she was becoming comfortable in her new life.

Leaning over the fire, she peered into the iron pot of boiling meat to make sure it was not being overcooked. Without looking back, she sensed his presence. He was standing behind her, silently watching as she prepared his morning meal. When she moved aside, looking up at him, he held her gaze for a long moment before nodding briefly to her. Black Elk seldom directed any words toward her, but she often caught him studying her intently as she worked under Moon Shadow's direction. What was he thinking behind those piercing dark eyes? Her life was so uncertain. She could only guess what would be her ultimate fate. Maybe, she told herself, it was time to think of escape again.

Sounds of the boys and some of the younger men,

driving the horses in, caught Black Elk's attention, and he looked away. She took that opportunity to study him. Tall and powerful, with his buffalo robe draped across broad shoulders, he stood watching the ponies as they romped and pranced before the drovers. In spite of her situation, Martha begrudgingly admitted that he was a magnificent specimen of a warrior—*handsome, even.* She immediately reprimanded herself for even thinking such a thought about a wild Indian.

Glancing briefly at the white captive, he moved briskly away toward the river's edge. Martha watched as he joined some of the other men of the village where they had gathered on the shore. He let the robe drop from his muscular shoulders, and with no further hesitation, plunged into the chilly water. Martha shivered at the thought, glad that Moon Shadow did not insist upon that ritual now that the mornings were getting colder. The two women heated water to cleanse themselves in the privacy of the tipi.

"He bathes in the river almost every morning. All of the men do. It toughens them for the winter months ahead."

Martha turned quickly. She had been so absorbed in watching Black Elk that she had failed to hear Moon Shadow come up beside her. Embarrassed at having been caught gazing so intently at Moon Shadow's husband, Martha at once turned her attention back to the pot of meat on the fire. "The meat is ready," she said, making an attempt to change the subject.

Moon Shadow smiled and nodded in reply. It pleased her that Martha admired her husband. Most of the women in the village admired the powerful war chief. Many, she suspected, were envious of her, especially since Black Elk seemed so devoted to her. It was common knowledge that he had taken her as a wife primarily as a favor to her father. Knowing that, it puzzled some of the maidens of the village that Black Elk had not seen fit to take another wife, as many of the other men had. It would have made the work easier for the fragile girl. That was the main reason she had welcomed Martha into her tipi, and encouraged Black Elk to keep the white woman when other men of the village made offers to trade for her. Moon Shadow smiled to herself when she thought of it. Reluctant at first, Black Elk quickly gave in, for he very seldom denied her anything that might please her. He teased her good naturedly about the price it had cost him. One of the more ardent young men had offered six horses for her, and that was why Black Elk gave Martha her Blackfoot name, *Six Horses*. While he always referred to her as Six Horses, Moon Shadow called her Marta.

"Moon Shadow, what will Black Elk do with me?" Martha suddenly asked.

Moon Shadow knew that Martha feared she might be traded to someone not as kind as Black Elk. She was quick to reassure her. "Black Elk will not trade you," she said softly. "He will keep you because I want him to. You are now my sister." She gave Martha a little squeeze, and said, "Now, let us get ready for the hunt. Black Elk will be finished with his bath and ready to eat."

There were other, more ominous parties interested in the Blackfoot village's preparations for the buffalo hunt on that chilly morning. Lying close to the ground in the high grass on the eastern ridge above the camp, a Crow raiding party watched the men of Bloody Axe's village as they went to fetch their favorite ponies, and the women as they caught the packhorses and hitched the travois.

The Crow warriors waited patiently. Led by the fierce war chief, Gray Wolf, they lay concealed in the high buffalo grass, watching as the Blackfoot village prepared for the hunt. Outnumbered more than tenfold, the Crows were not so foolish as to attack. Their mission was to steal horses from their hated enemy, and Gray Wolf knew that most of the fighting men would be gone from the village, and the huge horse herd would be left to be guarded by a handful of men and boys. They only had to wait until the Blackfoot hunters, and their women behind them, were beyond the sound of their gunfire.

The sun was high overhead now. It had been more than an hour since the last of the Blackfoot hunting party had disappeared beyond the ridge. Gray Wolf's Crow warriors were tense, impatient to act, lying still for so long. He held them hidden there in the high grass while he stole silently down the bluff overlooking the river to take a closer look at the Blackfoot village. After a few moments more, when it appeared there was no one left other than young boys and old men, he slowly rose to his feet and signaled with his hand.

Eager to act, the Crow warriors immediately made their way down through the long grass to the bluffs. Leaving their horses in a narrow coulee, guarded by three of their youngest warriors, Gray Wolf's raiders descended the bluff and forded the shallow river. Using the riverbank for concealment, they made their way upstream until directly opposite the Blackfoot horse herd. There he halted them while he crawled to the lip of the riverbank to locate the guards. There were three young boys; the closest to the river was a boy of fourteen summers. Gray Wolf planned to kill the boy with his bow, so as not to alert the peaceful camp. With hand signals, he instructed two of his best bowmen to take the other two when he signaled them.

Some distance downstream, young Crooked Lance guided his pony through the many gullies that had eroded down from the bluffs above. His prized possession, a Henry rifle, lay cradled in his arm. He had hoped to find some small game to shoot, but he had been unsuccessful in his hunt. Disappointed that Chief Bloody Axe had assigned him to stay in the village to guard the horses, Crooked Lance had decided to go out by himself in hopes of finding a deer or antelope. The three boys could watch the pony herd for a hour or two without his being there to direct them. Besides there were many of the older men who had remained in the camp as well.

Walking his pony along the water's edge, watching for signs of muskrats, Crooked Lance moved comfortably with the animal's easy motion when suddenly his senses were alerted. *Listen! A splash! Just beyond the crook in the river—from the sound of it, a large muskrat, perhaps a larger animal.* Crooked Lance nudged his pony with his heels. As his horse scrambled up the bank to a higher point above the river, the young Blackfoot warrior pulled him up short. What he saw crouched behind the opposite bank, no more than one hundred yards distant, almost made his heart stop. *Crow raiding party!* Without hesitating, Crooked Lance cocked his rifle and fired three times in rapid succession, aiming at the center of the line of raiders. One of the enemy yelped in pain, clutched his chest, then tumbled down the bank into the water.

On the far bank, Gray Wolf was startled. About to drop his hand to signal his bowmen to strike, he turned to see one of his warriors killed. Now the Blackfoot warrior who had spotted them was shouting the alarm to the rest of the village. His face twisted with rage at having lost the element of surprise, Gray Wolf desperately signaled his warriors to go for the horses. It was too late. The Blackfoot camp reacted immediately. The young boys guarding the ponies were quick to drive the herd away from the river. Yelling and whistling, they raced their ponies back and forth, stampeding the milling herd toward the hills beyond the village. From the circle of lodges, old men and women, even children, came running to defend the village. Well armed, they soon leveled a hailstorm of rifle fire upon the intruders, forcing the Crows to seek the cover of the riverbank once more.

The unexpected show of force caused Gray Wolf to reconsider his plan to storm the village. He had not counted on so many guns in the Blackfoot camp. And now, pinned down behind the riverbank, he found that he could not charge the lodges. Already, two more of his warriors had been hit—one of them dead. He was going to have to retreat, fearing that the noise of the battle might carry to the Blackfoot buffalo hunters. He had counted heavily upon surprise—striking the pony herd quickly, running off most of the horses before the village was aware of what was happening. The hated Blackfeet had too many guns. Now he had to be concerned about being cut off from his own horses.

"Back!" he cried out. "Get back to the horses. They are too many!"

The Crow raiders needed no further encouragement, for the shallow riverbank was alive with bullets, snapping like angry wasps flying overhead. They picked up their wounded and dead, and as quickly as they could manage, retreated across the river. The Blackfeet, encouraged by the rout of the enemy raiders, ran after them, filling the air with bullets and arrows. Young Crooked Lance, still on his pony, fired his rifle until the iron forearm became too hot to hold. Staying after the vanquished enemy until the Crows had scurried up the bluffs and disappeared over the ridge, the elders and boys of the village still fired their weapons in the air, chanting and singing of victory. Not one pony had been stolen.

Unaware of the battle just waged back in their village, the Blackfoot women were hard at work butchering the fallen buffalo. Like dark mounds scattered across the broad valley floor, dead and wounded animals lay waiting the knives of the excited swarm that would expertly skin them and carve them into slabs of meat. Moon Shadow looked up at Martha and smiled. "Finish packing the meat onto the travois. I'll start to work on this one over here." Martha nodded and continued loading the meat from the young cow while Moon Shadow picked up her knife again and started toward the carcass of a large bull some fifty yards away.

It had been a good hunt. The people should want for nothing in the coming winter. Today's kill should be enough to more than fill the food caches that would nourish them through the cold months ahead. Moon Shadow looked far off toward the point where the valley narrowed. Black Elk and most of the other hunters were somewhere beyond the point, still following the stampeding buffalo. Here and there some of the men rode among the fallen buffalo, killing those still not dead, while small groups of women followed behind them, ready to butcher the huge beasts. Moon Shadow smiled to herself, taking pride in the fact that she and Martha could work as fast as any of the others. Black Elk would be pleased to see how much Martha had learned.

Swift Runner, one of her husband's closest friends,

guided his pony toward her as she approached the
massive hulk of the fallen bull. "Moon Shadow," he
called out. "Be careful, that one is still breathing."

She smiled. Unable to hear what he said, she waved
cheerfully, and continued to walk toward the wounded
animal. Sitting upright, the bull's legs had crumpled
under his body, and he was unable to move. With his
life's blood seeping from his nostrils and mouth, he
sat helplessly awaiting his fate. Moon Shadow did not
realize he was still alive until she saw the wild glaze
of his eyeballs as they suddenly focused upon her. She
immediately jumped backward, but she was not quick
enough. With one desperate sweep of his massive
head, he tossed the unsuspecting Indian girl several
feet in the air, one deadly horn tearing a slash into
her side.

Hearing Moon Shadow cry out in pain, Martha
looked back to see the fragile body flung aside, like a
rag doll thrown by a bored child. "Moon Shadow!"
she screamed, and ran to her. In that horrible moment,
Martha realized how close the two of them had become. Her heart beating wildly, she knelt by Moon
Shadow's side and took the frail Blackfoot girl into
her arms. Already blood was seeping through the ragged hole in Moon Shadow's dress as Martha tried to
comfort her, rocking her like a baby while she tried
to stop the flow of blood now staining the brown prairie grass beneath her.

Within moments, the other women—those within
sight of the incident—converged around the wounded
girl. One crack of rifle fire startled Martha when Swift
Runner finished the bull, and a moment later, he was
standing over her. Moon Shadow's eyelids fluttered
open, then closed, and Martha feared her little sister
was gone.

"Lay her flat," an older woman said, and Martha

lowered Moon Shadow gently back on the grass. Then the woman used her skinning knife to widen the hole in Moon Shadow's dress, exposing the jagged tear in the young girl's side. Martha inhaled sharply at the sight of the bloody wound, and she suddenly realized how desperately she wanted Moon Shadow to live. Helping to hold the wound closed while one of the women wrapped it tightly with a strip of cowhide, Martha cooed softly to the stricken girl. After a few moments, Moon Shadow opened her eyes again and attempted a weak smile.

"We must get her back to the village," the woman who had cut her dress said. "Where is Black Elk?"

"Beyond the far end of the valley," Swift Runner replied.

"Someone must go to find him," one of the other women said.

The others nodded agreement, but the gray-haired woman insisted, "She cannot wait. Someone go and find Black Elk. I and Six Horses will start back right away. He can overtake us."

"I'll go," Swift Runner said, and leaped upon his pony.

Together with several of the other women, Martha carried Moon Shadow and placed her on a travois loaded with a small stack of hides, tying her on securely with a strip of rawhide. "Don't worry, little sister, I will take care of you," she whispered softly. Moon Shadow tried to smile. Martha gave her hand a little squeeze, then quickly scrambled up on the horse's back. The gray-haired woman caught up another pony, and they started out for the Blackfoot village.

Gray Wolf was angry. The raid on the Blackfoot pony herd had been spoiled by the unlucky arrival of one Blackfoot hunter. A few seconds more and they would have struck the herd before the village knew they were even there. They captured no horses, but worse than that, they had suffered one dead and two wounded. It was a humiliating defeat at the hands of some old men and boys, and a damaging blow to his status as a war chief.

After beating their shameful retreat from the Blackfoot village, the Crow party made their way across a low line of hills, staying close to the treeline until reaching a deep ravine that offered both water and concealment. It was here they stopped to decide what they should do. Scouts were sent out to ride the ridges, and watch for any enemy that might be near. Gray Wolf, anxious to regain his prestige in the eyes of the others, petitioned to remain in enemy country a few days longer and wait for another opportunity to steal horses. His appeal was met with a general lack of enthusiasm, and there was a definite lack of confidence for any further raids on a Blackfoot village of such underestimated strength. It was felt that Gray Wolf's medicine was not strong, and this was the reason for their failure. Most of the warriors agreed that it would be better to return to their own land, and wait for another time to raid an enemy as dangerous as the hated Blackfeet.

The discussion continued on into the afternoon, with Gray Wolf speaking passionately on the necessity to return to their village victoriously, with stolen horses to prove their bravery and skill. Some were in agreement with him, but the majority felt the same as the eldest of the group, High Hump, who said, "Gray Wolf, you are a mighty warrior. Your medicine has been strong in the past. It may be strong again. But it is my feeling that this raid was not favored by Man Above at this time, and it may anger him if we continue. It would be wise to leave this country before the Blackfoot hunters return to their camp. There are too many for us to fight." There being nothing more to be said on the matter, the Crow raiding party prepared to start back, and the scouts were called in. It was a painful rebuke for Gray Wolf, but he had no choice but to accept the decision of the majority.

One of the scouts on the ridge north of the ravine did not come in with the others. Instead, he appeared in a clearing above the ravine and rode his pony around in a circle, signaling. "Follows The Wind has spotted something," High Hump said.

"I'll go and see what he has found," Gray Wolf quickly replied, and jumped on his pony. Anxious to atone in some way after having lost face with the others, he galloped up the side of the ravine toward Follows The Wind.

Follows The Wind waited for a moment until Gray Wolf had almost reached the clearing. Then he wheeled his pony and bolted off along the ridge. When Gray Wolf caught up to him, he had dismounted and was kneeling upon a long flat rock that jutted out over the edge of the steep slope. When Gray Wolf came up beside him, he pointed to the valley far below. There on the valley floor, Gray Wolf spotted two horses—a rider on each horse, and one pulling a travois.

"Women," Follows The Wind said. "I think the one on the travois is a woman, too. At this distance, it's hard to tell."

Gray Wolf did not speak for a few moments, his mind still laden with frustration and anger over the failed raid on the Blackfoot pony herd. He watched the women intently, scanning the trail before and behind them, looking for any indication that there were others. While he watched, he could feel the blood beginning to boil in his veins as the desperate need for revenge bored into his brain like a weevil. When he spoke, his voice was low and husky with condemnation. "They shall pay with their lives for the Crow warriors their men shot."

"Maybe we should talk of this to High Hump and the others," Follows The Wind suggested. While the idea of killing the three Blackfoot women was appealing to him, he wasn't sure it was worth the risk of having the entire Blackfoot camp on their trail. "It might be best to let them go in peace."

"You would not avenge our dead and wounded?" Gray Wolf had already made his decision; he would not be swayed from his lust for blood. Without hesitating further, he moved back off the rock and leaped on his pony. He had no intention of waiting for the others in case they felt the same as Follows The Wind. Quirting his horse viciously, he raced down across the slope on a course that would intercept the unsuspecting women near the narrow pass that led out of the valley.

Following along behind the gray-haired woman, Martha sent many anxious glances back toward Moon Shadow, lying motionless on the travois. The frail Indian girl made no sound, even when occasionally jostled roughly whenever the trail became broken and uneven. Martha feared her friend might be mortally wounded, and she wished they could hurry the horses along. But knowing the rough ride might cause Moon Shadow's bleeding to start anew, she was forced to endure the slow pace set by the old woman on the horse ahead.

It happened so suddenly that Martha was not sure what had occurred. The old woman was sitting rigidly straight on the horse before her when Martha took another quick glance at Moon Shadow. It was only a moment, but when she looked forward again, the old woman suddenly jerked her head back sharply, crying out in pain. At almost the same time she saw the arrow in the old woman's side, Martha heard the pounding of flying hooves behind her. Still baffled, she turned to discover the charging horse exploding from the trees, and already almost upon her. Terrified, she tried to pull her horse aside, but it was too late. Both horses bolted to escape the charging Crow pony. Grabbing the travois poles to keep from being thrown, she was only vaguely aware of seeing the gray-haired woman land heavily upon the ground. There was no time for rational thought. Her instinct for survival— for herself and Moon Shadow—was all that was keeping her on the horse's back. But the Crow warrior was upon the hapless woman before she could control the startled pony. Using the bone handle of his quirt as a club, Gray Wolf landed a blow beside Martha's ear that knocked her from the pony's back, and the frightened beast galloped away wildly, dragging the travois bumping and bouncing along the rough trail.

Stunned, unable to stagger to her feet, Martha struggled to get up on her hands and knees, her vision blurred and fuzzy as she tried to see her assailant. Unable to defend against an attack that came from her blind side, she screamed when her hair was suddenly snatched back, lifting her head and arching her neck. It was only then that her eyes, wide with fright, focused on her attacker. At that terrifying moment, Martha looked into a face so twisted by rage that she was convinced it belonged to a demon from hell itself. Knowing she was helpless to defend herself, she prepared to die.

His knife poised inches from the pale throat, Gray Wolf hesitated. His fury only partially under control, the soft auburn hair he clutched caught his attention.

A white woman! Yanking back harder on her hair in order to get a better look at Martha's face, the anger in his face turned to one of smug surprise. This was an unexpected catch, one that pleased Gray Wolf's revengeful state of mind. Still clutching a handful of Martha's hair, he pulled her up until she was on her knees. Looking his prize over more carefully for a few moments, he then placed his foot in the middle of her breast and kicked her over on the ground.

Lying flat on her back, Martha was too frightened to move as the half-naked savage stood over her, the long knife still in his hand. Not sure what was about to happen to her, she tried to draw away from him as he took a step closer. As punishment for drawing away, he struck her hard across the face, shouting an order she did not understand. Then he reached down and pulled her skirt—the soft antelope skirt that Moon Shadow had helped her make—up almost to her waist to expose the creamy white thighs above her leggings. He stared at her for a long moment while she trembled with fright for what she feared was to come next. But the assault she dreaded did not come. Instead, he simply seemed fascinated by the whiteness of her skin.

Then as if suddenly aware of his surroundings, he backed away a step and looked around him. The horse pulling the travois had already disappeared through the narrow pass at the end of the valley. Some twenty or thirty yards away, the pony ridden by the old woman stood watching him. He glanced briefly at the gray-haired woman a few yards away, struggling to pull the arrow from her side, her hands drenched in her own blood. He watched her struggles for a moment, as if only curious. Then, warning Martha not to move, he walked over to the wounded woman, jerked her head back, and drew the knife across her throat.

While she gasped for her last breaths, he considered the thin gray scalp. After a moment's contemplation, he decided it would only bring derision from the other warriors, so he released her hair and let the old woman drop in the grass.

Thinking now of his own safety, Gray Wolf decided it best not to linger in the open valley. Taking a length of rope from his saddle, he quickly tied Martha's hands together and drew a hasty loop around her feet. Content that she would be unable to free herself for a few minutes, he then slowly walked over to retrieve the old woman's horse. The horse offered no resistance, which pleased Gray Wolf, for now he had a horse as well as a white captive. Collecting his prisoner, he led her back up the slope into the trees to rejoin his band of warriors.

High Hump was openly disturbed when Gray Wolf returned with the white captive. Facing the fiery war chief, however, he maintained a courteous demeanor, befitting a Crow warrior. "Gray Wolf, I am pleased that you were able to attack the Blackfoot women and return without making our presence known to the enemy. I am wondering why you brought this woman with you."

Gray Wolf could not repress a smirk. He knew full well that behind High Hump's polite inquiry there was a subtle reprimand. In matching tones of politeness, he responded. "She is a white woman. She will amuse me for a while. Then, maybe I will kill her. She has fine-looking hair. It will look good on my shield."

There was a low rumble of murmurs among the warriors gathered around Gray Wolf and his captive. Many of them were concerned that the missing woman and the body of the other one would trigger an all-out war party of Blackfoot warriors. High Hump spoke for them all.

"We have been at peace with the white men for

some time now. I think it might be a mistake to keep this woman. Maybe we should take her to the soldier fort." Most of the warriors nodded agreement with High Hump's words. Many of them had served as scouts for the army and feared that the presence of a white captive in their village might be discovered by the soldiers, and would mean trouble for them all.

Gray Wolf stood defiantly before High Hump. "The woman is mine to do with as I wish. I alone was brave enough to ride down into the valley and take this woman and this horse. I have no fear of the white soldiers." Still inflamed by his loss of prestige for the ill-fated raid on the Blackfoot village, Gray Wolf saw High Hump's opposition to his prisoner as another rebuke. He was determined to have his own way.

High Hump could readily see that to try to persuade Gray Wolf to release the woman was useless. "I would rather that you had just killed the woman and left her there with the other one. That would have been better than taking her as a captive." He shrugged his shoulders. "But I will speak no more on the subject. You will do as you think you must do." He took one long look at Martha before he turned toward the rest of the warriors. "We must leave this place now and cover our trail carefully. When the Blackfeet find the dead woman in the valley, they will try to track us down."

Wasting no more time, the Crow raiding party set out for their village on the Yellowstone River. The journey would take three days, and High Hump was anxious to cover as much distance as possible before the coming night. Being no more than thirty warriors, they could not afford to be caught on the open prairie by a larger force of Blackfeet.

With scouts out on either side, and two riding behind the main body to watch their backtrail, they hurried through the mountain passes, intend upon gaining the low hills before darkness dictated a stop. Astride the gray-haired woman's pony, Martha sat—her hands tied together and bound to the crosspiece of the Indian saddle. Her body swaying slightly with the horse's uneven gait, she remained in a daze—partially from the blows she had received from the sullen Gray Wolf, and partially due to the mental devastation at having been captured. She dared not imagine what her fate might be at the hands of the scowling Gray Wolf. Each time he looked at her, his eyes promised unthinkable horrors awaiting her.

Her thoughts shifted now to Moon Shadow and what might have happened to her. Knocked from her horse by Gray Wolf, Martha had been rendered senseless for a few minutes, but she was somehow aware that the horse had bolted, dragging the helpless Blackfoot girl on the travois. Martha feared that the stampeding horse might cause Moon Shadow's wound to bleed profusely. Her only hope was that Swift Runner had found Black Elk soon enough to track Moon Shadow and take her back to the village where she could be cared for.

The Crow warriors pushed their ponies hard, continuing to ride until it was almost dark before making their camp where a small stream nurtured a stand of willows at the bottom of a shallow ravine. As the Indians prepared to make camp, Martha was dragged roughly from her horse by Gray Wolf. Stumbling, trying to maintain her balance, she cursed the sullen Crow. Whether he understood her words or not, he definitely understood the tone, and slapped her hard across the mouth for her insolence. The thin trickle of blood that resulted seemed to please him, for an evil grin played upon his ugly face. He ignored her defiant stance while he took a length of rope and tied one end of it around her neck. Holding the other in his hand, he jerked hard on it, almost causing her to fall as he led her to a place under a willow a little apart from the rest of the warriors.

Using gestures and sign language, Gray Wolf directed Martha to gather wood for a fire and then to get water from the stream. He followed along after her as she did his bidding, holding the rope tied around her neck as if she were a dog or a mule. Whenever she misunderstood a command, or failed to act quickly enough, he administered a hard yank on the rope, causing it to cut into her throat. When at last he sat down to eat some dried meat, she had a few moments' peace. Even then, however, he tormented her with his eyes and his insolent stare. She was terrified even more than the first time she had been captured by Black Elk. For then she had no idea what lay in store for her. This time, there was no doubt in her mind what lay ahead. The thought of the squat, sneering savage putting his hands on her—bloody hands that had callously slashed the gray-haired woman's throat—reviled her to the point where she was not certain she could hang onto her sanity. As she sat waiting for her fate, she tried not to think about it, but she found she could not put it out of her mind. She did not realize she was crying until a tear dropped onto her hands, which were still tied together. The tiny drop of moisture seemed to capture her attention, and she stared at it as if it were her life's blood. *You will . . . you must live through this,* she tried to tell herself, knowing deep in her soul that the brute would kill her when she no longer amused him.

Black Elk drove his white war pony hard in an effort to catch up to Moon Shadow and Six Horses as quickly as he could. Swift Runner rode close behind. Knowing his wife was not a strong woman, Black Elk feared that she might be mortally wounded, for Swift Runner had said that she lost a great deal of blood. He was glad that Six Horses was with her. Moon Shadow was very fond of Six Horses—Marta, as she called her—and the white woman seemed to be genuinely fond of Moon Shadow. He knew she would do her best to care for his wife.

Galloping through a narrow valley, Black Elk suddenly pulled his horse to a sliding stop when he spotted something in the trail ahead, near the pass. Looking right and left, to either side of him, he scanned the slopes, looking for any suspicious signs. Then he looked back at the object in the trail. It appeared to be a body. The next moment, Swift Runner slid to a stop beside him.

"Careful," Black Elk warned, and pointed to the body. Then he nudged his pony with his heels, and approached the body, alert to the possibility of an ambush.

"Two Willows!" Swift Runner exclaimed, recognizing the gray-haired woman who had accompanied Moon Shadow and Six Horses.

Both men quickly slid from their ponies and rushed to her side, only to find that they were too late to help the poor woman. Black Elk looked at the arrow in her side. "Crow," he uttered, his tone filled with an age-old hatred. Then, alarmed, he stood up and looked around, expecting to see other bodies. There were none, a fact that offered only temporary hope. Had Moon Shadow and Six Horses managed to get away? Or were they captives of the Crows? Black Elk had to caution himself to calm his emotions and do what must be done. He and Swift Runner scouted the area around Two Willows's body carefully. The story was plainly written on the grassy floor of the valley. The horse pulling the travois had bolted toward the pass. Other tracks showed only two other horses. One would be the horse Two Willows rode. That meant there was only one Crow pony. A single Crow warrior in Blackfoot country? This seemed highly unlikely to Black Elk, and the thought immediately occurred that a Crow raiding party may have attacked the village.

"The two ponies went that way, up the slope toward the ridge," Swift Runner said. "He did not go after the travois."

"Maybe he killed the old woman for her horse, and let the others go," Black Elk replied. "Come, we mustn't waste any more time." He leaped upon his horse, then looked back at Swift Runner. "I'm going after Moon Shadow. Put Two Willows on your horse and take her to the village. But be careful, the rest of the Crows may be nearby. Maybe I will see you there before too long."

He had not ridden more than two miles before he spotted the horse grazing at the foot of a low hill, the travois still intact. Black Elk slowed his horse to a walk as he approached the nervous pony. It appeared that Moon Shadow was still on the travois, but he could not determine if she were all right or not. He could see no movement as he slowly closed the distance between them, speaking calmly to the pony all the while. Six Horses was nowhere in sight. This did not look good. He felt a sharp spike in his heart as the fear of what he might find filled him with dread.

He cooed softly to the horse, which was now eyeing him suspiciously. Although nervously stamping his front hooves, and snorting his distrust, the horse did not bolt, but remained where he stood, letting Black Elk approach. Taking only seconds to get the horse under control, Black Elk hurried to Moon Shadow. At once alarmed by the blood-soaked blanket that was wrapped around her frail body, he feared he was too late. She did not move when he first whispered her name. But when she felt his gentle touch on her cheek, her eyes flickered open to gaze upon his face.

"Don't look so worried," she whispered. "I'm all right." But he could see that she was not. She paused, the strain of talking obviously demanding extreme effort. She managed a slight hint of a smile in an effort to reassure her husband, which almost immediately turned into a worried frown. "Mar-ta," she gasped. "Is she all right?"

Black Elk shook his head. "I think the Crow warrior took her away. You must lie still now while I look at your wound."

"You must find her . . ." Moon Shadow started, but Black Elk placed a finger on her lips to shush her.

"I will find her, but now I have to take care of you." He removed the bloody strip of cowhide binding the wound in her side to reveal the jagged hole in her fragile body. He had to stifle his reaction so as not to alarm her. The wound was deep and still bleeding, and he feared the bull's horn had damaged the organs deep inside. Seeing there was nothing he could do for her now, he could only bind the wound tightly again, hoping to stop the flow of blood.

Moon Shadow tried to smile for him. "I think I am dying."

"Don't say that!" he exclaimed. "You will not die. I'll take you back to the village, and Red Wing will make you well."

Moon Shadow closed her eyes, but the weak smile remained upon her face. He was immediately alarmed, but after a moment's rest, she spoke again. "You must find Mar-ta. She will take care of me."

"I will, I will," he quickly assured her, while working feverishly to remove the straps that had held her to the travois. Time was important to him now, and he didn't want to waste any of it on a slow-moving horse pulling a travois. He didn't bother untying the travois poles. It would be simple enough for one of the others to catch the horse later on. Now it was important to get Moon Shadow to the old medicine woman in the village as quickly as possible. And on his swift white war pony, he could make it there in a few hours' time. Lifting her tiny body in his powerful arms, he easily held her while he climbed on the horse's back. With no thought toward sparing the horse, he set out for the village, his wife cradled in his arms.

Chapter 6

Long shadows spread dark fingers across the narrow trail as the new moon floated above the treetops on the eastern ridge. Witnessed only by a somber gray owl, a lone Indian warrior passed almost silently beneath the winged night hunter, almost as much at home in the darkness as the great bird above him. Pushing on through the moonlit night, Black Elk's mind was a cauldron of conflicting thoughts. He had been reluctant to leave Moon Shadow's side, but she had pleaded with him to bring Six Horses back, urging him to hurry before the Crow raiding party was through the mountain passes and closer to Crow country. It was only after Red Wing had practically pushed him from the tipi that he agreed to leave. The old medicine woman said Moon Shadow was so worried about her white friend that she would not rest until she knew she was safe. Even then, the old woman had to promise Black Elk that Moon Shadow was not going to die. "If you want to help her get well," Red Wing had said, "bring back the white woman." Confident that his wife would be all right, he didn't wait for the other young men to return from the hunt, and set out on a fresh horse alone.

So now, as he rode the dark passages, trails he knew

by heart, he told himself that this desperate feeling of urgency was entirely due to his need to fulfill his wife's wishes. He dared not admit that there was any concern for the white woman herself, not willing to acknowledge the empty feeling that clutched the pit of his stomach when he discovered that she had been stolen. Lately, it seemed, every time he returned to the village after hunting, and saw the auburn-haired woman helping Moon Shadow in her chores, the sight of her immediately triggered troubling thoughts. These thoughts worried Black Elk. The white man was an inferior race, was he not? Almost all the white men he had been in contact with were dirty, hair-faced men, smelling of whiskey and unwashed bodies. The few white women he had seen at Fort Union looked to be as bad as their grimy husbands. Yet, Six Horses did not seem to be that way. She seemed to be more like the women of his village. Sometimes this confusion she caused in his thoughts made him wish he had left her at her burned-out cabin in the Black Hills. Still, he had rejected all offers for her from other men in the village—because of Moon Shadow's fondness for her, he told himself. And now, his mind was tormenting him with pictures of what might be happening to her at the hands of the hated Crows.

He had followed the raiding party's trail from the ridge, through the pass, to their first campsite in a shallow ravine near a small stream. Much to his relief, there was no blood in the sand near the banks where their blankets had been spread. As soon as he felt certain they were following the old buffalo trail to the open plains beyond the mountains, he felt confident that he could close the distance between himself and the Crow party by riding on through the night.

Alert and tireless, he needed no rest as he was driven on by the urgency inside him. Stopping only to rest his horse for a couple of hours at daybreak, he was back on the trail again, knowing now that he was rapidly gaining on the Crows. Judging by the freshness of the horse droppings he examined at their last campsite, he could only be hours behind them. He would catch them at their next camp.

Martha sat with her back to a tree, her hands tied around the slender trunk behind her. Tired to the point of exhaustion, and weak from hunger, she was rapidly losing the will to survive. Three days they had ridden, following an old game trail through the mountains, wasting no time in leaving the Blackfoot land behind. Now, on the third night, she was aware of a lighter mood on the part of the Crow warriors, and she assumed that they must feel there was less danger now. It was a frightening thought for her, for she now feared that her scowling captor might feel it was safe to indulge his savage appetites and fulfill the carnal threats his leering eyes had promised.

Her head down, she could not see Gray Wolf, but she could hear him talking with several of the other warriors. They seemed to be arguing about something. She couldn't understand their words, but she was terrified by a feeling that she was the cause of the discussion, and she feared that her fate was being decided. The simple fact that Gray Wolf had not seen the necessity to waste even a scrap of food on her was indication enough that they planned to kill her soon. At this point, she no longer feared death. It was the thought of the tortures before death took her that filled her with terror. She wished they had done whatever they planned to do to her when she was first captured, instead of forcing her to agonize over the thought of it for three days. But she knew the only reason she had been spared this long was because the

Crow warriors were more concerned with reaching the safety of their own land.

Lost in her despair, she did not realize the discussion had ended. Suddenly, she cried out in pain, jolted from her anguished reverie when Gray Wolf yanked on the rope around her throat. When she looked up to meet his leering face, broad and cruel, his eyes told her what she had feared most in her heart. Her time had come. Complete terror, like a cold clammy hand, clutched at her heart and throat, threatening to choke off her windpipe. *Got to resist till my last breath*, she told herself as Gray Wolf untied her hands. But she knew she was almost helpless to resist. Too weak from hunger and fatigue, battered from the many cuffings and beatings, she knew that he could have his way with her.

Disapproving of their comrade's behavior, the other Crow warriors withdrew to a spot across the creek opposite a small meadow where their horses were grazing, not wishing to witness the scene about to take place. Torturing and raping women of their enemies was a common practice, but the Crows were allied with the white soldiers now. The woman should be taken to the soldier fort. But Gray Wolf was bitter over the shame he had felt at the Blackfoot village, and he was determined that someone would suffer for it. The woman, in High Hump's opinion, was a bad choice. There was too much at stake if the soldiers found out. The woman would have to be killed after Gray Wolf had satisfied his vengeful lust.

Back up the creek some forty or fifty yards, Gray Wolf dragged Martha roughly away from the tree. She tried to hold on to the slender trunk, but he easily overcame her weak attempt, growling in low guttural grunts as he pulled her to him. Untying the rawhide thongs that had bound her ankles together, he favored her with an evil grin, pleased with the fear he saw in her eyes. Her ankles free, he shoved her legs apart, and thrust a rough hand up into her crotch. She could not suppress the scream that resulted. The other warriors downstream merely glanced in her direction before turning their attention back to the discussion around their campfire.

Gray Wolf readied himself to take her, removing his shirt and breechclout, taking great pleasure in her efforts to look away from him. Her brain was on fire with fear and revulsion, and she heard herself begging for mercy when he jerked her skirt up over her hips, even though she had not consciously spoken. Knowing that she could not resist him physically, she tried to fight him mentally, trying desperately to delay the sickening violence that she must surely endure.

"Dirty!" she cried, speaking in the Blackfoot dialect she was now familiar with, hoping the Crow brute understood. He paused for a moment, a puzzled look upon his face, then continued to pull her toward him. "Dirty! Need to wash myself," she blurted frantically, using sign language to try to make him understand.

Finally he understood, for he suddenly halted his efforts to pull her legs around him. Remembering then the hard travel for the past three days, when he had not permitted her to clean herself, even forcing her to relieve herself where she was tied for the night under the watchful glare of his eyes. He wrinkled his nose and sniffed contemptuously. "I'll clean you, dirty coyote bitch." With that, he got to his feet and dragged her down the bank into the chilly waters of the creek, almost drowning her before he let her up for air. "Wash!" he commanded, while he stood over her in the dark chest-deep water.

While tears of terror streamed down her face, she dutifully went through the motions of cleaning herself.

Impatient now, he waited only a few moments before he decided she had done enough, and ordered her up the bank. When she didn't respond quickly enough, he slapped her hard, and grabbing her arm, dragged her out of the creek. Absorbed by the raging lust within him now, he paid little heed to the shouts downstream when the pony herd suddenly stampeded. His mind barely registered the warriors running after their horses, trying to stop them before they scattered in the trees beyond the creek.

Slammed down hard on her back, she somehow summoned the strength for one last attempt to protect herself. Easily avoiding her flailing arms, the Crow brute taunted her efforts before slapping her again and again until she succumbed and lay back in surrender. Pulling her wet skirt up over her hips again, he leered at her triumphantly. The look he saw in return was one of wonder—as if she had seen a vision. It was so strange that he turned to look behind him to discover the source of her vision.

For a moment, he was paralyzed by what he thought was an apparition. Then, too late to leap for his weapons, which were still by the tree where the woman had been tied, he realized that the terrifying sight that filled his eyes was real. In full stride, a lethal combination of muscle and sinew was bearing down on him with the speed of a deer, his eyes burning with the fury raging inside him. Gray Wolf was not a coward, but he experienced genuine terror for the first time in his life. Scrambling to his feet, he turned to meet the attack just in time to catch the full force of Black Elk's charge. The impact took Gray Wolf off his feet, knocking him backward several yards. A lightninglike flash of firelight on Black Elk's knife was all Gray Wolf saw of the fatal thrust before the enraged Blackfoot warrior drove the blade up under his rib cage, tearing at his insides. The hand clamped quickly over his mouth muffled his scream of pain when he felt the knife—white hot in his organs—rip its way out of his body to plunge in once more. He felt his life draining out of him as his eyes were transfixed on the searing gaze of Black Elk.

"Black Elk!" Martha gasped in wonder, hardly believing her eyes, yet somehow deep inside her she had known that he would come for her. He helped her to her feet, and she immediately came into his arms, her arms locked around his neck, her face pressed against his massive chest.

He held her close for a few moments, letting her cling to him while tears of relief streamed down her cheeks. Then he gently took her shoulders and whispered, "Come, we haven't much time." Springing into action once more, he swept her up into his arms, and sprinted toward a willow brake at the bend of the creek where his horse was tied. Behind them they could hear the distant cries of the Crow warriors as they chased after their horses, still unaware at this point of the daring rescue upstream. Placing Martha gently upon his horse's back, he then led the animal down through the willows into the creek. Making his way upstream in waist-deep water, the tall Blackfoot warrior led the pony almost a hundred yards before reaching a rocky shelf that offered a trackless exit. Once out of the creek, Black Elk quickly leaped up behind Martha, and urged the pony into a gallop.

Making no effort to avoid open ground or hide his tracks, Black Elk held his pony to a hard run, in a straight line that led back to his village—the same trail traveled by the Crow raiding party the day before. Holding Martha tight against him, he urged the laboring pony on and on. Having relaxed completely moments earlier, knowing she was now safe in Black

Elk's arms, she now began to worry that they were
not yet out of danger. The Crows would surely give
chase when they discovered what had happened. It
was a long way back to the village, and the horse
could not last long at this pace. As powerful as Black
Elk was, he could not fight all of the Crow warriors.

After a mile or so of hard riding, they once again
crossed the creek. As before, Black Elk dismounted
and led the horse into the water. But instead of continuing across to pick up the trail again, this time he
led them back the way they had just come, remaining
in the water for a short distance until he found a
grassy place where the horse's tracks would not be
easily spotted. Then, selecting a line directly east, he
led the horse up through a tree-covered slope in a
direction that would take them ninety degrees away
from the old trail.

"We should have time for the horse to get his wind
back now," Black Elk said. "There are too many
Crows to outrun, but it will take them a long time to
find our trail. I think they will soon stop looking for
it and just keep on the old hunting trail, hoping to
catch us before we can get back to the village."

She saw the wisdom in his actions then. Instead of
heading straight for home, he was going in another
direction, probably to find a place to hide far away
from the trail the Crows would be searching. Once
again, she felt safe, and could sense her body relaxing
from the tension that had claimed her. It did not regis-
ter in her mind at that moment, but in her earlier
fears that they would be overtaken by the Crows, and
she might never see home again—*home* had brought
to mind a Blackfoot lodge—not a cabin in the Black
Hills, nor a frame house in Virginia.

She had barely spoken during the race away from
the Crow camp, but now that they seemed out of im-

mediate danger, Martha was anxious to know about Moon Shadow. For a brief time, when fleeing for their lives, she had forgotten about her injured friend. Now she worried for her Blackfoot sister. "Moon Shadow?" she asked as Black Elk lifted her from his horse.

He waited to answer until he had gently settled her upon the ground. Then, shaking his head slowly, he spoke. "Red Wing is taking care of her, but she was gored badly. She is so weak that I fear she will not . . ." His voice trailed off as the image of the fragile Blackfoot girl filled his mind.

Seeing the concern in his eyes, she reached out to him, laying her hand on his forearm. "I will take care of her."

He did not reply, but the steady gaze of his dark eyes told her that he was grateful. Meeting his gaze, she looked deep into his eyes, and she thought she could almost feel the compassion he felt for his wife. Eyes that had harbored the menacing warning of an eagle when he had swept down on Gray Wolf, cold calculating eyes that had registered total indifference when she first confronted him in her cabin, were now filled with a defenseless plea for her help. She could not help but wonder how her world had become so confused. Robert Vinings had not crossed her mind in weeks, and she wondered if she should feel guilty about that. Maybe her capture by the Crows provided the shock that made her realize how content she had become living with Black Elk and Moon Shadow. And one crystal-clear truth struck her then, one that she had denied until this very moment: She had no desire to return to her life with Robert.

Realizing that they had been gazing intently into each other's eyes for a long moment, Black Elk quickly looked away. "I must find some food for you," he finally said. "There is a little pemmican in my parfleche. That will give you some strength until I can find some fresh meat. After we rest for a while, we'll circle around the Crow war party and go home."

She nodded and smiled, then lay back, content in the knowledge that he would watch over her. She was hungry, but there was a greater need for rest. Released from the terrifying tension of the last three days, she immediately relaxed, and soon her eyes closed. Kneeling beside her, Black Elk lingered for a few minutes, watching the exhausted girl, aware of the strange emotions stirring inside him once again. *Why do I have these confusing thoughts whenever I look at her? She is white, and not worthy of a Blackfoot warrior.* He worried over it for a moment, then thought, *But Moon Shadow treats her as an equal, even calls her sister.* After another moment, he could not resist reaching out and gently stroking her hair. She smiled, although her eyes remained closed. Soon she was asleep.

Chapter 7

There was more than a hint of fall in the air when Clay and Badger reached the confluence of the Yellowstone and the Missouri Rivers. The mornings had been chilly ever since they had left the Black Hills, struck the Powder and followed it to the Yellowstone, then followed that river to the point where Clay now stood. Now, even the afternoons were chilly, cooled by almost constant breezes that promised icy winds soon. His homespun garments having been discarded in favor of buckskins sewn for him by Gray Bird, he looked almost as wild as Badger. Looks only counted for so much, however, for Clay had come to believe that Badger was more timberwolf than human—and certainly more Indian than white. Over the past several days, as they crossed through country that filled Clay's mind with wonder, he had acquired an enormous respect for the old mountain man's cunning.

Almost as soon as they had struck the Yellowstone, they came upon a large Crow village. Badger deemed it prudent to skirt the village, even though the Crows were supposed to be friends to the white man. "They may be friends to a detachment of cavalry," he had explained. "But that don't mean they're gonna cozy up to every stray white man that passes through their

territory. Besides, I reckon I got too much Lakota
scent on me. We'd best give 'em a wide berth." Clay
still remembered the strange rush of excitement he
felt on that moonless night when he and Badger
passed the Crow camp. There was a ruby glow that
had hung over the peaceful village like a rose-colored
canopy, lit by more than three hundred individual
cookfires. It was a strange sensation, passing so close
to potential danger. Clay liked the feeling.

Now, as he stood on this small rise, waiting for Badger to tighten a loose strap on his packhorse, he
looked across the river at Fort Union. Glancing up at
the sun, he judged it to be close to noontime, and the
walled structure looked to be as busy as a city market.
Outside the formidable walls with their twin guard
towers on opposite corners, he could see many small
camps gathered in the plains around the fort. It reminded him of a mother hen, surrounded by her
baby chicks.

Badger told him that the fort, built by the Upper
Missouri Outfit of the American Fur Company, had
been doing most of the trading with the Indians since
the late twenties. It had been established mostly as a
post for the Assiniboin, but other tribes had traded
there—Blackfoot as well. "As a matter of fact," he
had said, "a feller by the name of Culbertson used to
be the *booshway* at Fort Union—and he was married
to a Blackfoot woman, name of Natawista. Right
handsome woman as I recall." Badger paused as if
trying to remember. "Near as I can recollect, he was
the *booshway* at Fort Benton, too."

Impatient to go now, Clay looked back at Badger,
wondering how long he was going to fiddle with that
pack. He was anxious to reach the fort and find Badger's friend Pete Dubois to see if there was any information about Martha. Badger had cautioned Clay not

to get his hopes up too high. At best, Pete might be able to give them a place to start looking for Martha. At worse, he would have found out that she was dead. In spite of the warning, Clay was counting on some positive information about his sister's whereabouts, and now he was getting a bit irritated at Badger's seemingly blasé attitude about reaching their destination.

Glancing up at his young friend, Badger guessed what Clay was thinking. "Just hold your horses, young feller. I don't wanna lose this here pack in that river yonder. There's a place to ford upstream a'ways—even so, the horses is gonna have to swim a little piece."

Clay nodded. Still impatient, but knowing that Badger was just making sure they didn't lose part of their food supply as well as a couple of buffalo robes that would come in mighty handy in a few weeks, Clay decided to check his own packs. "This friend of yours," he asked, "does he work in the fort?"

"Nah," Badger said, "Pete don't hardly work no-where. He's got a little shack 'bout a mile upriver he stays in when he ain't livin' with one band or another. I expect we'll find him there this time of year."

Badger figured correctly. Pete was there all right. They found him sitting on a wooden stool in front of his cabin. A squat little man, wearing buckskins blackened with age and hundreds of campfires, he sat skinning a rabbit before a small fire. He didn't bother to get up as the two riders approached his cabin—just cocked his head and squinted, trying to make out who his visitors could be. He gave no indication of recognition even when they pulled up before the cabin and dismounted, continuing to work on his rabbit while he waited for his visitors to state the purpose of their visit. It was Badger who broke the silence.

"Hey, you old bastard, can't you even get up off your ass to say howdy to a friend?"

Pete hesitated for just a moment before the dingy-gray whiskers parted in a crooked smile. "Badger? Well, I'll be go to hell . . ." He laid the rabbit carcass on the skin just cut away and stood up to greet his old friend.

Clay stood by smiling as the two old mountain men pounded each other on the back and shoulders. He had never tried to guess how old Badger might be. He was obviously quite a few years away from a rocking chair. But Pete Dubois looked as old as the distant hills. Like the scrubby pines near the peaks of the mountains, his spine was permanently bent from the cold north winds, giving him a hunched-over look even when standing. While the two friends brought each other up to date on the twists and turns of their separate trails, Clay looked around him at Pete's camp. The tiny log cabin appeared to be as run-down as its owner. It had a definite lean toward one side—probably in the direction of the prevailing winds, Clay speculated. The yard was strewn about with antlers of various sizes, and several deer or antelope hooves were scattered here and there—probably as far as the old man had been able to throw them. A tiny corral was attached to the back wall of the cabin where two horses stood staring over the top rail. Clay was reminded of a packrat's nest as he surveyed the little Frenchman's abode. "This young feller's Clay Culver," he heard Badger say, and he turned to grasp the outstretched hand.

"Pleased to meet you, Mr. Dubois," Clay said as he felt the iron in Pete's grip.

Dubois said nothing, squinting hard at him for a long moment before nodding. Then he released his hand and immediately turned back to Badger. "I'da shore thought you was dead by now. Last I heered of you, you was nestin' with a Sioux woman."

Badger laughed. "Still am." Looking over Pete's shoulder toward the cabin, he asked, "Where's that Blackfoot woman you was married to? Little Feet, weren't it?"

"Light Foot," Pete corrected. "She took sick winter before last. Carried on somethin' fierce for about a month before she went under."

"Well, that's a shame, I declare," Badger commiserated. "She was a fine little woman, as I recollect." He paused to take a look around at the general state of disarray. He should have guessed the absence of a woman. "Reckon you'll be lookin' for another'n now."

Pete chuckled at the thought. "Reckon I'm a mite too old to go after another'n. Nah, I reckon I'm 'bout near the end of my string. I can't see no more. Hell, I didn't know who you was till you 'bout stepped on my toes. Fact of the matter is I just come back here to die. No, I sure ain't lookin' for another woman. I couldn't do her no good, and I reckon I've got used to quiet, anyway. I don't know that I could stand to hear a woman chatterin' around me no more."

"Hell, Pete," Badger scoffed, showing no sign of sympathy for the old man, "you been talkin' 'bout dying for the last ten years."

"Is that a fact? Well, this time I mean it. When a man gits where he don't wanna leave the campfire no more, he's as good as dead, anyway. Hell, I can't hunt no more—nothin' besides trappin' rabbits and such. Hell, it's time to go."

Listening to the conversation, Clay was not at all

optimistic that Badger's old friend could be of any
help in finding Martha. From the looks of things, it
appeared the old man was now nothing more than a
hermit, waiting to wither away like the weathered old
cabin he called home. For that reason, when Badger
stated the purpose of their visit, Clay was relieved to
hear that Pete had spent most of the summer with
Light Foot's people on the Milk River. Maybe he
could tell them where to start looking for Martha
after all.

"I did hear there's a white woman livin' with
Bloody Axe's band," Pete continued. "A huntin' party
come into the camp one day, and they was talkin'
about it. I don't rightly know where Bloody Axe's
people is now. This time of year, they're most likely
gone into winter camp somewhere; weather's fixin' to
turn any day now. Bloody Axe ain't what I'd call real
sociable, anyway. He likes to keep as far away from
the tradin' posts as he can. I know he ain't come to
Fort Union in at least a year or two."

Clay could feel the increase in his heartbeat at the
mention of a white woman in Bloody Axe's camp. It
had to be Martha. He looked at Badger and the old
scout nodded in return. Turning his attention back to
Pete, Badger pressed for more information. "You got
any idea where Bloody Axe is most likely to winter?"

"Well, like I said, I ain't had no dealings with that
particular band of Blackfoot. But I know that he keeps
pretty much to the north of the Milk in the summer-
time. I wouldn't have any idea where he winters.
Maybe the mountains to the west, I couldn't say." He
paused to pull at his chin whiskers for a moment while
he thought.

It wasn't much to go on. The excitement Clay had
felt moments before was rapidly giving way to discour-
agement. Even though Badger had cautioned him

against getting his hopes up too high, Clay had counted on Pete Dubois to be able to tell them exactly where to find Martha. The thought of winter snows that might close the mountain passes was especially discouraging, and the nagging urge to hurry was upon him once more.

Having given the question more thought, something else occurred to Pete. "There's a good possibility that Crow Fighter—that's Light Foot's brother—he might know where Bloody Axe is camped."

This was at least a possibility. "Where can we find Crow Fighter?" Badger asked.

"He's with the band I summered with, old Black Shirt's bunch. They weren't even fixin' to move back up in the hills when I left to come back here to die. Black Shirt's got two or three favorite places to camp in the winter, but he don't generally go to 'em before the first signs of snow. If he's moved before you git there, I expect you'll find him in one of his regular winter camps."

Badger scratched his chin thoughtfully. "I reckon I can find him right enough. That ain't the part that worries me. You know, them dang Blackfoot ain't too friendly to many white men. It don't hold that we can just ride in to their camp and ask 'em where we can find Bloody Axe. We might not ride out again."

Pete nodded in silent agreement. "That is a consideration," he allowed. The two mountain men continued to look at each other for a moment, Pete still nodding his head as he thought. "Hell," he finally blurted, "I'll go with you. They won't give you no trouble if I'm with you."

Badger grunted. "Huh, I thought you come back here to die."

"Well, I expect I can die just as good up above the Milk as I can here," he shot back. "Matter of fact, I was just thinkin' what a sorry place to die this is, anyway. Most of the folks I've knowed at the fort are gone. The ones that are there now don't give a damn about us trappers that was here when beaver was shining. New man, name of Marlowe—mean son of a bitch—told me not to hang around there no more unless I had somethin' to trade." He snorted his contempt. "Word has it that he ain't gonna be around long hisself. There's talk that the army is plannin' to buy Fort Union." He snorted again for emphasis. "And there ain't nothin' to hunt around here anymore, 'cept rabbits and prairie dogs. Hell, I was thinkin' on eatin' my horses when you boys showed up."

"Well, if you come with us, it would make things a mite easier at that," Badger said. "But are you sure you're up to it?"

"Oh hell yeah," Pete tossed off, "it'll be better'n settin' around here wonderin' when this damn shack is gonna fall over."

It was settled then. Clay suspected that the opportunity to hit the trail again was a tonic that might lift the old man out of his fatal melancholy. He certainly appeared spry enough as he collected his possibles and prepared to leave his cabin. After talking it over further, they decided to stay there for the night and go to the fort in the morning for some extra supplies before setting out for the Milk. Badger and Clay had a few buffalo hides to trade, and there might not be another opportunity before winter set in.

Supper that night was a combination of rabbit, dried buffalo meat, and some pemmican that Gray Bird had packed for them. Pete fell asleep while Badger was still reminiscing about a time when they had spent the winter at Three Forks. He hardly stirred when Badger and Clay carried him inside the cabin and spread his blanket over him. The two of them elected to bed down outside by the fire. Both said they preferred the night air. But Clay suspected that, like himself, that Badger was afraid the rotten old cabin might collapse during the night.

The next morning, after a breakfast of buffalo jerky, the three travelers saddled up and prepared to depart. In a fitting gesture of finality, Pete Dubois set fire to his cabin, which pretty much answered the question of whether or not he planned to return.

They arrived at the fort just as the huge doors were opening, anxious to get what supplies they needed and be on their way as quickly as possible. After trading for some dried beans and coffee to supplement their rations of buffalo and deer jerky, the rest was used to buy extra cartridges for their rifles. Clay left Badger and Pete to indulge in one last shot of whiskey before leaving this final outpost of civilization, while he took Red over to the blacksmith to be reshod.

"Shore you don't want one?" Badger called after him as he led the big sorrel away. When Clay shook his head, Badger stood watching him for a moment. Then he turned to Pete and said, "We're gonna have to trade that damn horse for one that don't wear shoes. Even a drunk Injun could track that big ol' horse." Pete only grunted in reply. They both turned their attention back to the glasses on the counter before them, but Badger was thinking that it was something he was going to have to take up with Clay real soon. In the territory they were going to be traveling in, a shod horse would most likely lead a war party straight to a person. Clay thought a lot of that big red horse. They could just take the shoes off, but Badger knew it would take about a year before Red's feet would toughen up enough to go barefoot, especially over rocky ground. Clay wasn't gonna like it.

"It's gonna be a little while yet before that horse is shod," Badger said. "And that first drink burned a gully down my throat that oughta make another'n feel about right." Pete was in agreement, since Badger was buying. So they ordered up another round.

"Has that old fool got the money to pay for them drinks?"

Badger and Pete turned to find a large, heavyset man standing in the doorway behind them. His deep-set eyes, glowering contemptuously from beneath heavy black eyebrows, were locked on the two mountain men. "Marlowe," Pete mumbled almost below a whisper.

"They paid for 'em, Mr. Marlowe," the bartender offered.

This seemed to disappoint Marlowe. He pushed on through the doorway, filling up a sizable portion of the room. "Well, drink up and be on your way. I've done told you I'm tired of you hanging around here, wearing out my clerks' ears with all those stories about the good old days." He moved over to the end of the counter where he paused to look Badger over thoroughly. "I reckon this is another dirt-poor trapper looking for a handout. Take him with you."

Badger didn't say anything at first. In fact, he was too taken aback by the big man's uncalled-for attitude. In all his years as a trapper and a guide, he could never remember being told he wasn't welcome at any trading post. To the contrary, he was accustomed to a certain amount of respect—for surviving this long without losing his scalp, if for no other reason. It took a moment for the insult to settle in before he responded.

"Mister," he started slowly, "I don't know what kind of gravel you got in your craw—and I don't really give a good goddamn. But me and my friend here is gonna take our own sweet time finishing our drinks, and I'll thank you to mind your own damn business."

Marlowe was in a surly mood already. He wasn't about to tolerate anybody talking to him that way. As far as he was concerned, he was the boss in this place, and he would decide who could stay and who was not welcome. "Why, you old worn-out son of a bitch. You don't get away with that sass in my store." With that, he suddenly grabbed Badger by the collar and jerked him away from the counter. With his other hand, he swept the two drink glasses off the bar, sending them flying up against the wall, leaving two long streaks of whiskey to mark the spot where they landed.

Badger tried to tear away from the big man, but Marlowe's grip on the back of his collar was too powerful. Angry and frustrated, he pulled his pistol from his belt, and stuck it in Marlowe's belly. In a move surprisingly quick for a man of his size, Marlowe grabbed the barrel of the pistol and forced it away from him. Smirking with the confidence of a bully who was accustomed to overpowering his adversaries, Marlowe looked Badger right in the eye as he slowly forced the pistol down toward the floor. Badger knew the man had him right where he wanted him.

"Now, you son of a bitch," Marlowe growled, "I'll teach you to pull a gun on me." Locking both arms around Badger in a crushing bear hug, he started slowly bending the scout over backward. Badger strained with all the strength he possessed, but Marlowe was too powerful. He could feel the pain racing along the length of his spine as he fought to resist the overpowering force.

"Let's see how far you bend before your backbone snaps," Marlowe grunted as he increased the pressure on the helpless trapper.

"Let's see how big a hole this Winchester makes in your head."

Feeling the solid thump of the rifle barrel against the back of his skull, Marlowe released his hold on Badger. His face twisted with rage, he whirled around to confront his assailant, freeing Badger to stagger a few feet away. Surprised to encounter a calm but determined young man in buckskins standing there with a Winchester leveled at him, Marlowe took a step backward. Sizing him up, he determined that this deliberate stranger might be a bit more to handle than the old trapper. Still, Marlowe had never met a man with the physical strength to get the best of him. Though tall and sturdy, Clay was still outweighed by a good many pounds. It was enough to give Marlowe confidence in his ability to bully.

"You got gall, coming in here holding a gun on me. You fire that rifle, and there'll be fifty men in here," Marlowe growled.

"They won't do you much good with a hole in your belly," Clay replied calmly. "Now as soon as your man there pours two more drinks for my friends, we'll be leaving your hospitality." He motioned toward the clerk with his rifle barrel. The clerk didn't wait for Marlowe to approve, producing two more glasses in a wink.

Marlowe didn't move. Although he was burning with the fury inside him, he said nothing while Badger and Pete hurriedly tossed their whiskey down. "It was nice talkin' to you agin, Marlowe," Pete taunted as he and Badger headed for the door, while Clay kept the rifle on the fuming giant.

"I can see what you're thinking," Clay stated, his voice level and quiet. "I wouldn't advise it." He began to slowly back away, following his two partners.

The rage and indignation was too much for Marlowe to allow. He waited for his chance, and it came when Clay turned to go through the doorway. Marlowe charged. Like a wounded buffalo bull, he stormed through the door after Clay. Into the open courtyard he exploded, intent upon crushing the life from the tall young man. With no show of excitement, Clay turned to meet the attack. When Marlowe's massive hands were inches from his face, Clay deftly stepped to one side, and using his rifle as a spear, plunged the barrel deep into Marlowe's belly. Marlowe, bent double by the blow, wheezed like a winded mule as the breath was knocked out of him. Spurred on by this added insult to his rage, he recovered quickly enough to spring at Clay once again. This time, Clay easily avoided the wildly swinging fists, and brought the barrel of his rifle across the side of Marlowe's face with sufficient force to lay him out cold on the hard-baked clay of the courtyard.

Watching spellbound from a short distance away, Badger and Pete could only marvel at the swift efficiency with which Clay defused the situation. There was not a word spoken between them for a few seconds, then Pete observed aloud, "He's mighty handy to have around, ain't he?"

Figuring they had pretty much worn out their welcome at Fort Union, they wasted no time in leaving, heading for more peaceful country. Badger had a hint of a smile on his face as he considered the confrontation with Marlowe. He silently congratulated himself on his judge of character. *I knowed he was cut from the right tree the first time I saw him at Fort Laramie.*

Chapter 8

Encouraged by the fact that he was at last venturing into the territories frequented by the band of savages that had abducted his sister, Clay Culver rode easily in the saddle, his body moving in perfect partnership with Red's gait. Up ahead, Badger guided his dingy gray Indian pony around the many cuts and defiles that broke away from the prairie toward the wide river they had followed since sunup that morning. Following Pete's directions, the little party had set out to the west on the north side of the Missouri.

Watching the old scout rocking gently in the saddle before him, Clay realized how fortunate he had been to run into Badger. And he still puzzled over the fact that the crusty old mountain man would choose to guide him into hostile country, leaving his wife and friends behind, with no apparent reward for his services. Clay had yet to learn of the irresistible calling the mountains had on a man like Badger, and the constant craving to see what might lie beyond the next ridge.

Moving his head constantly from side to side, sniffing the air as he did, Badger reminded Clay of a prairie dog, scanning the plain for signs of danger. The peril—some men might call it folly—of three lone white men riding deep into Blackfoot country caused no concern in Clay's mind. He had the utmost confidence in Badger's ability as a scout and his own efficiency with his Winchester rifle. If there were trouble, he was confident that he could make it extremely expensive for any hostiles who might consider attacking them.

Bringing up the rear of their tiny caravan, Pete Dubois rode a shaggy brown mount that walked, head down, behind Clay's packhorse. His eyes dulled by too many winters in the high mountains, Pete was content to let Badger lead the way, after he had advised Badger on the most direct trail to one of Black Shirt's favorite campsites. Glancing back occasionally at the old Frenchman, Clay couldn't help but question the wisdom in bringing Pete along. Badger felt it critical that Pete should accompany them since he was known by the Blackfeet and considered a friend, but Clay wondered if the old man was going to make it to Black Shirt's winter camp. Like his horse, Pete rode slumped over, his head down as if each mile might be his last. Clay questioned the advisability of arriving at the Blackfoot camp with a dead man. Badger only laughed when Clay expressed his doubts, saying, "Don't let his looks fool ya. That old buzzard might outlive the both of us."

The weather was getting colder as each day passed, and the cool morning air promised the possibility of an early winter. The animals seemed to know it. Already there were signs that antelope were moving away from the open plains toward more sheltered valleys and beaver had already returned to their dams. Game was still abundant on the prairie, however. There should be no scarcity of fresh meat to be killed whenever they needed it.

The very vastness of the prairie seemed to capture

Clay's mind. He had seen the ocean at Portsmouth, and this country he was now crossing made much the same impression as when he had stood on the Atlantic shore, gazing out at an endless horizon. The long buffalo grass, bronzed by the summer sun, swaying in the chilly wind, reminded him of the ceaseless movement of the ocean. He stood up in the stirrups for a few moments, and looked all around him. There was no sign of life in any direction except for a small herd of antelope some four or five miles distant. There was a great emptiness about the country that gave him the feeling that he was the first to set foot upon that rolling plain. Settling in the saddle again, he was aware of a sense of complete serenity, content to be where he was, feeling the rhythmic motion of his horse as Red followed dutifully behind Badger's packhorse. For a brief moment he would almost swear he could hear his name whispered on the restless wind that parted the long grass before him. Behind him, Pete glanced up briefly, watching the young man's reaction to the country, and a faint smile creased his lips. It had been many years ago that he had felt the same sensations, but he still remembered.

They rode from sunup to near sundown, following the Missouri without sighting another human being until they left the wide river when it took a more southwesterly course after striking the Milk. There were eight of them, a small roving band of Blackfeet, camped in a grove of cottonwoods that bordered a stream Pete identified as Porcupine Creek. It was early afternoon on the fifth day on the trail, and Badger had planned to make camp in the same spot that was now occupied by the Blackfeet. He pulled up when he spotted the Indian ponies among the trees, and waited for Clay and Pete to catch up to him.

"Well, I don't know," Badger started when the others were beside him. "Maybe my eyes is gittin' too old, too." He directed his statement at Pete. "I'da damn sure rode around them devils if I'd seen 'em a mite sooner."

Pete shaded his eyes with one hand while he strained to make out the party in the trees. "I can't see nuthin' at this distance. How many is there?"

"Eight, near as I can tell," Badger replied.

"Why *don't* we just ride around them?" Clay wondered aloud.

"Too late for that," Badger said. "They've done spotted us. The worse thing we could do is to let 'em think we're runnin' from 'em. We'd best just ride on in and say howdy—let 'em know we ain't a'scared of them." He glanced at Pete. "Ain't that what you say, Pete?"

"Reckon you're right," Pete agreed. "Can't show no fear. Blackfoot'll sneak up on you at night, or early morning if he's gonna raid you. But if you show any sign of runnin', he'll chase you all the way to St. Louie."

Badger nudged his horse and started out again. Glancing back at Clay, he said, "Keep that rifle of your'n handy. You might have to use it."

"Maybe they're some of that bunch I know," Pete said, "and there might not be no fuss a'tall."

"Maybe," Badger replied with more than a hint of skepticism in his voice. He could remember a few past encounters with Blackfeet—none of them pleasant.

Clay reached down and eased his Winchester up a little to make sure it was riding free and easy in its elkskin scabbard. He would not hesitate to break it out if the Indians showed any indication of aggression. In spite of Badger's opinion, he was not convinced that they had been spotted by the party at the creek. There was no sign of activity. They appeared to be seated around a fire, taking no notice of the three approaching white men. Close enough now to clearly see into the cottonwoods, Clay could count only seven warriors. Just as he was about to decide that Badger had miscounted, a lone warrior rode up out of a coulee off to their left, and paralleled them as they approached the camp, pacing them on his pony. *Reckon that's why Badger was sure they spotted us,* Clay thought, and smiled to himself. *I guess I've got a lot to learn about this country.*

When they had closed to within fifty yards of the cottonwoods, Badger raised his arm and called out a greeting, asking if they could enter the camp. He was immediately answered by one of the Indians, politely inviting the three white men to approach. The warriors who had been seated around the fire showed no signs of excitement beyond getting to their feet. The white men continued on toward the camp. As they neared the creekbank, both parties were intent upon sizing up the other. Clay noted the absence of repeating rifles among the warriors. A couple of them carried what appeared to be army Springfields, some were armed with old Hudson's Bay fusees, an unreliable musket at best. From the polite reception, he could guess that the Blackfoot warriors had taken note of the white men's superior weaponry.

A tall hawk-faced warrior stepped forward to meet them, eyeing the three visitors curiously. He glanced from one to the other several times as if trying to recognize them. "Welcome," he finally said. "It's strange to see white men this far from the fort."

"You know any of 'em?" Badger asked under his breath.

"Nope," Pete quickly returned. Then speaking out to the Blackfoot warrior, he said, "We are on our way to find Black Shirt's camp."

"Ah . . . Black Shirt," Hawk Face replied, nodding his head solemnly. He paused for a moment, then: "You have business with Black Shirt? Maybe guns and whiskey to trade?" He craned his neck to look around Pete, curious about the loaded packhorses. The others in his party now became more interested in the conversation, and some of them moved slowly to positions on both sides of the white men. Clay pulled gently on the reins, backing Red up a few paces to make sure all eight of the Indians remained in front of him just in case they might harbor some ideas about closing in behind them. The precautionary move did not go unnoticed by the warriors, and the hand resting on the butt of his Winchester tended to discourage any further thoughts along those lines.

"No," Pete answered. "We have no whiskey. We carry only food for our journey. We go to visit our friends. My wife was a member of Black Shirt's village. She is in the land of the spirits now. We go as friends to visit the great chief."

Hawk Face considered this for a moment. "I think Black Shirt's village is many days ride that way." He pointed toward the west. "It might be dangerous for only three men to ride there alone. Perhaps it would be wise to travel with us." He was talking to Pete, but his eyes were on Clay's horse. The handsome chestnut had attracted the gaze of most of the other warriors as well, causing Clay to draw back another step to keep all eight in view.

Badger answered for Pete. "We thank you for your hospitality," he started in the Blackfoot tongue, not so fluent as Pete's, and supplemented with sign language, "but we have to move on. We don't plan to stop while the sun is still high."

There was a genuine expression of disappointment in Hawk Face's eyes, accompanied by a low murmur of half whispered comments among his brothers. Hawk Face's frown immediately turned to a contrived smile, and he waved his arm in a welcoming gesture. "Come. Get off your ponies. We will have something to eat. Then we can trade. We have many fine pelts to trade. I'll trade you for that horse."

I knew that damn horse was gonna attract attention, Badger thought. To the Blackfoot he said, "That horse is big white man medicine. We cannot trade him." He glanced briefly at Clay, knowing his young friend could not understand a word being said.

"Ah . . . I see," Hawk Face replied softly, his head nodding again in confirmation. "Too bad, he is an unusual pony. But no matter, you must eat with us before you go on. We have fresh-killed buffalo."

Pete and Badger exchanged cautious glances, both knowing it would be considered extremely impolite to refuse the invitation. "Thank you," Pete replied. "We are honored to accept your hospitality."

The three white men dismounted and joined the Blackfoot warriors by the fire. Clay didn't have to be told to keep his rifle with him. He wasn't sure if by doing so he might be insulting his hosts, but he didn't think it was worth the risk to leave it on his saddle. Then he noticed that Badger and Pete both cradled their weapons in their arms. If the Indians were offended, they made no sign of it. In return for the feast of buffalo hump, Badger supplied some coffee and a little sack of dried apples. The apples especially seemed to please the hawk-faced Blackfoot, who introduced himself as Many Scalps.

While the strips of meat sizzled over the flames, Clay looked around the half circle of warriors seated on the other side of the fire. Blank expressions greeted him as he looked from one man to the next, but all eyes seemed to be locked on the shiny Winchester cradled in his arms. He was waiting for one of them to ask to examine it, knowing that he was damn sure going to refuse. And he wondered if that was going to be the fuse that would ignite a rather volatile situation. But to his surprise, no request came to handle the weapon.

Many Scalps suggested that the white men should unsaddle their horses and let them graze with their small herd of Indian ponies. Badger declined, explaining once again that the three of them must hurry on their way. When they had eaten the meat offered them, they wasted no time in expressing their thanks, and were back in the saddle as soon as politeness allowed. Crossing the creek and leaving the cottonwoods behind, all three continued to look back, waving good-bye to their dinner companions until they felt it was safe to turn their backs and gallop.

When they had put considerable distance between them and Porcupine Creek, Badger reined back to let the horses rest. "Well, that was right tasty buffalo hump," he allowed.

"Maybe somebody ought to explain to me how we got away from that surly-looking bunch without a fight," Clay said. He had read the treachery in their hosts' eyes as well as anyone.

Badger snorted, "Oh, we ain't done with that bunch yet. They'll be payin' us a little visit tonight, if'n they can find us." He unconsciously glanced toward their backtrail as if they might already be coming. "I was plannin' on campin' back yonder tonight, but there's daylight left yet. We can make the forks of the Milk before dark if we push these horses a little harder." If Pete had a better idea, he didn't express it, so they spurred their mounts on to cover the additional twelve or fourteen miles to reach the Milk River.

Flat and endless, the plain behind them showed no

signs of pursuit for as far as Clay could see, and he began to wonder if Badger might be a bit overcautious. He didn't doubt the Blackfeet's capacity for treachery, but Many Scalps would be careless indeed to lead his warriors into the field of fire he and Badger could lay down with their repeating rifles. Still, he had learned not to question Badger's wisdom in matters pertaining to hostiles.

It was a little before dark when the three riders approached the line of scrubby trees that marked the Milk River. Badger continued on until he came to a small island, formed by a fork in the river. "I reckon this is as good a place as we're likely to find. This way, they're gonna have to cross water to git to us from any direction, and it'll be damn hard to sneak in and run our horses off."

In the twilight of the evening, they crossed the horses over and hobbled them, which Clay thought a bit unnecessary; they were on an island, after all. But Badger said he wasn't about to take a chance that one of the damn-fool horses might decide to cross over to get to some better-looking grass on the other bank.

Pete nodded approval. "I lost a mule one night, seven or eight years ago on the Missouri. He just decided to go for a swim, I reckon. Just set out toward the middle and floated downstream. There wasn't no way I could git to him before the current washed him 'round a bend in the river. I climbed on my horse and rode down around the bend, but there warn't no sign of mule or anything else. He either drowned or wound up in St. Louie, I reckon. 'Course that was a mule. Mules can be mighty peculiar at times."

"Amen to that," Badger agreed. "Some says they're smarter'n horses, though. Ain't neither one of 'em got much sense, to my way of thinkin'."

"You really think those Blackfeet will try to attack

us tonight?" Clay asked, as he checked his rifle to make sure it didn't get wet crossing the river.

"I expect so," Badger answered, busy checking his own weapon. He cocked a mischievous eye at Clay. "It'd be against their religion not to make a try for that fancy horse of your'n—that, and help theirselves to our rifles and the rest of our plunder."

"I expect they ain't gonna be too happy when they find out we're camped on this little island," Pete offered. "It's gonna make their work a mite harder for 'em. They'd like to come sneakin' up on us at night on foot, and two or three of 'em run the horses off while the rest jump us in our blankets."

"Well, they're gonna have to swim fer it tonight," Badger said. "Clay, that log out near the point is a good spot for that rifle of your'n." Clay nodded and immediately started toward the water's edge where an old log lay half submerged. "Keep your eyes peeled, son," Badger called after him. "They'll be comin' after dark. I'll be between them two willows yonder." He pointed them out, and Clay nodded again. Pete positioned himself on the backside of the tiny island so they were deployed in a triangle with the horses in the middle. With each man in position, and each man knowing where the other two were so there wouldn't be any danger of accidentally shooting each other, there was nothing left to do but wait for the visitors Badger was certain would come.

Clay spent a few minutes fashioning a rifle pit for himself behind the eight-foot piece of tree trunk by scooping some of the dirt from behind the log. When he was satisfied that he had enough cover from any shots from across the narrow channel of water, he propped his rifle against the log and settled back to watch the opposite bank. Already it was getting dark, but he could still see Badger about thirty yards off to

his left, digging sand away from the base of the larger
of the two willows. Fixing the exact spot in his mind
before it became too dark to see clearly, he then
looked to his right to verify Pete's position. Confident
that he wouldn't shoot either of them in the heat of
battle, he then settled down to wait.

The lonesome call of a night bird signaled the end
of twilight. It seemed to quiet the humming and buzz-
ing of the daylight creatures that had gone unnoticed
until their busy chatter suddenly ceased. Silence descended upon the river. As the night deepened, the
gentle gurgling of the water seemed to become louder,
or perhaps it was simply because he had been unaware
of it before the chilly cloak of darkness brought it to
his ear.

Hours passed with no sound to disturb the gentle
night, except the occasional stomping of a horse's hoof
as the animals grew impatient with their hobbles. Clay
looked toward the two willows where Badger lay, unable to make his friend out in the dark shadows. *What
if he's asleep?* he wondered, then immediately rejected
the notion. Badger was in a position directly opposite
Clay's point on the island—these two the most likely
places to come under attack from the opposite shore—
while Pete was posted farther back toward the rearmost part of the little island. Badger did not express
it, but Clay knew that he and Badger would most
likely catch the brunt of an attack. He had stationed
Pete farther away because he could no longer trust the
old man's vision. This arrangement was fine with Clay.

Still more time passed with no threat of attack. Clay
looked up into a sky filled with tiny pinpricks of light,
a deep starry field of soft velvet. *No night could be
more peaceful,* he thought as he fished in his pocket
for a piece of dried buffalo jerky. He had not taken
the first bite when a dark object caught his eye. At

first he thought it was something floating on the water. But then he became immediately alert because the object did not drift downstream with the current. It was making a steady course straight across the river. *Muskrat?* he wondered. *Maybe.* He continued to stare at the dark stretch of water. After another second, a second object appeared, bobbing after the first, and it was clear to him then that the objects were heads. Badger had been right in his prediction.

Clay carefully replaced the jerky in the pocket of his buckskin shirt, and reached over to retrieve his rifle from its resting place against the log, never taking his eyes from the river. Laying the barrel across a notch in the log that had been formed by a broken limb, he waited. *Two of them,* he noted. *Wait, there's another coming out from under the shadow of a willow.* His eyes moved rapidly back and forth across the dark bank, searching the shadows. Still he waited. Finally, when he was certain there were no more than three, he returned his full attention to the two lead Blackfeet, by then no more than a few yards from the island.

He and Badger had not worked out any form of signal between themselves. In fact, there had been no discussion about what to do when the Blackfoot warriors actually made a try for the horses. Clay didn't give it much thought at the moment. There was little doubt in his mind that the Indians meant to murder the three of them if they got the chance. *My rifle will be signal enough,* he thought as he drew the Winchester's sights down on the leading head. A split second later, the gentle fabric of night was ripped apart by the roar of Clay's rifle. Almost before his first bullet smashed the unsuspecting warrior's skull, Clay shifted his aim to send the second Blackfoot to follow his brother to the spirit world. He quickly drew his rifle around for a third shot, but the third head had disappeared beneath the water. Across the tiny island, he heard Badger's rifle, barking out in the night—three, four times—and then there was quiet again.

"Clay!" Badger called out as Clay crawled to the other end of the log in case the remaining warriors had spotted his muzzle flash. "How many?"

"Three here," Clay returned. "I got two. The other one went underwater somewhere."

"Three come across here," Badger called back. "I got one fer sure. I ain't sure about the other two." That left two more of the Blackfoot party that weren't accounted for. "Pete!" Badger called again. "You all right?" There had been no rifle fire from that corner of the island.

Clay listened. There was no reply from the old Frenchman. He immediately swung around, ready to repel any attack from behind, but there was no one there. A quick look told him that the horses were all right, although the sudden shooting had caused them to raise a fuss. Clay quickly turned his attention back toward the river, anxious to try to spot the warrior who had ducked underwater. There was no sign of him, and Clay decided that he had evidently made it back into the shadows on the other side. Now his concern was for Pete, and the whereabouts of the two unaccounted-for Blackfeet.

"Pete!" Badger called out. Then he shouted the name again.

"Yeah," the reply finally came back, "I'm all right."

No more than an instant later, two musket flashes exploded from among the horses. Clay threw himself flat on the ground. Then he realized that the shots had been fired toward the rear of the island, where Pete was dug in. They were at the horses! Now the horses were bucking and screaming, having been startled by the two muskets fired practically from right under them. Clay didn't hesitate any longer. He was up and running in the wink of an eye. The other two Indians must have somehow gotten by Pete, unaware of his presence, and had shot at him when he answered Badger's call.

Rushing headlong into the thicket where the horses were hobbled, Clay surprised two dark forms in the shadows hurriedly trying to reload their muskets. When they heard him charging through the bushes, they turned to meet his attack. Unable to complete the loading of the old muskets, they stood ready to use them as clubs. One shot from Clay's rifle doubled over the one nearest him, and he crumpled to the ground. The other, recognizing the inevitable, sprang into the bushes, and ran for the river. Clay slowly raised his rifle and sighted on the running warrior. He held it there for a few seconds, then lowered it again, watching the fleeing Blackfoot until he dived into the river and began swimming for his life. There had been enough killing. "Pete!" he yelled.

"I'm all right," came the reply from the deep shadows near the rearmost point on the island.

"Well, keep low and keep your eyes peeled," Clay responded. "I'm gonna get back to my position." After making sure that the horses were safe, he went back to the log on the point to make sure there was no further assault from across the river. All was quiet.

"Clay! You and Pete all right?"

"We're all right," Clay answered. "Two of 'em got to the horses, but it didn't do 'em any good."

"I don't expect we'll see any more of them devils tonight. They've done lost too many—three for shore."

"Four," Clay corrected. "There's one laying over by the horses."

"Well, hell, I know they won't try us again now," Badger said. "We've done kilt half of 'em. It's still a couple hours till daylight. We'd best stay where we are till sunup. Then we can see what's what." Clay agreed. Then Badger called out to Pete once more. "You hear that, Pete? Just sit tight." As before, there was no answer from the old Frenchman. "Pete?" Still there was no answer. "Now what the hell . . . ?" Badger mumbled. Clay could hear him rustling around in the branches of the willows as he got to his feet. Then: "Pete!" This time it was almost a roar.

"Yeah?" a faint reply came from the darkness.

Exasperated, Badger repeated his instructions to stay put till sunup. Clay could still hear him mumbling as he situated himself between the two willows once more.

The morning broke, clear and chilly. From their defensive positions, the three embattled white men peered through the mist rising from the river. Watching carefully, his eyes lingering on every gully and defile on the opposite side before moving on, Clay scanned the empty riverbank. There was no sign of the Blackfoot war party.

"I reckon they run off during the night," he heard Badger saying behind him, and he turned to see his two partners leaving their positions and heading for the thicket where the horses were hobbled. Picking up his empty cartridges, he got to his feet and went to join them.

Badger was busy stacking a pile of sticks and small limbs to build a fire while Pete bent low over the Blackfoot corpse, still doubled over, frozen in his death agonies. "Many Scalps," Pete muttered when Clay walked up.

"Damned if it ain't," Clay responded. Then remembering the circumstances of the night before, he wondered aloud, "How the hell did those two get to the horses?"

Badger supplied the answer. "Hell, they strolled right by Pete, that's how."

"I didn't hear a thing," Pete protested. Badger's simple statement amounted to an insult to a mountain man. "It was too dark down in that pocket to see anything."

"Shit fire," Badger snorted. "That's the only thing that saved your worn-out hide. Them two didn't know you were there till I called you and you answered."

"Yeah," Pete replied indignantly. "And I can thank you for that. I got two lead balls whistling by my ass 'cause I answered you. I was just lucky they didn't have nuthin' but them cheap old guns."

Knowing the old man was mortified that the two Indians had walked right by him in the dark, Badger was not above chastising him nonetheless. "You was right about one thing, you're damn shore blind as a bat. But, I swear, I didn't know you was deef, too. We thought you was dead a couple of times. I had to holler like hell to git you to answer."

"Yeah? And you can kiss my gray-haired ass, too, Badger. You ain't that far from a rockin' chair yourself."

"Is that a fact? Well, when that day comes, I reckon I'll have sense enough to stay by the fire. I shoulda left you back at Fort Union."

"Why you ol' polecat," Pete huffed like a chicken with its feathers ruffled, "you're the one what wanted me to come with you 'cause you're afraid of the Blackfeet."

Badger was about to retort, but the argument was ended abruptly when a bullet smacked into the middle of the fire, sending flaming sticks flying. It was followed immediately by the sharp crack of a Springfield rifle. All three men dived for cover behind a low mound of sand. The first shot was followed by a second report that sent a lead ball ripping through the leaves over their heads. That was the start of a methodical barrage of fire from the two Springfields, firing as rapidly as the two warriors could reload.

"Damn. I reckon they didn't turn tail at that," Badger grunted as he hugged the sandy ground beneath him. He looked around him as best he could before deciding, "And this ain't the best of spots to defend." It was obvious that the two Blackfoot riflemen could keep them pinned down, even if they couldn't get a clean shot at the three behind the mound. "Maybe they're just givin' us a little farewell salute before takin' off."

Pete disagreed. "Blackfoot don't take kindly to white folks to begin with, and we've kilt four of their warriors. I expect them four that's left is bent on taking some revenge for the ones we kilt. They'll wait us out—till we starve or make a run fer it."

After a short while, the Blackfeet grew tired of wasting their ammunition firing at the sandy mound. Impatient for some form of retaliation for the loss of their four brothers, they shifted their fire to concentrate on the thicket where the horses were hobbled. "Hellfire," Badger swore, "I didn't think they'd shoot at the horses!" Without waiting for anyone to give the order, all three beat a hasty retreat toward the thicket, crawling, running, and scrambling to make the cover of the thick bushes before a rifle ball caught them in the open.

"Put 'em down!" Badger yelled as he reached for his horse's head, and wrestled the animal to the ground. "Lay on his neck!"

The packhorses would have to be left to take their

chances on being hit. Each man went for his best horse. In a few short moments, Pete was lying across the neck of his horse, but Clay was having difficulty with Red. Unlike the two smaller Indian ponies, the big chestnut was frightened by his master's sudden wrenching of his neck, and his inclination was to fight it. With bullets ripping through the leaves around him, Clay struggled with the confused horse. In a panic created by the gunfire from the opposite bank and his master's strange assault upon him, Red jerked his head free and reared up on his hind legs, knocking Clay flat on his back. He was a target the Blackfoot rifles could not miss. One bullet crashed through the ribcage of the screaming horse while the second drove deep into his broad chest.

Stunned by the sight of his magnificent sorrel crumpling in a heap among the tangle of brush and vines, Clay could only cry out in shocked disbelief. "Red! Red!" he wailed. The big horse managed to pull himself up once more before sinking to the ground again, his legs collapsing under him. Clay crawled quickly over to him, trying to get Red on his feet, but the handsome chestnut stallion slowly rolled over on his side, and Clay knew he had lost him.

Ignoring Badger's shouts to put his packhorse down to keep it from getting shot, Clay just sat there for a long moment, half in disbelief, half mourning the loss of the best horse he had ever owned—and the only one he had ever stolen. Sitting there with Red's head in his lap, Clay was oblivious to the continuous rifle fire from across the river, even the occasional round that found the carcass of his horse. He barely registered the sound of Badger's voice, seemingly in the distance, as the old trapper pleaded, "Clay, git down! Dammit! Git down!"

Clay looked around at Badger and Pete, pinned to

the ground, laying across their horses' necks, then back at his own dead horse. Suddenly the sense of great loss was replaced by one of anger, pure white-hot anger, over the senseless killing of such a fine animal. He grabbed his Winchester and cocked it.

"Clay! For God's sake, what are you doin'? Tryin' to git yourself kilt?" Badger thought his young friend had lost his senses.

"They shot my damn horse," was all Clay answered as he climbed up over the sand mound and started running toward the log he had spent the night behind. Ignoring the shouts of both Badger and Pete to come back, he ran, zig-zagging across the open bank, daring the Blackfeet to hit him. With bullets kicking up sand on either side of him, he dived for cover behind the fallen tree.

With no uncertainty of purpose, he started rocking the log to loosen the end resting in the sand until he was able to move it. Once it was free, he rolled it into the water, sliding his body into the chilly current behind it. There was a momentary pause in the firing from the opposite bank while the Blackfeet puzzled over the stange behavior of the white man. Assuming that he was making an attempt to escape by floating downstream, the warriors suddenly emerged from a long coulee where they had been hidden from view. Amid loud war whoops of excitement, the two carrying the Springfields rushed down toward the water to get a better shot at the white man in the river. Not to miss out on an apparent turkey shoot, the other two warriors ran downstream to be in position with their bows when Clay floated by. All four were taken by surprise when the man behind the log pushed straight across, heading directly for them.

From behind the sand mound in the center of the little island, Badger and Pete inched their heads up enough to find out what was going on. What they saw would be a story that Badger would recount many times over during the coming years. Pushing the log ahead of him in the narrow channel, Clay was charging straight for the Indians, his rifle held safely above the water. On the opposite bank, the two Blackfeet with rifles were firing and reloading as fast as they could. Huge chunks of rotten wood were sent flying in the air as the bullets struck the log, but Clay never wavered. With his head low in the water behind the log, he was almost across when he paused, waiting for the impact of two more shots in the log. Then, while the Indians were reloading, he suddenly appeared from around one end of his floating fortress. Standing waist-deep in the water, he drew down on the closest warrior. The Winchester spoke, knocking the surprised Blackfoot backward, shot through the chest. Clay quickly cocked the rifle and turned to settle with the other rifle—just in time to see that warrior double over with a shot in the belly from Badger's rifle. Hesitating for only an instant, Clay pushed the log aside and waded ashore, his sights set on the two remaining Indians some fifty yards downstream.

With no thought for his own safety, Clay charged out of the shallow water, his shoulders slightly hunched and his head thrust defiantly forward like a mountain lion closing in for the kill. The two young warriors each notched their arrows and sent them flying, but they lost their will to fight when their arrows landed harmlessly at the feet of the wild man bearing down on them with no apparent regard for his life. It was clear to them that this was no ordinary white man—perhaps he was a demon of supernatural powers—and they decided it prudent to run for their lives.

While Clay chased after the retreating Blackfeet,

Badger and Pete brought the horses across from the island. After calmly assessing the situation, Badger surmised that two things were certain. Clay, in his water-soaked buckskins, wasn't going to catch the two Indians before they reached their horses; and Clay was now in need of a horse himself. With that in mind, Badger kicked his pony into a gallop, making a run to cut the two warriors off. He spotted the ponies standing in a clump of willows but not in time to intercept the two sprinting warriors. However, it was a close contest. And seeing Badger boring down on them, the two Blackfeet quickly concluded that they didn't have time to save the rest of the horses. They were already disappearing over a rise in the prairie when Badger reined his horse to a stop. A few minutes later, a breathless Clay charged into the willows.

The two men didn't say a word for a few moments while Clay caught his breath and Badger just sat in the saddle, looking at his young friend, a wide grin on his face. When Pete rode up, leading the pack animals, Badger turned to flash his grin on the old man. "Well, Pete, looks like our young grizzly here is done run off all the Injuns. He wasn't plannin' on savin' any of 'em for me and you."

Pete matched Badger's grin with one of his own. "Looks like," he replied. "I thought I'd seen 'bout ever' way a man could commit suicide. That was one I hadn't thought about, though."

Clay, still fuming, looked up at the old man, and simply mumbled, "They shot my horse."

"Don't pay to rile him too much, does it?" Pete remarked, shaking his head in amazement.

"Peers not," Badger replied. Turning back to Clay, he said, "Well, you've got your pick of a new one." He motioned toward the half-dozen Indian ponies still standing among the willows.

Unimpressed with the selection left to him, Clay stared at the horses for a long moment. "They don't look like much," he finally remarked.

Badger, also looking over their newly acquired stock, was of a different opinion. "They may not look as sleek and pretty as that big ol' horse of your'n. But believe me, son, any one of them there ponies'll carry you a lot farther than that grain-fed dandy you just lost." Clay had seen enough evidence by then of the speed and stamina of Indian ponies to know that what Badger said was true. Still, he would miss the big horse that had carried him home from the war.

Chapter 9

Her legs crossed Indian fashion, Martha Vinings sat before the fire scwing the final ornamentation on the toes of a new pair of winter moccasins for Black Elk. At Moon Shadow's suggestion she had designed a three-pronged symbol representing the three major tribes of the Blackfoot nation. When she had finished, she held them up for Moon Shadow to see. The wounded Blackfoot girl had been lying quietly on the other side of the fire, watching Martha as she worked.

"Let me see," Moon Shadow said, holding out her hand. Martha got up and handed the moccasins to her. Moon Shadow smiled as she took them, turning them over and over, admiring Martha's obvious skill with a bone needle. "Black Elk will be pleased. They are better than the moccasins I made him last winter."

"No, little one," Martha replied, smiling warmly. "They may be different, but not better."

Moon Shadow did not reply, merely smiling in response. She knew that her white friend was very modest about her sewing talent. She also knew that Black Elk was very fortunate to have a woman with Martha's skills to take care of him while his wife was too weak to perform her duties. It was a good thing when *Na'pi*—Old Man—the creator of the Blackfoot people, sent Martha to them. She was a strong woman, strong enough to take care of Black Elk and Moon Shadow.

"It's beginning to get a little chilly out here," Martha decided. "I'd better take you inside now." She helped Moon Shadow to her feet. Supporting most of the young girl's weight, she walked her slowly back inside the tipi, and settled her on the soft buffalo robes that served as a bed. Moon Shadow lay back, exhausted from the simple effort required to return to her bed.

"Thank you, Marta," she said softly. "You are a good friend to take care of me so well."

"You would do the same for me," Martha said, smiling down at her. "When you get well, I will lay by the fire and watch you work," she joked. Moon Shadow smiled and nodded slightly. Martha strived to maintain a cheerful and optimistic attitude in Moon Shadow's presence. But inwardly she worried about her friend. There had been no improvement in the fragile girl's condition. In spite of the herbs administered by Red Wing, and the gentle care given by Martha, the wound in Moon Shadow's side appeared to worsen, leaving her weak and in almost constant pain. Martha feared the bull's horn had done irreparable damage to some of the organs inside, because she was unable to hold any food down. Every time she tried to eat any solid food, it immediately came back up, and there was always blood in her vomit. Martha feared she was losing the best friend she had ever known—and the only true friend among the other women of the village.

It had been a truly unexpected blessing that the two women had become so close in the time since Martha's capture. And now, Martha could not bear the thought of losing her. Although she tried not to let such thoughts occupy her mind, it was impossible not to think about what her fate might be if Moon Shadow did not recover. Would Black Elk keep her? Or would he trade her to one of the other men of the village while he mourned for his wife? The Blackfoot customs were strange in some ways. Martha had learned that there could be long and extensive periods of mourning when a man died, or was killed in battle. And usually there was some physical sign of grieving: a finger cut off, hair cut short, scarring of legs. But this was almost never done when a woman died. What would Black Elk do if Moon Shadow died? He possessed such obvious affection for his wife that Martha felt certain he would be devastated to lose her. These were troubling thoughts indeed for Martha, for she had to admit that her affections were strong for both of them.

"You must take good care of Black Elk when I am gone."

Moon Shadow's softly murmured command startled Martha, and she wondered if her young friend had somehow read her thoughts. Fearing that her embarrassment might be evident in her face, she quickly responded, "Don't say such things. You will soon start to get well."

Moon Shadow smiled, but her eyes told of her weariness and pain. "He should have already taken you as a wife. I had no sisters till you came. Now I have a sister, and you will make him a good wife. I have told him this."

Martha was outwardly flustered by Moon Shadow's frankness in a subject she felt was extremely delicate. She hardly knew how to respond. The custom among the Blackfoot people, for a man to take more than one wife, was not an easy concept for Martha to accept. Admittedly, she had all but forgotten what her life had been before her capture, having fit comfortably into the life forced upon her. But there was a strong aversion toward sharing one's mate with another. An instant flashback rekindled a picture of Charley Vinings's leering grin when he used to watch her climb the hill to the cabin. At the same time, she knew there was no correlation between the two circumstances. Black Elk had shown her nothing but kindness, almost from the beginning. She was his property. He could do what he would with her. Yet he treated her like a sister to Moon Shadow. Still, she knew there were deeper feelings in the heart of the proud warrior. She could not help but sense them. There had been a pronounced change in his bearing around her since he rescued her from the Crow war party, and she knew that Moon Shadow was too astute not to notice it as well.

"Let's not talk of such things," Martha finally responded. "You are the only wife Black Elk needs." Seeing Moon Shadow about to protest, she hurried to interrupt. "But don't worry. If something happens to you, I'll take care of Black Elk." She paused, still flustered. "He wouldn't have to marry me."

Martha stood over Moon Shadow for a moment, studying the stricken girl intensely. Fragile to begin with, her face now showed the effects of her injury. The natural brightness of her dark eyes seemed somehow dulled by the pain that was with her constantly, and her cheeks were drawn and ashen. There was nothing more she could do to help her little sister, and it was becoming painfully evident that Moon Shadow was not strong enough to do it on her own. Afraid the frail Blackfoot girl might read the fear in her eyes, Martha turned away from her. "I must go to get more wood for the fire. You must try to rest now. Black Elk will be back soon, and you know you want to be fresh for him."

Outside the lodge, Martha made her way along the

path by the river. The walk to fetch firewood was getting longer and longer each day as the women of the village were rapidly using up all of the usable wood close by. Martha carried a hand axe to chop the larger pieces and a deerhide flap to bundle her wood. The fact that she was allowed to carry an axe and go unchallenged anywhere she pleased was no longer novel to her. It no longer occurred to her to try to escape. She was content here where daily life was an uncomplicated search for food and water. In a land where buffalo, elk, deer, antelope, and even bears were plentiful, there was a never-ending source for food and hides for warmth. It was little wonder that the Blackfeet were a happy people.

She had not gone far down the path when she met two women returning with their bundles of firewood. She stepped off of the path to let them pass. "How is it with you, Six Horses?" the first woman asked, calling Martha by the name Black Elk had given her.

"I am fine, and you?" Martha returned.

The second woman, the wife of Swift Runner, asked, "How is Moon Shadow? Is she any better?"

Martha told them of her concern for Moon Shadow, and the fact that she seemed to be getting weaker as each day passed. Both women nodded solemnly, showing their own concern. "We will be leaving this place within a day or so," Swift Runner's wife said. "I hope she will be strong enough to travel."

This was something that had also worried Martha. As she left the two women and continued down the path, thoughts of the coming days filled her mind. The weather was beginning to get cold now. Already there had been frost in the mornings, so Bloody Axe had called for the people to ready themselves to move farther west into the mountains for winter camp. It had been a good and bountiful summer. The food caches were filled with ample supplies of dried meat as well as dried sarvis berries, bull berries, dried and ground chokecherries, bitterroot, and camas roots. It was time to move before the snows came to the prairie, but Martha feared that Moon Shadow might be too weak to travel. She knew that Black Elk shared her concern.

Bringing her mind back to the task at hand, she moved among the trees that lined the river, picking up dead branches and fallen limbs. It was late in the afternoon, and she was alone in her search for firewood, so she worked quickly to fill her bundle. When she had gathered all she could carry, she walked down to the water's edge to wash her hands. There was still no one else close by, and as she splashed the cold water over her hands she was tempted to take the opportunity to take a bath. She had often marveled that the men of the village found the cold river water refreshing, no matter the temperature. And it would soon be too cold for her to even consider bathing outside the tipi. She was a couple hundred yards from the village, and she was sure she could hear anyone coming down the path in plenty of time. The decision made, she laid her bundle of wood down by the water while she hurriedly removed her leggings, pulled her cowskin shirt off over her head, and pulled her long skirt up, tucking it into the tie at her waist.

The water felt icy as she cautiously placed one foot in and then the other. A chill ran the length of her spine, and she almost changed her mind about bathing, thinking it might be wiser to wait until morning and wash in the warm lodge. Still, she was drawn by the freedom of splashing in the gently moving river. *I've come this far,* she thought, *I might as well go through with it.*

Shivering with each step, she waded in up to her

knees before deciding that was as far as she dared.
Splashing a little on her exposed thighs in an effort to
acclimate her body to the cold, she couldn't help but
utter a smothered squeal as each handful of the icy
water chilled her, raising goosebumps all over her
body. Taking a deep breath to strengthen her resolve,
she cupped her hands and doused her face and shoulders with the frigid water. After the initial shock of
it, she didn't permit herself to pause, splashing water
upon her chest and arms, rubbing vigorously. By the
time she considered it enough, she was gasping to
catch her breath.

Moving back to the bank, she stood there shaking
and rubbing herself, wishing she had a towel. Glancing
down at her naked breasts, she laughed to see her
nipples standing cold and hard in the chilled air. *Martha, girl, I believe you've taken leave of your senses.*
Suddenly her smile froze as a feeling swept over her
that she was not alone. She was at once alarmed. She
could not explain the sensation. She had heard no
sound. In fact, the whole riverbank was silent. Turning
slowly, she looked down the path toward the village.
There was no one there. Then turning back toward
the opposite bank, she saw him.

Black Elk stood motionless, his eyes captured by
the vision across the narrow river. Unblinking, he
gazed at the nearly naked woman no more than a few
yards distant. Startled, but making no effort to hide
her nakedness, Martha gazed back at the powerful
Blackfoot warrior. There was a long moment when
the world stood still, and they were held in a silent
embrace. Abruptly, the stunned warrior seemed to recover his senses, and without saying a word, suddenly
turned and walked toward the village, leading his
horse behind him. Exhaling finally, Martha felt
strangely calm. She could not explain why she had

simply stood there under his intense gaze, making no move to cover herself, meeting his eyes with hers. She stared at his broad back as he strode gracefully along the riverbank, and she began to shiver again, but not from the chilly air.

Still standing in ankle-deep water, she watched him until he and his horse finally disappeared in the trees. Only then did she seem to be released from the fiery hand that had clutched her emotions. Having no desire to explore feelings that ran contradictory to her sense of propriety, she labored to put the incident out of her mind. Still, she could not deny the strange sensation that she felt in her bosom. There had been a silent message between them. She could not deny that, and it frightened her.

Martha returned to the lodge to find Black Elk kneeling beside Moon Shadow, stroking her hair. He didn't turn to look at Martha when she entered the tipi and placed her bundle of wood beside the fire. Her voice weak and halting, Moon Shadow strained to tell her husband something, but he gently shushed her. "Do not try to talk, little one. You must rest." Still without turning his head, he said, "Six Horses, there is an antelope on my pony." Without a word, Martha turned and left the lodge.

It was almost dark by the time Martha managed to drag the antelope carcass from Black Elk's horse. She began to skin the animal. Due to the rapidly fading light, it was necessary to put more wood on the fire outside the tipi to provide some light to work by. Working as quickly as she could, she carefully slit the hide so as not to damage it, laying it back so she could butcher the meat. After a short while, Black Elk emerged from the lodge, and stood looking down at her for a few moments.

"I'm sorry that I got back so late. I had to travel a

long way today to find this animal. It is late. I'll help you butcher." With that said, he drew his knife and knelt down beside her. "We will leave this camp tomorrow, so there will be no time to dry the meat properly." She nodded silently, afraid to look at him, although she could feel his eyes upon her, watching her as she carved the portions away. "We will eat the fresh meat tonight and share with the others," he continued.

With the butchering not yet finished, Black Elk left her to complete the task while he walked among the lodges calling for friends to come and take portions of the meat. The offer was graciously accepted, and soon the carcass was disposed of. When the last of Black Elk's friends departed, Martha picked up the remains of the butchering—what bones and entrails the dogs did not take—and put them in the fire to burn. *I should have known,* she thought when she looked at her hands and arms, covered with the blood of the antelope. Having just recently exposed her body to the chilling waters of the river, she had no choice but to visit the river again.

Kneeling upon a flat rock that jutted out over the edge of the water, Martha scrubbed her hands and arms until the last of the dried blood and soot from the fire had disappeared. Her mind wandered to the last time she bathed in the river, only a few hours before, and she trembled when she remembered the sensation she had felt. Then a picture of Moon Shadow, lying frail beside the fire, came to her mind. When their friends had come for the fresh meat Black Elk had offered, he had carried Moon Shadow outside by the fire so she could enjoy the social gathering. Martha had roasted a strip of the meat for her to chew on, but Moon Shadow showed little interest in eating. Although her little sister smiled bravely when greeted

by her friends, Martha knew she was in great pain.
After a short time, Black Elk carried his ailing wife
back inside to rest. The dullness in Moon Shadow's
eyes worried Martha, and once again Martha allowed
herself to acknowledge the tragic possibility that her
newfound sister might not survive the terrible wound
she had suffered. She suddenly shook her head, trying
to rid her mind of such depressing thoughts.

"I am worried, too."

Startled, she uttered, "What?" She had not heard
Black Elk until he was right behind her.

"You worry for Moon Shadow," he said softly. "I
am worried, too. The camp will be moving tomorrow,
and I'm afraid Moon Shadow is too weak to move."

"I know," she replied, rubbing her arms to help dry
them. "What will you do?" She stood up to face him.

"I'll stay here until she is well enough to join the
others."

"Good," Martha said. She had been afraid Black
Elk might have been planning to pack the failing girl
on a travois and have her endure the rough trip to
the higher country. "We can care for her until she's
able to make the trip."

He did not comment right away. He continued to
look deep into her eyes with the probing gaze that
Martha had felt so often in the last few days. She
trembled, feeling that he could see into the depths of
her soul, reading her innermost thoughts. She started
to turn aside, but he placed his hands upon her shoulders and held her. "You have been a good friend to
Moon Shadow," he said softly. "I have been thinking
about you a great deal, and I think that maybe I will
let you return to your home . . ." He hesitated slightly.
". . . and your husband."

His words stunned her. The thought of being returned to the white world had flown beyond the

boundaries of possibility in her mind. She found it difficult to believe that Black Elk would even consider taking her back to her husband. She was even more startled by her own response, a statement from her subconscious, uttered before she had time to think.

"I don't want to go back. I want to stay with you." Her gaze, until that moment meeting his, now dropped to her feet, as if ashamed of what she had just said.

She felt a slight increase in the pressure of his hands upon her shoulders—nothing more than this for what seemed a long time—until he moved a hand to gently lift her chin up so that he could look into her eyes again. "I had hoped with all my heart that you would say this," he whispered, then pulled her close to his body. She trembled at the touch of his muscular arms as they enclosed her, and she melted against his broad chest.

She told herself that she had no choice in what happened on the bank of the river. She was a captive, and Black Elk was a powerful warrior, too strong to resist. What could she do to protect her virtue? It would be useless to try to fight him. Although these thoughts raced through her mind, she could not deny the eagerness with which she received him, matching his passion with a yearning for him that was overpowering. Martha found herself giving her body and soul with an intensity she had never dreamed could exist. And at the supreme moment, she was startled to hear her own savage cry, as it burst forth from deep within her.

When it was over, he lay in her arms. They lay there for a long time, not moving until she began to feel the chill of the autumn wind's gentle kiss upon her bare skin. He lay so still that she thought he might be asleep, so she pulled a corner of the buffalo robe they laid upon over his shoulders.

"I am not cold," he said softly, but he pulled more of the robe up to cover her.

Feeling contentment that she had never known, Martha closed her eyes and lay back in the afterglow of a passion that had awakened her innermost lusts. She would admit it to herself now. She had wanted this man, this child of nature, whose dark head now lay exhausted upon her naked shoulder. At that moment, all thoughts of home, family, Robert—all were forgotten. There was nothing but the two of them. And she was content.

It was late when they returned to the tipi. Thinking Moon Shadow was asleep, they entered, taking care not to disturb her, but her eyelids flickered briefly before opening wide at the sound of the entrance flap being pulled aside. When she saw them, her face relaxed, and she smiled, nodding slowly. Martha was certain that the frail Indian girl somehow knew what had happened, and that she was pleased.

"Your forehead feels very warm," Martha said as she bent over her little sister, her hand on her brow. Looking up at Black Elk, she said, "I fear her fever has returned. I'll wet a cloth to bath her face." She started to get up, but Moon Shadow caught her arm and pulled her close again.

"Marta," she whispered. "You are where you belong. You must take good care of our husband."

"I will," she whispered in return, knowing that Moon Shadow was sincere in her hopes that Black Elk would take her as a wife. She glanced up at Black Elk, who was standing over them. He nodded solemnly when he met her eye. Looking back at the feverish girl, she gave her an affectionate squeeze, and whispered, "Now I must get a cloth to cool your fever."

The fire was nothing more than a bed of glowing coals by the time Moon Shadow finally drifted into sleep beside Black Elk. He held her in his arms as she slept, pressed close against him, her face reflecting the inner peace she had found. In the early hours of the morning, she slipped into that peaceful world beyond, knowing that she had left her husband in good hands.

Chapter 10

"How you makin' out, old man?"

"Don't worry 'bout me," Pete Dubois replied haughtily as Badger reined his horse back alongside him. "I'm makin' out all right."

"I didn't wanna tire you out, what with you being in the saddle since sunup . . . a man of your age," Badger chided, a thin smile on his face.

"Tire me out?" Pete snorted indignantly. "Moose shit! That'll be the day when I can't ride you into the ground."

"Is that so?" Badger teased. "That shaggy overgrown dog you're ridin' looks like he's gonna break down any minute." He winked at Clay, who had just caught up to them. "Ain't that right, Clay?"

Clay laughed, shaking his head. "Don't try to draw me into that argument. Both of you look pretty worn out to me."

"Is that so?" Badger replied, laughing. "Well, if this old coon knows what he's talkin' about, Black Shirt's camp oughta be less than a half day's ride now."

The camp was right where Pete had said they would find it, and, as he had predicted, the village had yet to leave the open country for a more sheltered location for the winter. Clay wondered at their good fortune because already the mornings were frosty and there was a smell of snow in the air. The sun was low on the far horizon when they crested a rise in the prairie and first saw the lodges clustered near the fork of the Big Sandy where it joined the Milk. Clay estimated over two hundred tipis nestled under a thin blanket of smoke, created by the many cookfires tended by the women. The sight inspired a peaceful feeling until Badger reminded him that it was a Blackfoot village, and consequently, potentially dangerous to a white man—this even while Pete protested that while that might be true, it was his village, too.

"Hell, them's my people down there," Pete said. "I got a lot of friends in that camp."

"Yeah, maybe so," Badger replied. "I reckon we'll find out soon enough, won't we? I hope to hell that bunch we tangled with back at the river didn't come from this camp. Clay, you keep that rifle of your'n handy." He gave his horse a little kick with his heels and led out again.

The close proximity of the Blackfoot camp was enough to create a tenseness in Clay Culver. He had thought a lot about Martha the night before, the old thoughts that had at times caused sleepless nights—when he would permit his mind to create images of his sister living under the cruel hand of some savage Blackfoot warrior. He could picture her face, crying out for someone to rescue her, and it tormented him at times thinking that she might be lying cold and afraid, maybe tied hand and foot in a Blackfoot camp. And although he knew there had probably been nothing Robert or Charley could have done to prevent Martha's abduction, still he blamed them for letting it happen.

He closed his eyes tightly for a few moments and shook his head, trying to clear these thoughts from his mind. It was a time for positive thoughts now, he told himself. Someone in Black Shirt's camp might be able to tell him where Martha was. He reminded himself that there was no guarantee of this. Pete had only said that his brother-in-law, Crow Fighter, would probably know where Bloody Axe's band was camped. Still, Clay had to have faith that he would find her. *Maybe,* he thought, *Robert and Charley Vinings are searching for her, too.* He had no notion of their whereabouts, only that they had left for Montana territory with a wagon train of miners. O.C. Owens at Fort Laramie had assured Clay that Robert and Charley had no intentions of going after Martha when they left there. But he could be dead wrong. After all, Martha was Robert's wife. How could a man not go after his own wife? *I'm going to find out the truth of it,* he promised himself.

"Come on up here, Pete, so your friends can see you," Badger said. "Them devils is just as likely to shoot at the first white man they don't recognize." He glanced back at Clay. "Might be it's a good thing we caught 'em right at suppertime. Maybe they'll be in a friendly mood."

Glancing at Badger, Pete shook his head impatiently as he prodded his mangy horse to the front. "Hell, Badger, Black Shirt's as friendly as any Injun. It's just *some* white men he don't like."

"Is that a fact? Well, just tell him I'm married to a Lakota woman, and see how much he likes me."

"We best not tell him that," Pete conceded.

The dogs were the first to notice the arrival of the three strangers. First one, then several others alerted the people in the village to the presence of the riders skirting the large pony herd on the east side of the river. Clay's gaze darted quickly back and forth from one side of the Blackfoot camp to the other. So far, there was no indication of alarm. Most of the people were eating their evening meal, and only a handful of men were curious enough to leave their fires to see what had set the dogs off. When the visitors were spotted, there was a good deal more activity among the lodges nestled near the river, and soon a group had gathered near the center of the camp. Still there was no sign of alarm or hostility, merely curiosity as the people watched them approach.

Pete guided his horse to a shallow ford in the river and started across with Clay and Badger close behind. When he reached the west bank, he held up his hand in a sign of peace and called out, "Peace, my friends, how is it with Black Shirt's village?"

Recognizing the old trapper at once, several of the people returned his greeting, all smiling cheerfully, for they had assumed they had seen the last of the old mountain man. Black Shirt himself called out, "Welcome, Gray Otter. I did not expect to see you again so soon."

"Gray Otter?" Badger whispered to Clay. "More like Gray Muskrat."

If Pete overheard the chiding comment, he ignored it. "I've come back to the people," he said. "There is no longer a place for me at the white man's fort."

"Ahh . . . ." Black Shirt responded, nodding his head knowingly.

As they pulled up before the growing assembly of men, women, children, and dogs, one of the Indians strode forward to greet them. Pete dismounted and the man clasped his forearm, shaking it vigorously. "It's good to see you again, my friend," Crow Fighter said, a wide smile covering his face, and the two men pounded each other on the back heartily. The rest of the gathering crowded around the old man, laughing and chattering away in good-natured welcome. Clay was amazed to compare this reception to the one experienced at the hands of the first group of Blackfeet they had encountered at Porcupine Creek. He wondered if Badger might be mistaken in his assessment of the Blackfoot disposition. There might be a different reception, he allowed, if they knew they had killed several of their tribesmen in the fight at Porcupine Creek.

Badger and Clay sat upon their horses, silently watching the homecoming of their companion until Black Shirt, who had been eyeing them intently, spoke. "You have brought some friends with you."

Pete, having forgotten Clay and Badger for the moment, turned away from an old woman who was pounding him on the back joyously. "These two are friends. They come hoping to find news of a white woman captive, maybe the one I heard about in Bloody Axe's camp this past summer."

Black Shirt shrugged. "There was talk about a white woman in Bloody Axe's camp, but I can't say for certain. I did not see Bloody Axe this year. He stays far to the north of us."

"He always winters in the mountains where the sun goes," Crow Fighter volunteered, gesturing toward the northwest, "near the land of the Kutenai."

Upon hearing this, Clay was ready to start out immediately for the mountains, but Badger convinced him that it was best to remain there for a day or two to rest the horses. "We might as well enjoy the hospitality of the camp as well. Looks like ol' Pete was right—they ain't gonna scalp us right off."

Pete was evidently highly thought of by the Blackfoot people, for he was certainly received graciously. At Crow Fighter's invitation, Pete moved into his lodge with him and his wife, who seemed as pleased as Crow Fighter to welcome the old man. Clay and

Badger declined an invitation to join them, preferring to bed down outside with their horses. That night, there was little time to prepare anything beyond a simple supper of boiled meat, but Crow Fighter promised a feast the following day. Feeling no threat of treachery, even though they were in the midst of over two hundred Blackfoot lodges, Clay and Badger went to sleep beside a cozy fire close by the herd of Indian ponies.

Clay awakened the next morning to discover a light blanket of new-fallen snow upon his buffalo robe, and the fire was out. The weather Badger had been predicting for the past week had finally come.

Reluctant to stir from his warm burrow of thick buffalo robes, Clay continued to lay there for a while, listening to the sounds of the waking village. Close by his head, he could hear the horses pawing and scraping the light snow away searching for the grass beneath. Across the narrow river, the women were stirring up their cookfires in preparation for making breakfast. Clay glanced over at Badger, still snoring under a white mound of snow and showing no signs of arousing. *I guess it's up to me,* he thought, and crawled out of his bed to rebuild the fire. Hearing what he first thought were war whoops, Clay looked quickly back toward the Blackfoot camp to see several of the men gathered by the water's edge. While he watched, first one and then another threw off their robes and plunged into the icy water. "Damn fool thing to do," he heard Badger say behind him, and he turned to find the old trapper sitting up in his bed, shaking the snow from his robe.

"Thinks it makes 'em strong," Badger continued, displaying his contempt for the practice. "It's a wonder it don't kill 'em."

Clay laughed and resumed his patient labor with his

flint and steel until he succeeded in causing a weak flame in the dried moss he had carried in his parfleche. Nursing it lovingly, he fanned it into a healthy flame as he added small twigs and grass, and soon he had the fire rekindled.

Coffee and a little dried venison served as breakfast, since they anticipated a feast of roasted buffalo hump, promised by Crow Fighter. Afterward, when they went in search of Pete, they found the elders of the village discussing the wisdom in delaying the move to winter camp. The early snow was definitely a sign to many of them that they may have lingered on the plains longer than they should have. Others, Black Shirt foremost among them, felt that the hunting had been too good to leave before now, and there was still plenty of time to travel to the sheltered valleys to the west. All were in agreement that it would be unwise to wait any longer, however, so it was decided to strike the tipis and get on the trail the following day.

The rest of that day was spent in preparing to move. It was a busy time for the women of the camp, but Crow Fighter's wife still managed to roast a large portion of buffalo hump in honor of their guests. It was a typical Blackfoot feast. Each invited guest was served a portion of the roasted meat. It was a generous portion, and if a person couldn't eat it all, he took the remainder with him. No second servings were offered. Clay found it to be plenty for one man. Counting Clay, Badger, and Pete, there were eight invited guests. Since Crow Fighter was the host, he did not eat. When all had finished eating, Crow Fighter lit a pipe and passed it to Pete on his left. Pete took a long draw, blowing the smoke out slowly, then passed it on to the man on his left. The pipe continued around in this fashion until it reached Clay, who was seated by the door. After Clay smoked, Pete told him to pass the pipe back the way it had come to him, to be passed all the way around to the man seated on the opposite side of the door.

There was conversation and laughing often, but Clay had no notion what was being said. Several times he was certain some of the talking was about him because of the way everyone looked his way. Once, Badger looked directly at him and nodded his head as if to let him know something significant had been said. But when Clay started to question him, Badger held up his hand to silence him. Clay then realized that only one man spoke at a time, and all others listened until he was finished. It was decidedly different from a group of soldiers around a fire with everyone talking at once. There was a certain dignity about it that Clay couldn't help but admire. When the last pipe was smoked, three in all, Crow Fighter announced the end of the feast, and everyone got up and filed out of the lodge.

Once outside, Clay was quick to press Badger and Pete for anything that had been said about the whereabouts of Bloody Axe's winter camp. "Well," Badger began. "There's definite sign, all right. Didn't none of 'em know for sure where Bloody Axe went this year. One feller, though, the one with the scar across his face, he said he visited Bloody Axe's camp this past summer. He seen the white woman, said she belonged to a buck called Black Elk. Can't say for certain she's your sister, but chances are she is."

The very words sent an icy chill through the length of Clay's spinal cord, and he felt the muscles in his forearms tighten. *Black Elk*, the savage that had haunted his imagination now had a name. Trying not to show the tension in his brain, Clay asked in a calm voice, "Do you have any idea where to look for my sister?"

"Well . . ." Badger hesitated. "I do and I don't." He scratched his beard while he thought about it. "Accordin' to Crow Fighter, Bloody Axe favors a camp in the foothills of the Rockies, usually not too far from the Milk River."

"Then I reckon we'd better get started," Clay said.

"Hold on a minute," Badger warned. "That's a lot of territory. He could be anywhere along the east slope of the Rockies. There's hundreds of little creeks and valleys where he could camp in that country. In the first place, it's nigh on to ten or twelve days' ride from here. And that's just to git someplace where we can start lookin'. And I don't like the looks of this weather. I feel a real spell of winter coming on." He rubbed his shoulder as if to confirm his joints' agreement with the forecast.

Clay gazed thoughtfully into the old trapper's eyes, evaluating his opinions. He wasn't sure he was ready to rely upon Badger's signals from his aching joints. The way he saw it, the weather might turn bad, and it might not. And with thoughts of Martha waiting for him to come, he decided he'd prefer to gamble on the chance that the weather would not worsen. The decision made, he said, "I'm going on. You can stay here with Pete if you want. But maybe you can tell me how to get there."

Badger just shook his head, exasperated. He glanced at Pete, looking for confirmation, then back at his young friend. "Clay, I reckon I know how anxious you are to find your sister, but it don't make a lot of sense for you to set out on your own in country you ain't never seen before—especially if a hard winter hits all of a sudden. There ain't nuthin like a hard winter snow on the plains. Snow up to your horse's belly, sky solid gray, wind sharp enough to cut leather—a day or two of that and you likely wouldn't

know east from west, north from south." He paused
to judge the effect of his words on the determined
young man. He could see right away that Clay was
not swayed. "Another thing, son, don't be fooled by
all this *fofurraw* here. These Injuns might seem
friendly enough right now, but I swear to you it's only
'cause Pete's with us. Blackfeet ain't never got along
with no white men 'cept the Hudson's Bay people—
like Pete. The best piece of advice I can give you is
to wait out the winter. Then, if your sister's still alive,
we'll find her."

Clay didn't say anything for a long moment. It was
obvious that he was weighing the advice just offered.
Finally he spoke. "I'm much obliged for your concern,
but I guess I'll still be going."

"Damnation!" Badger cursed. "If you ain't the
hardheadedest damn pilgrim I've ever seen." He
looked at Pete, who was shaking his head in disbelief.
"I reckon we're settin' out for the mountains in the
morning."

"Clay, wake up."

Clay felt Badger's hand on his shoulder, and he was
immediately alert. Bolting upright, he reached for his
rifle. "What is it?" he whispered, looking right and
left in the black night, ready to defend himself.

"Shhh . . ." Badger commanded in a voice barely
above a whisper. "Git your possibles together and saddle your horse while I start loadin' the packhorses."

Fully alert now, Clay threw his robe back and got
to his feet. Looking around him again, he realized that
it was still in the middle of the night. "What's the
matter?" he asked. "What's going on?" He could see
no sign of trouble from any direction. The Blackfoot
camp was still asleep. Not a sound could be heard
from across the river.

Badger continued drawing up the straps on his packhorse while he explained his strange behavior. "I wanna git a good start outta here before them bucks know we're gone. That whole camp is packin' up in the morning and pullin' out—Pete with 'em. You and me is headin' north and west, all by our lonesomes. And take my word for it, partner, the only reason we was tolerated was because we was friends of Pete's. Come mornin', we'll just be two white men in Blackfoot country."

Clay found it hard to believe there could be any threat from the people who had been so gracious the day before, and he said as much. "Damn, Badger, surely you don't believe these people would harm us. We smoked with them yesterday, shared their food. Why, I don't doubt the honor of Black Shirt or Crow Fighter for a minute."

"It ain't them I'm worried about," Badger replied impatiently, as he finished securing his packs. "I expect you're dead right about them. If we stayed with them, we'd most likely be all right. But we ain't staying with them. You're dead set on headin' out alone, and that's mighty temptin' to some of them younger bucks. Repeatin' rifles, like that Winchester of your'n, ain't that easy to come by. So if you don't mind, I'd a'heap druther have a few hours' head start on any of 'em that might have ideas about trailin' us. With this snow on the ground, there ain't no way we can hide our trail, so outrunnin' 'em is the only choice we got."

Clay didn't argue further. He got his things together, and while the Blackfoot village slept on through the cold night, the two white men led their horses quietly down the river several hundred yards before crossing over and striking out for the distant mountains. Clay felt a little regret for not having an opportunity to say good-bye to Pete, and to thank the old man for helping him search for Martha. But Badger assured him that Pete would understand their midnight departure—he had even advised it. "At least the old fart will spend his last days with his wife's people," Badger said. "It's a sight better than waitin' to die in that damn run-down shack back at Fort Union."

Later that morning, the sun broke through for a little while. It was a welcome sight to Clay at first, but after no more than an hour, he began to wish it would go away again. The brilliant glare of sunlight upon the endless sea of stark white snow threatened to blind him. In desperation, he pulled his fur hat down on his eyebrows and wrapped his extra shirt around his face, leaving no more than a slit to peer through. He still could not help closing his eyes for long periods at a time, trusting Badger's lead as he followed blindly behind him.

The discomfort was eased somewhat soon after midday, for apparently the sun had merely popped in to say good-bye for a period that was to last for several days. Clay began to respect the ability of Badger's joints to predict the weather when the sky turned again to slate, and the wind switched, bringing chilly air from the north. Taking shelter in a coulee deep enough to get the horses out of the wind, they stopped to build a small fire to make some coffee. It was the first time they had stopped since stealing out of the Blackfoot camp.

Crawling back up to the rim of the coulee, Clay looked back over the endless white plain behind them. There was no sign of anyone trailing them. Feeling their early departure had successfully discouraged pursuit by any of Black Shirt's hot-blooded young warriors, they took a little extra time to eat and rest the horses. Before pushing on across the silent white prairie, Badger mixed some ashes with a little grease, making a black paste. "Here," he said, "rub this under your eyes. It'll help with the glare off of the snow."

For the next two days they continued on a westerly course across lonely prairies seemingly devoid of any other living thing. The whiteness of the gentle snowfall blending into the milky clouds made Clay sometimes feel he and his horses were suspended between earth and sky. Bundled against the freezing snow, he sat in the saddle all day, his joints stiff and cold, blindly following the ghostly figure of Badger several yards ahead. After only the first day, he had realized the truth of Badger's warning that he could not start out after Bloody Axe's camp alone. For, in fact, he could not tell which direction they were riding in—there was no sun, no stars at night. He could only hope that Badger knew where he was going.

On the third morning, the clouds darkened and the constant wind increased in velocity until it became an unending howl. They had barely gotten underway when it began to snow again. Soon it became painfully evident to Clay that to go on made no sense. In the swirling snow, they could have passed within twenty yards of Bloody Axe's village and never have known it. So when Badger called a halt to rest the horses, Clay was not surprised to hear his guide declare it folly to continue.

"Son," Badger began, "I know you got your mind set on finding your sister, but the weather's turned on us. You couldn't find a bull buffalo in a tipi in this kind of weather, and it's only gonna git worse. I'm gittin' a mite worried about the horses. I'm thinkin' this winter's gonna be a hard one. We ain't seen hide nor hair of nothin' to hunt in three days. That tells me that all the animals has sensed the hard winter, and they've already headed for shelter. I'm afraid

we're gonna have to go to shelter, too." He looked
expectantly at Clay, waiting for his objections.

Clay nodded slowly, as if considering what his partner was telling him, then replied. "You're right, I am
anxious to find Martha. But I know enough to call it
quits when we can't see two feet in front of us. What
do you think we oughta do?"

Relieved to see that his young friend was going to
be reasonable about their situation, Badger said,
"Well, we can't stay in this open country, that's for
sure. We've got to get to some real shelter. The closest
place I know of is Fort Benton. If we head south from
here, we ought to strike the Marias in a day or two.
We can follow it down to the Missouri. Fort Benton
ain't no more'n a half a day or so from there."

Clay solemnly nodded. It was not necessary for Badger to spell it out that this was not just a temporary
delay. Clay had heard enough about winter on the
high plains to know that the search was over until
spring. He couldn't help but feel a sinking sensation
in his heart, as he clenched his teeth against the disappointment and frustration, but he knew there was
nothing more he could do. He had prepared himself
to fight Indians if they tried to stand in his way, but
there wasn't much he could do against the weather.
Climbing up into the saddle once again, he followed
Badger out of the coulee where they had taken shelter, his horse stepping heavily through snow already a
foot deep.

It took about a half day longer than Badger had
estimated to reach the Marias River because of the
constant snowfall. After an icy crossing, they started
out in a southeasterly direction until they again struck
the river on its southern leg. From this point, Badger
deemed it best to follow the Marias south to its con-

fluence with the Missouri. Although it appeared that they had ridden out of the heavy snowstorm that had slowed them for the past few days, there was still a fair amount of snow on the ground before them. The journey was made a good deal easier by following the river, for the trees along the banks offered sheltered campsites at night.

During the hard ride, Clay became concerned about the condition of his horses. They looked thin and trail-worn, although they never faltered as they made their way, surefooted and steady, around the gullies and ridges. Badger assured him that the horses were tough enough. They were Indian ponies and accustomed to the hardships of the prairie winter. "Now that there fancy red horse of your'n, he might not have cared for this weather too much. We mighta had to carry him on one of the packhorses."

It was late afternoon on the fourth day after first striking the Marias when the two half-frozen riders sighted the structures that made up the town of Fort Benton. Although a bustling little town on the Missouri during the warm months of the year, it now rose above the prairie as a bleak, almost lifeless collection of buildings around the fort on this cold snowy day. It was difficult to imagine this sleepy town as the busy port it became during the summer, when steamboats pulled up to the levees, unloading the supplies into the freight wagons that would deliver them throughout the territory.

When they had huddled before their campfire the night before, Badger had talked about the old days at Fort Benton, when beaver pelts were the trapper's bread and butter. "Hell," he recalled. "Beaver played out. Now it's buffalo hides. Them big ol' steamboats come all the way from St. Louis, loaded with ever'thing you can think of and go back loaded with hides."

"What about the Blackfeet?" Clay wondered, knowing the fierce tribe's dislike for the white man. "Wasn't there trouble with them?"

"Well, sure—some—but it was the Blackfeet that asked the American Fur Company to build a trading post there in the first place. Hell, they git along with white men when white men got somethin' they need."

Clay thought about Badger's comments of the night before as they now rode toward the solid adobe walls of the fort. It might have been built as a trading post to trade with the Indians, but it also looked to be formidable enough to withstand any attack. Walls, fourteen feet high, connected all the buildings inside the compound, and it was further protected by two blockhouses at odd corners of the fort, giving the defenders a clear line of fire in any direction. Clay figured the presence of the fort more or less guaranteed the peaceful existence of the town that had sprung up around it.

"Well, I'll be . . ." Johnny MacGruder uttered when the two trail-worn travelers stepped into the trade store. "Badger, is that you?"

Badger was stopped in his tracks. Taken by surprise, he looked hard at the man behind the high wooden counter while he shucked his heavy buffalo coat. Then recognizing an old friend, his whiskered face broke into a wide smile. "Johnny MacGruder," he announced. "If you ain't a sight for sore eyes. I swear, I almost didn't know who you was." The two friends grasped hands and pounded each other on the back, laughing joyously. "What the hell are you doin' behind that counter?" Badger asked. Then, not waiting for an answer, he said, "Looks like you fattened up a little since the last time I saw you."

Johnny laughed. "Hell, I been eatin' regular since I quit tryin' to make a livin' offen animal hides." Looking beyond Badger, he cocked an eye at Clay. "Who's this here young grizzly?"

"Clay Culver, Mr. MacGruder," Clay volunteered, and stepped forward to offer his hand.

MacGruder stepped back in mock surprise, then took Clay's hand and shook it enthusiastically. "Damn, a talkin' grizzly." Then he laughed good naturedly.

The man's reaction left Clay slightly baffled. Badger seemed to enjoy the joke as well, joining in the laughter. He might have seen the humor in MacGruder's comments had he been able to see himself in a mirror. Taller than the average man, Clay was indeed a formidable figure with his heavy buffalo robe draped across wide shoulders, and a full crop of whiskers bristling out from under a foxskin cap.

"This here's a friend of mine," Badger told MacGruder. "We sorta found ourselves out in the middle of the prairie when the winter come in kind of suddenlike. So I says to Clay, let's ride on down to Fort Benton and visit my old friend Johnny MacGruder."

Johnny grinned, a twinkle in his eye, as he looked from Badger to Clay, then back at Badger. "You lyin' ol' buzzard—you didn't have no idea I was here."

Badger laughed. "You're right about that. Hell, I thought you was dead. The last I heard of you, you was hightailin' it outta that camp above Horse Creek on the Green River with some little Snake gal's papa on your trail." Badger laughed again as he thought about it. "I see you got away, though."

Johnny scratched his head thoughtfully, a wry grin still in place. "Well, I reckon you could say that. Ol'

Many Horses caught up with me before I could clear the valley. Reckon it was the best thing coulda happened to me. I'd probably still be with that little gal if she hadn't run off with another feller." He winked at Clay and added, "I didn't learn my lesson, though. I hitched up with another one right after I come here—a Blackfoot woman."

"Well, I'll be . . ." Badger exclaimed, shaking his head. "So you're a squaw man, too."

Johnny looked surprised. "Don't tell me you took a wife."

"Sure did—a little Lakota gal—and she's a dandy. Ain't she, Clay?"

Clay smiled and nodded. "She sure is. She's a fine woman."

Clay stood by while the two old friends relived some past times spent in the mountains and brought each other up to date on the present. Badger explained why he and Clay came to be looking for a place to hole up until spring, instead of sitting by the fire with Gray Bird in Little Hawk's camp.

"Stole your sister, huh?" Johnny sympathized. "Well, I reckon Badger's told you the straight of it. You'd not likely find Bloody Axe now that the snows have come." He raised his eyebrows slightly as he fixed Clay with an unblinking stare. "It ain't gonna be easy to find that renegade come spring. I can't say that I know much about that particular band of Blackfoot—only what I hear from some of the Injuns that come in here to trade. But from what I hear, his people keep pretty much to theirselves and don't have much to do with white folks if they can help it. He ain't one to take to the reservation. Bloody Axe stays pretty far to the north, especially since the army sent soldiers to set up a camp on the Judith this past summer. My woman might be able to find out a little more for you, but I don't know if I'd git my hopes up too much, young fellow."

Like Badger, Johnny soon discovered that Clay Culver was not a man easily discouraged. So he offered to help in any way he could. "You'll be needin' a place to stay till spring. I'm pretty sure I can fix it up with the *booshway* so's you can bunk in the Engages' Quarters." Clay was about to protest that he had no money to pay for his keep when Johnny anticipated his concern. "Won't cost you nothin' to stay. You can hunt to pay for your keep—maybe help cut firewood, tend the livestock. There's plenty of room since most of the upstairs is empty now, what with the furs and hides mostly played out."

So Clay and Badger took care of their horses, then moved their possessions into the Engages' Quarters where they shared living quarters with the half-dozen French-Canadians who remained to do the hard labor required to maintain the fort. It was a warm place to wait out the coming of spring, what with a large fireplace at the end of the building—and the blacksmith shop located directly beneath them.

Chapter 11

Charley Vinings bolted upright in his bed. In a fit of panic, his heart beating wildly, he looked around him in the darkness. "Robert?" he called, searching the darkened tent.

"What?" a groggy response came back from the cot at the other end.

Realizing he had been dreaming, Charley replied gruffly, "Nothing. Go on back to sleep." The voice grunted once more then was quiet again. It had been another one of those dreams. *Damn you, Robert,* he thought, *why don't you stay in hell and leave me alone?* This was the second time in the past week Charley had seen his dead brother in his dreams, and the second time he had awakened in a cold sweat. He thought he was done with those dreams, the ones where he would see Robert walking toward him, the side of his skull crushed, his bloody hand outstretched as if pleading for help—and that damned eye bulging out of the socket. But the dream had come back to haunt him in the last few weeks. Charley didn't believe in ghosts, especially when it was broad daylight. But those damnable dreams tormented his sleep so that sometimes he wondered if Robert really was trying to reach him from the grave. *Well, it ain't gonna do you no good. You're dead and you're gonna stay dead. You might as well leave me be.*

Too awake now to go back to sleep—and reluctant to return to that veiled realm where Robert might still await him—Charley threw his legs over the side of the cot and slipped his feet into his boots. He didn't have to glance at the little stove in the center of the tent to know that it had gone out during the night. The chill of the new day about to dawn told him that Marlowe had not banked the fire sufficiently the night before.

He pulled his blanket close around him and stood up. Pausing for a moment to consider the steady snoring of the huge man in the other cot, he entertained a notion to douse him with a cup of cold water for letting the fire go out. *I would, too,* Charley thought, *if you weren't such a big son of a bitch.* Marlowe *was* big, and was possessed of an especially nasty disposition—qualities that Charley found useful in his particular brand of the freighting business.

He had seen the value in the hulking Marlowe as soon as he showed up at Pea Vine Gulch, looking for work. It didn't take but one bottle of raw frontier whiskey to reveal Marlowe to be a man of opportunity, the same as Charley. All Charley was able to learn about the man's recent past was that he had spent some time working at Fort Union. Charley suspected there had been some trouble there, enough to warrant his leaving. Just what the trouble was, Charley didn't really care. The fact that the man was willing to crack a few skulls for ill-gained profit was all Charley needed to know.

Outside the tent, Charley stood shivering against the early spring chill, despite the heavy blanket draped around his shoulders. He looked out over the dingy collection of tents and shacks that comprised the little community of Pea Vine Diggings—half of them now unoccupied, their former tenants having given up and moved on to another gulch in their search for the elusive fortune. The green lumber used to hurriedly fashion the shacks had already weathered to gray. And here and there a broken screendoor banged open and shut at the will of the raw spring breeze as it whistled through the deserted windows.

This place is dead as hell, he thought, as he casually unbuttoned the fly in his long underwear and urinated. *Piss on this town,* he thought, smiling at the pun. He made up his mind right then that it was time to move on to riper pickings.

Charley had established himself as a freighter in German Gulch, and had done quite well until some of the leading citizens began to wonder about the coincidental prospering of his business paralleling several tragic accidents that had taken the lives of several miners. In spite of the suspicions, nobody had any proof that he had anything to do with it. Still, when the local citizens committee started asking too many questions, Charley decided to move on to new pickings. Now Pea Vine had petered out as far as the gold was concerned, but not before he had acquired a sizable portion of the profits from the hard labor of the honest men who worked the mines.

Charley was determined not to make the same mistake he had made at German Gulch and overstay his welcome. He couldn't help but laugh when he thought about it. *I'll be leaving Pea Vine before anybody has time to ask questions.* For a moment, his dream of the night just past came back to mind. It did not trouble his mind so much now, for now there was a low band of light inching its way up the mountains to the east. It would soon be dawn, and Charley didn't worry about his dead brother in the light of day. He had never feared Robert when he was alive. Why, he won-dered, did he fear him since he was dead? *Robert be damned!* he thought. *He's better off dead. He'd just be in my way.* "Yessir," he mumbled, "it's time to move on. The snow's mostly gone from the mountain passes. I best git while the gitting's good."

Marlowe bragged a great deal about his dealings with some of the wilder Blackfoot bands north of the Milk. So Charley decided that was the best place to be until the stench of some of his past dealings had time to die away in the goldfields. He paused to con-sider the ill-tempered man still snoring inside the tent. *Marlowe will be useful, especially if he knows the Blackfeet like he says he does. But I expect, when we get done with this trip, it'll be time to put a bullet in the back of his head before he gets the notion to do the job on me.* With that thought in mind, he turned and went back inside to rebuild the fire in the stove.

The weather on this morning looked even better than the day before, leaving no doubt that winter's long frigid grip had been broken. Charley and Mar-lowe spent most of the morning loading the two big freight wagons with the trinkets and supplies that Charley had accumulated while at the short-lived dig-gings. One wagon was loaded with twenty-two gallon-sized jugs of whiskey, originally meant for a saloon in Alder Gulch, but had somehow gotten sidetracked on the way from Virginia City, the driver's body lying at the bottom of a gully with a bullet in his back. Charley figured the whiskey, once it was watered down suffi-ciently, could bring a nice profit in hides and furs from the Indians. When they had cooled down enough, the stove and stovepipe were the last things loaded, and the two unlikely partners were ready to hitch the teams.

"Reckon that's it," Marlowe declared.

"All right, then," Charley acknowledged. "You lead out, since you say you know the way."

"Oh, I know the way all right," Marlowe was quick to reply. "I've knowed a bunch of them Blackfoot—traded with 'em for years." So they started out, leaving the small settlement of Pea Vine behind them, setting a course toward Three Forks and the Missouri country beyond.

Spring could not come soon enough for Clay Culver. There had been times during the long hard winter when he had again entertained thoughts of setting out to find Martha before waiting for the thaw. Only his common sense—and Badger's constant assurance that he would wind up frozen to death in some snowbound canyon—enabled him to control his impatience.

It was not a time of idle waiting, however, for there was plenty of work to do to keep the fort supplied with firewood, as well as livestock to look after. Clay more than earned his keep. When there was time, he would sometimes venture out to hunt. Although there was very little game to find that winter on the frozen plains, still Clay managed to find the occasional elk or buffalo. On one such hunting trip, he was fortunate to discover a small herd of buffalo more than twenty miles west of the fort. There were only about thirty of the shaggy beasts, and they were all following along behind one lead bull in a single file as he broke trail through the waist-high snow. It was a simple matter to cut down the last four buffalo in the line. The real work came when they had to be butchered and packed all the way back to Fort Benton.

The long winter nights were the hardest for Clay, since this was when his imagination would torment him with thoughts of his sister's suffering. To occupy his mind with other tasks, he decided to learn the

Blackfoot language. He had willing teachers in Johnny MacGruder and his Blackfoot wife Silent Woman, and they soon discovered that he was an exceptional student. By the time the first signs of spring began to appear, Clay conversed quite competently with Johnny's wife, sometimes speaking in nothing but the Blackfoot language. His diligence in learning her native tongue delighted Silent Woman and she would nod approvingly as he recited the day's lesson.

As each day brought them closer to spring, Clay's mind was filled more and more with thoughts of Martha, and he wondered if she had given up hope of rescue, *if she were even still alive.* He tried not to imagine what it must be like for her. He found it impossible to avoid forming a mental image of the face of her captor. *Black Elk*, they had said he was called. Often, when Clay was sitting alone before the fire, listening to Badger's steady snoring behind him, he would picture that face. It was the cruel unforgiving face of a savage, and he promised himself that he would rid the world of the heathen devil.

On the rare occasion when he would give voice to his anxiety over the inhumane treatment surely being suffered by his sister, Badger would remind him that Johnny's wife Silent Woman was a Blackfoot Indian. "And she ain't so damned savage, is she?" he would insist. "There's mean Injuns, and savage ones, but for the most part, I expect they's just about like most folks." Clay found Badger's counsel pretty strange for one who so suspected the Blackfoot people of treachery. But he appreciated his partner's efforts to ease his mind.

When it appeared that spring was finally going to come, Clay wondered if Badger might be thinking about how long it had been since he had seen his own wife, and he feared the old mountain man might decide to head back to the Powder River country looking for her. But Badger assured him that he had promised him he would help him find his sister, and he was a man of his word.

With the change in the seasons, spring also brought a trickle of Indian visitors to the trading post. Among these were several families from Silent Woman's tribe who brought a message from her father. The old man was not up to making the journey himself, but he wanted her to know that he and her mother hoped she would come to visit them.

"I reckon I'm gonna have to take Silent Woman to see her folks this summer." Johnny MacGruder winced as he said it, causing Badger to laugh.

"Hell, you're lucky her relatives ain't come to live with you," Badger snorted. "That's the trouble with hitchin' up with a woman so much younger than you are: All their dang folks are still livin'." He cocked a mischievous eye at Clay, and added, "That's the main reason I set out with Clay—just to git away from Gray Bird's relatives for a spell."

Clay raised an eyebrow at that remark. "When I first talked to you at Laramie, you were complaining about being away from your wife too long, and you wanted to spend some time with your family."

"Oh, I warn't lying. I wanted to see my wife right enough, but at my age, son, it don't take long to git caught up, even less time to git caught up visitin' her relatives."

Johnny shook his head and grinned knowingly. "It's hell, ain't it? You take a shine to some little gal. You ain't interested in takin' on no new relatives; you just want a wife. Then you wake up one mornin' and find out she didn't just spring up from the earth like a stalk of corn. She come with a mammy and pap, brothers and sisters, uncles, aunts—and they all expect you to be part of the family. And all you wanted was a wife. Hell, you already had enough damn relatives of your own."

Silent Woman's visitors unknowingly brought some additional news, however, news that was of the utmost concern to Clay. Prompted by Johnny, Silent Woman asked her guests if they had any information as to the whereabouts of Bloody Axe's village. One of them, a man called Little Bear, told her that his brother had encountered a hunting party from Bloody Axe's camp no more than a week before. They told him that Bloody Axe was moving his camp to Willow Creek above the Teton River. Upon hearing the news from Silent Woman, Badger glanced at Clay. The look in Clay's eye told him not to waste his breath asking. Clay was already preparing to leave. They bid farewell to Johnny and Silent Woman the following morning, heading for Willow Creek.

Chapter 12

"Well, this is a fine mess," Charley Vinings complained, standing, hands on hips, staring at the sheer rock walls on either side of the river. "Dammit, Marlowe, you led us into a blind draw. How the hell are we gonna get these wagons around this?"

"I told you I didn't know if we could git wagons through this stretch of the river," Marlowe snarled.

"You're the one that said you knew where to find your Blackfoot friends," Charley insisted, his frustration growing by the minute. With two wagons loaded down with trade goods and whiskey, apparently at a dead end, he was in no mood to be forgiving.

"I do know where to find 'em, by God, but I ain't never tried to follow this damn river up there. I told you that. I always come over from the Yellowstone country before. I told you back at Pea Vine that we probably oughtn't to try it with wagons."

Charley didn't say anything for a few seconds. He didn't recall any such advice from his sullen partner when they were loading the wagons. He stared at the narrow trail that wound up through the boulders before him, then to the right and left. "Well," he finally sighed, "what do we do now?"

"What I said we oughta do in the first place," Marlowe replied, his voice thick with sarcasm. "Unhitch them mules and start loadin' 'em up."

"Jesus Christ, man, we can't get all that load on these mules! We're gonna have to ride two of 'em. That don't leave but six mules to carry all this stuff."

"Well, I reckon we're gonna have to cache what we can't carry," Marlowe said, making no effort to disguise his own impatience with Charley's whining.

"Cache the rest . . ." Charley started, but was interrupted before he could finish his complaint.

"We got company," Marlowe growled, holding up his hand to silence Charley. He pointed to the bluff over Charley's right shoulder.

Charley turned to follow the direction pointed out by Marlowe. Stone still at the rim of the bluff, two Blackfoot warriors sat on their horses, watching the two white men arguing below them. Charley's entire body tensed, and his first reaction was to drop his hand on the handle of his pistol. Seeing the panic in Charley's eyes, Marlowe was quick to caution him.

"Don't make no sudden moves," he warned while keeping his eyes on the two Indians above them. "They might be friendly. They ain't got nothin' but bows. If they had rifles, they'da done shot us."

"A couple of shots with a rifle ought to scare 'em away," Charley said.

"No. Hell, no." Marlowe quickly replied. "We don't know how many more of 'em there are. We best act real friendly till we find out if there's any of their friends hangin' around." Without waiting for Charley's concurrence, he raised his arm and waved, calling out, "Come on down. We are friends."

High on the bluff, one of the Indians raised his arm in return. The two of them deliberated for a few seconds before reining their ponies back from the rim of the bluff and disappearing from view. In a few minutes, they reappeared on the narrow trail through the boulders. Charley moved over next to his wagon to make sure his rifle was handy while he watched their visitors descend.

"Don't look like there's but two of 'em," he said. "We can knock them off before they know what hit 'em."

"Just hold your horses," Marlowe shot back. "There might be two hundred of 'em within sound of a rifle shot. They look friendly enough. I think they're just lookin' for somethin' to trade." He shot another glance at Charley and grinned. "Besides, this might be a piece of good luck. They might be willin' to help us cache our goods for a drink of that whiskey." He started gathering some dead wood. "Might as well build a fire. We're probably gonna have to feed 'em."

"Maybe you're right," Charley reluctantly relented. After all, he conceded, that's what he came out here for, to trade with the Indians. He took a step away from the wagon and stood by Marlowe as the two warriors approached.

"Welcome, friends," Marlowe greeted them, getting up from the small fire that was just beginning to show signs of life. His Blackfoot-speaking skills, while not fluent, were sufficient to communicate, aided by use of sign language.

The two warriors were surprised to happen upon the likes of Charley and Marlowe to say the least. With glances of curiosity, first at the two white men, then at the two heavily loaded wagons, they introduced themselves and dismounted. After an exchange of greetings, one of the Blackfeet—a solidly built young man, called Heavy Owl—asked the obvious question, "How will you get your wagons over the rocks?"

Marlowe explained that the wagons were going to

be left behind, and the contents carried forward, packed on the mules. Heavy Owl nodded his understanding, but the expression on his face suggested that he doubted the mules' ability to carry all that he saw in the wagons. Thinking it impolite to point out the white men's faulty planning, Heavy Owl changed the subject. "We have a fresh-killed rabbit we can share with you."

"That would be good," Marlowe said. "We have coffee and some hardtack."

The white men and the Indians sat down together, the two Blackfeet on one side of the fire, and Charley and Marlowe on the other. While they waited for the rabbit to roast, Marlowe explained that they were going to have to cache a good portion of their goods, and he wondered if Heavy Owl and his friend knew of a good place where they would be safe. Taken aback by the white man's apparent naïveté, Heavy Owl eagerly responded that he did indeed know of such a place. Marlowe confided that he had a wagon filled with jugs of firewater, and that he would give one to each of them if they helped them hide the rest of their load.

"It's real strong firewater," Marlowe assured them, "I'll git you a taste to see for yourself."

He went to the back of the wagon and pulled one of the gallon containers out and poured a generous amount into a tin cup. Returning to the fire, he offered the cup to Heavy Owl who eagerly accepted it. Taking a sip of the raw liquid, he held it in his mouth for a few moments while he tasted it. He nodded briefly to his companion then spat the mouthful of whiskey into the fire, smiling with satisfaction when the potent brew caused a sudden burst of flame. *This buck's had some watered-down whiskey before,* Marlowe thought, grinning as he watched Heavy Owl's reaction. With proof that the whiskey was satisfactory, the two Blackfeet agreed to help unload the wagons.

With Heavy Owl and his friend's help, the two white men soon had a good portion of their merchandise, the stove and stovepipe, stored away under a ledge of solid rock. The two Blackfeet remained on hand to help fashion packs for the mules as well, never questioning the fact that Charley and Marlowe loaded all eight mules, apparently leaving the two white men to travel on foot. If their thoughts had not been occupied with the prospect of returning to the cache after the foolish white men had gone, the Indians might have suspected that Charley and Marlowe had no intention of walking.

When the wagons were empty except for two saddles, Heavy Owl asked if they were going to be left in the wagon. Marlowe grinned at Charley while he translated the Indian's question. Both men laughed at that. "No," Marlowe replied. "Them saddles go on your ponies." His response puzzled the two Indians for a moment, and before Heavy Owl could thank him for the generous gifts, Charley and Marlowe had their pistols out. Marlowe shot Heavy Owl's companion in the back of the head before the surprised Blackfoot warrior had time to react. Heavy Owl made a dash for his horse, but he had taken no more than five steps before Charley's bullet smashed into his spine.

"I thought for a minute there you was gonna let him git away," Marlowe commented dryly.

Charley smirked, calmly replacing the bullet he had fired. "I reckon I coulda shot quicker if I'd wanted to, but I wanted to see how fast he could run." He cocked a warning eye at Marlowe. "Don't ever worry about how quick I am." Receiving only an insolent grin in return, he locked eyes with his partner in crime for a brief second before breaking it off. "We've wasted enough time here. Let's drag these bodies over and throw them in the river." Reaching down to grab Heavy Owl by the heels, he glanced at Marlowe again and said, "I hope to hell these two weren't from the same village you're supposed to be leading us to."

"Matter of fact, they was," Marlowe casually replied. "Leastways they said they was from Black Shirt's village. I never seen 'em before, but, hell, I never went there. The only time I ever seen any of 'em was when they came to Fort Union."

"You never . . . Whaddaya mean?" Charley demanded. "You told me you and them Blackfoot was big friends. Now you're telling me you ain't ever been to their camp?" Charley was beginning to realize the folly in partnering with a liar.

"Hold on," Marlowe growled. He didn't care much for Charley's tone. "I said I knew where Black Shirt would likely be, and I do. We'll find him. Don't you worry about that."

"Well, we'd better," was all Charley said in return, but he had already made up his mind to settle Marlowe's hash when the time came.

After the bodies were disposed of and the wagons pulled into a deep ravine, the next order of business was the introduction of the Indian ponies to the heavy leather saddles Charley and Marlowe had brought along. As it turned out, the saddles themselves were not the biggest problem. The horses accepted them, although reluctantly, in exchange for the lighter Indian saddles. The trouble came when they were introduced to the bit. Their Blackfoot masters had simply fashioned a makeshift bridle, which consisted of a length of rope with a couple of half-hitches, and tied it around the pony's lower jaw. That was all that was necessary to guide the horse. When subjected to the leather bridle and the cruel metal bit, both horses

balked, refusing to take it. It was only after almost an
hour of combat between horse and man, that the two
Indian mounts were beaten into submission, and Charley and Marlowe set out once again—on ponies with
severely sore mouths, leading eight mules packed with
an odd assortment of trade goods and six gallon-size
jugs of whiskey.

Martha opened her eyes, blinking the sleep away.
It would be sunup pretty soon. She must rouse herself
and see to the fire, but she was reluctant to leave her
bed. It was snug and warm where she lay, pressed up
against Black Elk's back. She smiled when she thought
of her husband, and put her arm around him, pulling
herself even closer against his bare back. *He sleeps
like a dead man,* she thought, *never tossing, never turning.* It was true. Always, after he made love to her,
and whispered good night, he would turn on his side
and sleep like a stone, never moving from that position until rising the next morning. Martha sighed,
dreading to slide out from under the soft buffalo robe.
Finally, she forced herself to move. *I don't want the
other women to think Black Elk has a lazy wife.*

As she busied herself reviving the fire in preparation
for cooking Black Elk's breakfast, she couldn't help
but think about little Moon Shadow. The image of the
slight girl often came to mind whenever Martha was
busy with the daily chores that filled the life of every
Blackfoot woman. For Moon Shadow had taught her
everything. Every chore she now performed had been
patiently demonstrated by her adopted sister. Martha
paused for a moment to give the thought her full attention. She missed Moon Shadow.

Tomorrow would be a busy day for all the women
of the village, for Bloody Axe had said that it was
time to leave the mountains and move the camp to

the buffalo country. Martha looked forward to the journey. The winter just past had been the most enjoyable one she could remember, for she had embraced the simple straightforward life of the Blackfeet. And now spring would soon be here, a new spring for Martha, like no other spring before, in a new life without fear or shame.

She had come to terms with her conscience regarding Robert. In the early days after her capture, she had prayed for Robert to come for her, only because of the harm she feared might befall her. She realized now that she had never really loved Robert, and the two of them had drifted apart long before her abduction from the cabin in the Black Hills. How could she have foreseen the strange twist of fate that would open a whole new life for her. She had fretted with it at first, thinking it sinful to dishonor her husband with her lust for Black Elk, a lust that she had been unable to deny. But she had put all guilty thoughts out of her mind for good now.

Behind her, the soft rustle of the entrance flap told her that Black Elk was awake. She turned and looked up at him, smiling. "I wondered if I was going to have to wake you," she teased. "The sun is already high in the sky."

He smiled. "I was only waiting for my lazy wife to cook my breakfast. I think if it is not prepared by the time I come back from the river, I will have to give you a good beating."

She laughed delightedly. Springing to her feet, she picked up a small stick and playfully rapped him sharply across the buttocks. "We'll see who does the whipping around here."

"Yow!" he yelped in surprise when the blow was a little sharper than he expected. Then, embarrassed that he had uttered a sound, he grabbed Martha, locking his powerful arms around her so that her arms were pinned to her sides. He lifted her until her face was level with his. Affecting a fierce scowl, he said, "I think I'll throw you in the river and be done with you."

Giggling like a child, she kissed him, covering his face with kisses until, totally embarrassed, he put her down, quickly looking around to see if anyone had witnessed this foolish play between a man and his wife. "If you don't learn to behave, I'm going to give you back to the Crows," he said, trying hard to look annoyed.

She watched him as he strode through the circle of lodges on his way to the river to bathe. His long black hair, woven in two dark braids, rested lightly upon powerful shoulders that glistened bronze in the morning sun. She felt herself tremble with thoughts of those shoulders and the night just past. *You'd better get your mind on your chores,* she admonished, looking about her quickly, afraid someone might see the dreamy expression on her face.

"Six Horses."

Martha looked around to see who had called her name. She smiled when she saw Red Wing approaching. The old medicine woman had become a close friend since the two of them had tried to nurse Moon Shadow back to health. "It is a fine morning, Red Wing," Martha greeted her friend.

"Yes it is," Red Wing agreed. "I think it would be a fine morning to walk down the riverbank. I have been watching for the past few days, and I think I know where some ducks are nesting. We could have a nice feast of duck eggs tonight. Why don't you come with me after you have prepared Black Elk's breakfast?"

"Thank you. I would like that," Martha quickly replied. She knew it would please Black Elk, for he, like most of the people of the village, thought goose and duck eggs were a special treat. It would be a fitting banquet on their last night in this camp. Tomorrow the lodges would be taken down and packed on travois, along with all their other belongings. Martha's tipi was a small one, only twelve cowskins were required to make it. The larger tipi had been used as a burial wrap for Moon Shadow. Martha herself had sewn it around her little sister, with her favorite cooking pots and utensils for tanning hides inside. Black Elk would soon provide enough cowhides to make her new lodge. She wanted it to be a more fitting home for her husband—eighteen hides at least, and more for the inner lining. She wanted new backrests, too, and antelope skin to make herself a new dress. Black Elk needed new leggings, and a new shirt. There was a great deal to be done. She would be very busy this spring.

Chapter 13

"Git back!" Marlowe commanded, his voice a harsh whisper as he frantically motioned for Charley to hold the mules below the rim of the ridge. "Injuns!" he warned as he yanked his pony's head around, causing the animal to slide back down the incline, almost colliding with Charley's mount. Scrambling back up to the rim on his hands and knees, he flattened himself to avoid being seen.

"Who are they?" Charley called out in a loud whisper while he struggled to control the string of pack-mules, unsure if he should be drawing his weapons or not.

"How the hell should I know?" Marlowe shot back, more than a little concerned himself until he could manage to get a good look. "Looks like a huntin' party," he said a moment later. "Or maybe they're just on their way somewhere. Leastways, they ain't wearin' paint."

"How many?" Charley asked.

After a few moments, Marlowe answered. "I count six of 'em. Blackfoot."

"Well, what are we hiding for? I thought you were friends with the Blackfoot." Once again, Charley was beginning to question just how effective Marlowe was as a guide.

"I don't know every damn Blackfoot in the territory. Hell, man, it always pays to see any damn bunch of Injuns before they see you." There was a long pause while he continued to watch the party of Blackfeet. Then he volunteered, "Shit, I know this bunch. That's ol' Wolf Tail, biggest drunk in the Blackfoot nation." Marlowe got to his feet. "You can bring 'em on up," he said, waving Charley on.

While Charley brought the mules up to the top of the ridge, Marlowe yelled out to the line of riders, waving his arm back and forth to catch their eye. The Indians stopped immediately, and paused to consider who might be hailing them, exercising a natural caution at the sudden appearance of white men. Remaining motionless while they watched Marlowe and Charley lead the string of eight heavily loaded mules across the ridge, they constantly scanned the hillsides on either side, mindful of the possibility of flanking riders. When it was apparent that the white men were alone, the Indians' attention focused immediately upon the pack mules. Their interest fully awakened, they sat their ponies, waiting for the white men to approach.

"Wolf Tail, it's me, Marlowe. We was just on our way to do some tradin' with your people, our friends the Blackfeet."

Wolf Tail recognized the huge man on the Indian pony before he even spoke. He turned to his companions and told them that this was the man from Fort Union who sold him whiskey when the *bourgeois* said it was forbidden. Turning back to face the approaching white men, he held up his arm in greeting. "Marlowe, it is good to see you, my friend," he said in English.

While his companions gathered around the mules,

eyeing the securely bound jugs, Wolf Tail explained that they were returning to their village after visiting his uncle in Bloody Axe's camp on Willow Creek. For once, Charley could follow the conversation, since Wolf Tail was eager to demonstrate his mastery of the English language. The courteous exchange of greetings was dispensed with in short order, since Wolf Tail's interest was concentrated on the gallon-size jugs strapped on the mules. He was well familiar with the contents of jugs similar to these.

There was immediate talk of trade, but the six Blackfeet had very little to trade with them—nothing that Charley wanted, anyway—so they suggested that Charley and Marlowe accompany them to Black Shirt's village where they had many robes and furs. For now, however, Wolf Tail thought it would be a sign of good will if they were allowed to sample the whiskey. In exchange, he promised, he would lead them to Black Shirt's camp. Charley thought this an excellent suggestion since he had begun to doubt if Marlowe would ever find the village on his own.

"Keep your rifle handy," Marlowe whispered. "These boys might git the idea they wanna grab the whole shebang, and our scalps with it."

"I hope they do," Charley murmured in reply. "I'd enjoy sending them to meet their friends back at the cache."

"Let us sit down and eat together," Wolf Tail said, "we have the hindquarter of an antelope we killed yesterday. We are happy to share our food."

Yeah, and we provide the whiskey, Charley thought while affecting a smile as genuine as he could make it. While two of the Indians gathered wood to make a fire, Charley hobbled the mules in a thicket. He released one jug of whiskey from its straps, and set it down, along with a tin cup, in front of the fire just lit.

The six Blackfeet gathered around eagerly waiting to sample the firewater. Charley filled the cup to the brim, then corked the jug and pulled it back away from the fire. There was a simultaneous look of disappointment on all six faces when they realized that one cup was all that would be offered to sample. Wolf Tail shrugged and picked up the cup, taking a quick gulp, immediately followed by another before he passed it to the warrior on his left. By the time the cup came back around to Charley, it was empty, the last of Wolf Tail's companions having emptied it. This forced Charley to make a show of further generosity. He had not planned to donate more than the one cup of whiskey, but Marlowe whispered that it would be impolite not to drink with their guests, and at least one of the Blackfeet knew the cup was empty, so Charley couldn't pretend to take a drink. "What the hell," he muttered and uncorked the jug for one more round.

By the time the cup made another round, the strips of antelope were sizzling over the fire, and Marlowe persuaded Charley to fill the cup once more. In no time at all, the cautious atmosphere abated. Even the stoic companions of Wolf Tail were chattering among themselves as the glow of Charley's whiskey warmed their bellies.

Chewing thoughtfully on a tough strip of roasted meat, Wolf Tail eyed Marlowe's white companion, curious about a man who would team up with the notorious loner. As far as he knew, none of the other white men at Fort Union had much use for the sullen bully. And Wolf Tail held no illusions about the professed friendship Marlowe claimed for the Blackfoot people. Marlowe had been his only source for the white man's firewater. It was as simple as that—and Wolf Tail had a big craving for firewater. This stranger, Charley, appeared to be the owner of the whiskey, for he was the

one who decided when to fill the cup. In spite of the
white man's apparent friendliness, Wolf Tail decided
it would be wise to watch his back when Charley was
around. He had the look of a weasel, with eyes close
together and set back under heavy brows. After studying the man, Wolf Tail could finally curb his curiosity
no longer.

"You are new to this country," he stated, staring at
Charley. When Charley said that he was, Wolf Tail
nodded and said, "When we first saw you on the ridge,
we think maybe you came looking for the white
woman." He smiled. "But then we see Marlowe."

Charley's jaw went slack when he heard the words
white woman. He spat out the half-chewed piece of
meat he was eating, and shot back, "What white
woman?"

Wolf Tail shrugged indifferently, glancing at Marlowe, then back at Charley as if expecting everyone
to know about the woman captive. "The one taken by
Black Elk last summer," he answered.

Suddenly totally sober, Charley asked, "Took her
from a cabin in the Black Hills?"

Marlowe stopped chewing long enough to listen to
the conversation when he noticed Charley's rapt interest regarding the white woman. When Wolf Tail
seemed unsure about Charley's question, Marlowe
quickly supplied the Blackfoot words for Black Hills.
Understanding then, Wolf Tail nodded, "Yes, it was
there."

Charley sank back on his heels, stunned by the
news. *Martha!* he thought. Then a sly smile creased
his lips. *So the bitch is still alive. Now, ain't that something?* His thoughts flew back to the cabin in the Black
Hills, and the lust he had for his brother's wife. The
thought of her rebuking him, which angered him so
at the time, now only widened his smile. *Maybe this*

is one helluva twist of fate. She wouldn't stick her snooty nose up at me now, I reckon. With a sudden laugh, he dragged the jug from behind him. "Let's have another round, boys. Hand me that cup."

Staring at him with a suspicious eye, Marlowe asked, "You're gittin' mighty generous with that whiskey, ain'tcha, pardner?"

Charley just laughed again at the thought. "Seed stock, Marlowe. Hell, these boys has got something to trade now."

Marlowe didn't understand, so Charley stated his intention to offer all the whiskey they had packed on the mules if neccessary as an inducement for Wolf Tail and his friends to deliver Martha to him.

The announcement didn't set too well with Marlowe. "What the hell for?" he demanded. "What do you want with a woman, especially one that's been used up by a bunch of Injuns? We can git a helluva lot of furs for that whiskey. You wanna throw it away for a woman?" He shook his head, unable to believe what he was hearing. "Hell, if you need to plant your pickle that bad, you don't have to give away all our whiskey for it. We can steal you a squaw for nothin'."

The smile remained on Charley's face for a long moment before it gradually faded into a dark frown when he spoke. "In the first place, it ain't *our* whiskey. It's *my* whiskey, and I'll do what I damn well please with it." He paused to let that sink in while he glared into the angry face of his partner. "We've got sixteen more jugs back in the cache. I don't figure it'll take more than the five we got on the mules, plus a little piece of this one." When Marlowe just shook his head, still dismayed, Charley went on to explain. "This ain't no ordinary woman. Why, this is my dear sister-in-law," he said contemptuously.

Marlowe didn't like it, but he didn't protest further,

mollifying himself with the knowledge that the time would soon come when he would put a bullet in Charley's back. He sat still, holding his tongue while Charley proposed a trade that Wolf Tail was going to find difficult to resist.

At first, Wolf Tail did not understand. "Whiskey for the white woman? The woman is not mine. She belongs to Black Elk of Bloody Axe's village. I cannot trade a woman that is not mine."

"You can steal her, can't you?" Charley persisted. He motioned toward the packmules. "I would give you all this firewater for the woman."

Wolf Tail had a strong desire for the whiskey, but this thing Charley proposed was a bad thing indeed. He could not entertain thoughts of stealing from his own people, even when Charley explained that the woman was his sister-in-law. He gazed longingly at the jugs before giving his final answer. "This I cannot do. Black Elk is a blood brother." This was all he voiced, but he also knew that Black Elk was a fierce warrior, renowned for his bravery in battle, and would no doubt kill the man who stole his property.

Charley was rapidly losing his patience. If Wolf Tail was the drunk Marlowe stated him to be, he should be willing to cut his own mother's throat for that much whiskey. The thought of Martha was already burning a picture in his mind of the sweet revenge he would enjoy for her rejection of him. He tried further enticement by suggesting there might be even more whiskey to come in exchange for the white woman. The more Wolf Tail resisted, the stronger Charley's desire for Martha grew.

Disgusted with the foolish offerings of a sizable fortune in trade goods, Marlowe snorted his displeasure and withdrew from the campfire. Muttering that he was going to see to the mules, he walked over to his horse and pretended to check the girth strap. If Charley succeeded in talking Wolf Tail into trading the woman for the whiskey, Marlowe stood to lose a great deal, payment he figured was owed to him for putting up with Charley in the first place. The question before him now was, what would be the risk if he put a bullet in Charley's back right then? Would the six Blackfeet then rise up against him? Marlowe's hand slid down the barrel of his rifle until it rested just above the trigger guard. It was tempting. Charley's back was unprotected as he continued to haggle with Wolf Tail, but Marlowe didn't like the odds that would result: one white man with eight packmules, alone against six Blackfeet. It galled him to admit it, but he needed Charley.

Finally, Charley wore Wolf Tail down to a compromise, one that Marlowe found more to his liking. Wolf Tail agreed to take Charley to Bloody Axe's camp in exchange for one jug of whiskey, but that was all he would agree to. Charley was going to have to deal with Black Elk himself. Marlowe tried to convince Charley that he might be playing a dangerous game, but Charley was confident that a few jugs of whiskey could buy him most anything from any Indian.

Martha paused and sat back on her heels to listen. She thought for a moment that she had heard something, but decided that it was nothing more than the whinnying of the ponies on the other side of the creek. She was about to continue scraping the buffalo cow skin staked out before her when she heard the camp dogs begin to bark. Looking toward the center of the village, she saw Bloody Axe and a few of the other men staring out toward the prairie. Shielding her eyes against the afternoon sun, she turned to look in the direction they were watching, hoping it might be Black Elk returning early from the hunt.

Someone was coming, all right. She could see them now. But it was not Black Elk. Getting to her feet, she continued to stare out at the approaching riders until she could make out their features. It appeared to be Screech Owl's nephew Wolf Tail in the lead, a fact that aroused her curiosity, because he had just left the village to return to his own camp. The other five who had accompanied him were not with him now. She wondered if anything was wrong. Now they were close enough that she could make out the riders following Wolf Tail—two men, leading a string of pack mules. Suddenly a cold chill ran the length of her spine as she realized they were white men. *White men!* The thought struck her like a blow to her chest. Her heart threatened to explode inside her breast. The thoughts racing through her mind were thoughts of fear. *White men! What do they want?* Looking around her frantically, she wondered if she should hide. *Calm yourself!* she scolded, never thinking to question her reaction upon seeing people of her own skin for the first time since her capture. *There is nothing to fear. They lead packmules, loaded heavily. They are hoping to trade, that's all.* Although she was curious as to what trinkets they might have to trade, she decided to remain at a distance.

Several of those who had been standing with Bloody Axe walked toward the edge of the village to meet the riders. Screech Owl, Wolf Tail's uncle, was among the foremost. The two white men stopped at the edge of the water while Wolf Tail continued on. When he rode up from the creek, he slid off his pony and stood talking to Screech Owl. There followed an animated discussion between the two with much arm waving and gesturing toward the mounted white men. As she watched, standing beside the entrance to her lodge, Martha began to experience a feeling of dread. Something about the sudden appearance of these white men disturbed her greatly. She wished that Black Elk was there.

Finally, the discussion over, Wolf Tail motioned the white men over, and he and Screech Owl led them to meet Bloody Axe. Martha moved a few yards away from her tipi to get a better look at the visitors. What she saw stunned her, and for a moment, she felt that her knees were going to buckle. *Charley!* At first she thought her eyes were playing tricks on her, and she strained harder to see him. She closed her eyes tight for a few seconds then opened them again. It *was* Charley, but the other man was not Robert. Martha's mind was reeling! She had long ago accepted the fact that she would never see either of them again. Instead of joy at the sight of her brother-in-law, her impulse was to run, to hide from a part of her life that was no more. The thought of returning to a life with Robert made her almost sick with despair. She looked around frantically, seeking an avenue of escape, but there was none. So instead of running, she retreated inside her tipi, hoping that if she remained out of sight, maybe Bloody Axe would not tell Charley that she was there.

Seated at the back of her lodge, Martha tried to concentrate on the white antelope skin from which she would make a dress. But her stitching was slow and careless as she strained to listen to the sounds from the center of the circle of lodges. Then her heart began to beat wildly when she heard the soft pad of moccasined feet approaching outside, and she thrust her bone needle faster and faster through the soft hide. Dreading the summons that she anticipated, still she jumped as if she had suddenly heard a gunshot when she heard her name called.

"Six Horses." It was Bloody Axe's voice. "Come, I would speak with you."

For a moment, she considered not answering, hoping he would think her gone, but she knew that he had seen her working on the cow skin that morning. Reluctantly, she put her sewing aside and went to the entrance. Pushing the flap open no more than a few inches, she peered out cautiously, fearful that she might see Charley standing there. When, much to her relief, there was only Bloody Axe, standing waiting, she pushed the flap aside and went out.

"Six Horses," Bloody Axe began, "two white men have come to our camp. They are searching for a white woman that was captured, and they heard that we have one with us. I think it is you they search for." When he saw the look of alarm on her face, he hastened to assure her. "They look for a slave. I told them that Black Elk's wife is a white woman, but she is not a slave. I'm going to send them away because they have brought the white man's firewater to trade with our young men. It is an evil drink, and I will not let them bring it into our village."

Martha was greatly relieved by Bloody Axe's words, but when she looked toward the center of the camp, she saw Charley and the other white man still there, standing and watching. She felt a shiver skip along her spine. She looked into Bloody Axe's face, wondering why they still remained. "I don't want to see them," she said, her voice trembling as her eyes focused upon her feet.

Bloody Axe nodded patiently, understanding her reluctance, but he encouraged her to come with him. "I do not want them to bring the soldiers. I should kill them for bringing the firewater that sickens our young men. But if I kill them, the soldiers might still come to look for them. I think it is best if you tell them yourself that you are not a slave, and stay here by choice. Then maybe they will go in peace."

Martha listened to the chief. There was logic in Bloody Axe's words. There could be trouble if she did not face up to Charley and tell him that she preferred to remain with her Blackfoot family. It would be hard. She did not want to cause Robert any pain, but she knew that the choice she made was best for her and Robert. Knowing that it was not right to hide from the responsibility for the choice she had made, she finally relented. "I'll talk to them," she said.

Charley was not prepared for the change in his sister-in-law. He had expected to see a wretched shell of the wife of his late brother—downtrodden and abused, desperate to be rescued and consequently seeing him as her savior. Instead, he was stunned by the radiant vision, stepping softly in colorfully beaded moccasins behind Bloody Axe. For one brief moment, he wasn't even sure that it was Martha. He had not remembered her to be so tall and graceful. Little wonder he had lusted for her then. Maybe, he thought, he had forgotten what a handsome woman his brother had taken for a wife.

The small gathering of people parted to make way for her, eager to hear what would be said between Six Horses and the white men. As she approached, Charley started to step forward to meet her, but was immediately restrained by Screech Owl's hand on his arm. Marlowe's warning frown reminded him that the two of them might well be in peril.

"Martha," Charley began as soon as she had halted some ten paces from him, "I've come to rescue you." He affected a wide smile as he waited, anticipating an emotional outpouring of relief upon seeing he had

come to save her. But there was no sign of gratitude
in her expression. Instead, she stood close to Bloody
Axe as if seeking his protection. "It's all right, Martha,
I'm gonna take care of you now. You ain't gotta be
afraid no more," Charley went on, still baffled by her
unexpected lack of response.

Martha didn't answer at once, looking at her
brother-in-law and then at the dark menacing-looking
man with him. She thought it odd that Robert was
not with them, that there was no mention of Robert.
So she asked, "Where is Robert?"

"Well, now, that's a sad piece of news to have to
bring you," Charley replied, shaking his head sorrowfully. "Poor Robert's dead, murdered by outlaws."
When she drew her breath sharply, stunned by the
news, he hastened to assure her. "It's a mighty dis-
tressing thing to have to tell you, but it can't be helped
now. I'm gonna take care of you from now on. That's
the main thing." He looked around him at the gathering of people. "Which one of these bucks is Black
Elk?" he asked, ready to buy Martha's freedom with
one of his jugs of whiskey.

She ignored his question while she fought to control
her emotions. *Robert dead! Murdered!* Charley's
words so stunned her that she grabbed Bloody Axe's
arm to steady herself. There was an immediate murmur of angry voices in the circle of men and women
surrounding the white men. Thinking Martha had
been threatened by the strangers, the people pressed
closer, almost touching Charley and Marlowe. Some
of the men brandished weapons, causing Marlowe to
quickly plead their innocence. Speaking in his halting
Blackfoot, he explained that they had not threatened
Martha.

"What he says is true," Martha said, quieting the
angry voices. "He just brings sad news of someone's

death." In an emotional quicksand, confused by old feelings and new beginnings, she found it hard to know what to say to Charley. The news had shocked her, for she had once thought that she loved Robert. To think of him slain by a craven murderer was a horrifying thing to accept. *Poor Robert,* she thought, *he was never strong enough for this wild new country.* For a moment, she felt guilty for having been abducted, leaving him alone. It was difficult to understand why things happened the way they did, and she was truly saddened by the news of Robert's death. After a moment, it occurred to her that she was now free of the guilt she had lived with for embracing Black Elk as her husband while still legally married to Robert. It was not the way she would have chosen, but she could now close that chapter of her life.

Shifting nervously from one foot to the other, Marlowe continued to glance around him at the restless crowd of Indians. He was thinking that he and Charley should have stuck with their original plan to find Black Shirt's camp. He didn't know this Bloody Axe, only his fierce reputation. His prior thinking, that Wolf Tail would vouch for them, looked to be a mistake now. Bloody Axe had already forbidden them to bring their whiskey into his village. Charley was foolish to think he was going to buy the woman with it. *She don't look in no all-fired hurry to come with us, anyway.* Nudging Charley on the elbow, Marlowe whispered, "We'd best take our leave of this place while we still can."

Charley was less concerned. "Hell, they're not gonna jump us as long as we're holding these repeating rifles. They'd lose too many. Anyway, it looks to me like there ain't nobody in camp but old men, women, and boys." Looking back at Martha, and raising his voice again, he repeated his question. "Where's Black Elk?"

Meeting his eyes with a steady, straightforward

gaze, Martha said, "I'm sorry about Robert, and I'm sorry you have troubled yourself to come all this way to find me, but I can't go with you, Charley."

Finding it difficult to believe, Charley questioned her statement. "Can't come with me? Whaddaya mean, you can't come with me? Hell, I've got enough whiskey to buy you from this buck Black Elk. Don't you fret about that, he'll let you go. We'll go down-river and set up camp. That old chief ain't gonna be able to keep his young bucks from coming after that whiskey."

"You don't understand," Martha said calmly. "I *won't* go with you. I belong here with my husband's people."

Charley jerked his head back, aghast. "You what?" he sputtered, unable to believe his ears. Looking around him at the people crowding around them, he demanded, "You'd rather stay here with a bunch of heathen savages than go with your own kin?"

"You're not my kin, Charley. You never were. I have a new life now, here with my husband."

Charley was seething, having been rebuffed again by his brother's wife. His stare intensified as if to sear her with his gaze. "So that's how it is, is it?" Glancing around him again at the bodies pressing closer, he snarled, "I always knew you were a damn slut."

"I think you'd better go now," Martha replied.

"I think that's a good idea," Marlowe interjected. "Our business is done here." He was getting more and more nervous as he watched the faces around them. There was enough English in the group to begin to catch key words, and the crowd was showing signs of getting testy. If things got out of hand, Wolf Tail, who understood every word, might refuse to hold his tongue, figuring to get more than the one jug he had bargained for.

"I'll be damned . . ." Charley started to protest.

Marlowe cut him off. "Don't be a damn fool, Charley. They're lettin' us leave with our scalps. I'm ridin' outta here. You can stay if you want."

Charley's face was twisted with anger he made no attempt to hide. His deep-set eyes flashed with a renewed hatred for this woman who had held herself too good for him, choosing instead to live with a savage Indian. He was tempted to raise his rifle and clear out some of the crowd gathered around, but his instincts told him that the satisfaction would most likely cost him his life. Seeing Marlowe already backing away toward his horse, Charley reluctantly conceded. "I'm going," he snarled between clenched teeth. He shot one more threatening look in Martha's direction, a silent warning that this might not be the last of it, then he followed Marlowe.

Wolf Tail, after seeing the ill feelings that were spawned by the visit of the two white men, stood aside with his uncle, silently watching Charley and Marlowe cross the creek and pick up their packmules. Lest there be any question where his loyalties lay, he would bide there a while before leaving again for his own village. But he had no intentions of losing the jug of firewater that had been promised him for guiding the white men to Bloody Axe's village. As he watched Charley and Marlowe catch up the lead lines and start off downstream, he was thinking how fortunate it had been for them that most of the men were off hunting.

They had ridden no more than ten or twelve miles when Charley pointed toward a stand of trees along the riverbank. "That looks like a good place to camp."

Marlowe looked around, surprised. "It's a little early to set up camp, ain't it? There's a lot of daylight left, and we ain't far enough away from that Blackfoot camp to suit me."

A sly grin creased Charley's face. "We don't wanna be too far away when some of them bucks slip outta camp and come looking for their firewater. Besides, I saw which one of them tipis Martha came out of. I might just pay her a little social call tonight."

"Damn!" Marlowe swore, his patience with Charley's single-minded craving for Martha having just about run its course. "You're just bound and determined to git us kilt over a little piece of tail, ain'tcha? Well, I say hell no. We'll keep on ridin' if we know what's good for us, and the devil take that damn woman."

The grin on Charley's face immediately disappeared, and his dark brows pressed down until his eyes were no more than tiny black coals glaring out at his partner. When he spoke, there was more than a hint of warning in his voice. "You got no say in it. This ain't no partnership. I own every last scrap on these mules, and I reckon I'll decide where we camp."

The two men continued to glare at each other for a long moment, locked in a fierce battle of wills. There was no backing down by either man, so Marlowe decided right then and there that this would be Charley Vinings's last night above ground. That decision made, he affected a thin smile, and said, "I reckon you're right. It's your goods we're haulin'. I'm just sayin' it ain't healthy to camp this close to them Blackfeet."

"We'll take our chances," Charley replied, smug in his triumph in the battle of wills. Charley was not quite the fool Marlowe had labeled him, however. He would watch his back with extra diligence from this point on. The time had come, he figured, for the inevitable parting of the ways. Charley sorely needed Marlowe to guide him to Black Shirt's camp, but he had long ago decided that it would be better to be on his own than to have to constantly watch his back. He motioned for Marlowe to lead the way into the stand of trees by the water.

There was very little conversation between the two as they went about the business of setting up camp. Each man was careful to keep a wary eye on the other as the mules were unpacked and turned out to graze. When the animals had been taken care of, Charley took the one nearly empty whiskey jug down to the river and filled it half full of water. After adding more whiskey from one of the other jugs to bring the watered-down jug to the top, he set it aside. Satisfied with that, he then built a fire and sat down with his back against a tree, his rifle on the ground within handy reach of his right hand. Equally as cautious, Marlowe carried his rifle across his forearm when he took the coffeepot down to the river to fill it.

The sun was not yet resting upon the distant mountains when Wolf Tail showed up. "Well, lookee here," Marlowe smirked when he spotted him. "I didn't figure it'd be too long before ol' Wolf Tail come to collect his pay." The two partners sat where they were, chewing on their meager supper of dried buffalo meat, watching the familiar figure as he approached.

"Yeah," Charley said, "come for his jug. Well, I've got it ready for him."

Still some fifty yards distant, Wolf Tail hailed the camp, and was waved on in. The appearance of a third party served to relax the strain between the two partners for the moment as they sat watching Wolf Tail trot his pony into the clearing. After greetings were exchanged, the Blackfoot warrior wasted no time in inquiring about the whiskey Charley had promised him.

"It's right here," Charley said, "just like I said." He

patted the watered-down jug beside him. "Filled to the neck." When Wolf Tail started for it, Charley held up his hand to stop him. "Hell, it wouldn't be polite to drink up all your whiskey. Let's have a couple of drinks of mine, then you can take your jug with you."

This suited Wolf Tail just fine. So he sat down beside the fire and joined them. Charley poured a cup of whiskey, and before long, tongues were loosened and the conversation was flowing easily. Wolf Tail expressed his regrets that Charley and Marlowe were treated so coolly at Bloody Axe's camp, but reminded them that he had warned them before.

"Ah, there's no hard feelings. T'weren't your fault," Marlowe assured him.

"That's a fact," Charley chimed in, "it wasn't your fault." He passed the cup to Wolf Tail again. "I guess all the hunters are back in the village by now."

Wolf Tail shook his head. "No. They're not back yet—maybe in the morning."

This was the news Charley wanted to hear. He leaned back against the tree, a smug smile etched across his face, ignoring the scowl from Marlowe. He wasn't even disappointed when Wolf Tail told them that there would be no one from the village coming to find them. Bloody Axe was dead set against the evils of the white man's firewater, and none of the boys or older men left in camp cared to risk his disfavor by trading prime furs for the fiery liquid. *No matter,* Charley thought, *I'll still get what I came after.*

It was not yet dark when Wolf Tail finally succumbed to Charley's generosity—and passed out, very nearly falling face-first into the fire. Charley, sober as a hangman, got up and stood over the drunken Indian for a few minutes. "Let's get going," he tossed over his shoulder at Marlowe. "I want to get back to that village close after dark."

Marlowe's expression was like stone. "So you're still plannin' on goin' after the woman."

"Damn right," Charley replied. "That's what I came out here for." Marlowe didn't respond for a long moment, so Charley went on. "We'll go get the woman. Then we can take our goods to Black Shirt's camp, just like we started to in the first place."

"What about him?" Marlowe asked, nodding his head toward the unconscious Indian. "You just gonna leave him layin' there?"

Charley looked down at Wolf Tail as if seeing him for the first time. "Him? Hell, he ain't gonna bother nobody." He drew his knife from his belt, kneeling as he did, and in one quick motion, brought it up under Wolf Tail's chin, opening his throat from ear to ear.

"Damn!" Marlowe exclaimed, surprised by Charley's ruthlessness. "Damn," he repeated, this time with a note of disgust in his tone. "There weren't no need to do that. Wolf Tail's been tradin' with me for a long time."

"Did you think I was gonna leave that Injun here with all my goods while we go back to that camp?" He rolled the body over with his foot. "He ain't got no complaints. He died happy." He wiped his knife clean on Wolf Tail's shirt. "Let's go. I want to get there right after dark."

Marlowe remained seated. "I ain't goin' back to that Injun camp for no damn woman. You're takin' a mighty big chance of havin' that whole village on your tail. She don't wanna come with you, anyway. It sure as hell ain't worth stickin' my neck out just so's you can grab yourself a play-pretty."

Charley didn't say anything right away. He just stood there looking down at Marlowe as if giving his comments serious thought. It did not escape his attention that Marlowe's hand was resting close to the handle of the pistol in his belt. After a few moments, he said, "Well then, maybe I'll just go by myself. Maybe you can stay here and see that no mischief happens to my goods."

A sly smile creased Marlowe's lips. "Why, shore, I'll wait right here and keep an eye on things. I reckon that's the least I can do."

"I'm obliged," Charley said as he reached down and picked up the whiskey jug that Wolf Tail had paid for with his life. "Well, we saved us a jug of whiskey. Hold onto this." As soon as he said it, he tossed the jug to Marlowe.

Marlowe, forced to react quickly in order to catch the jug, reached out with both hands. Charley took that opportunity to pull his pistol from his belt, but the front sight caught on his belt, causing Charley to rush the shot. Consequently, his first bullet smashed the jug and sent Marlowe rolling over and over on the ground, trying desperately to pull his own weapon. Charley stepped quickly to stay right over him, firing point-blank at the huge man. Two shots caught Marlowe squarely in the back, causing him to yelp in pain. Still he tried to scramble away, fighting to gain enough room to get his own pistol out. Cursing wildly, spraying blood-flecked spittle with each oath, he managed to pull the stubborn weapon free of his belt, but Charley was too quick. He stomped Marlowe's wrist, pinning his gun hand to the ground, and fired another shot, this time hitting Marlowe in the neck. Marlowe's pistol fired off two shots as a result of the big man's struggle to free his hand. The bullets buried themselves harmlessly in a tree trunk.

"Damn you, die!" Charley grunted as he emptied the revolver into Marlowe's back. Finally the brute of a man ceased to struggle, lying still at last. Charley, his foot still planted on Marlowe's wrist, reached down and pulled the pistol from his hand.

Suddenly drained from the exertion, Charley stepped back to catch his breath. The big man had taken a lot of killing. Charley felt exhausted. Then, hearing a low groan from Marlowe, Charley realized that he was still alive. Bending low over the body again, he could hear Marlowe's heavy breathing. In a fit of exasperation, he emptied Marlowe's pistol into the back of his head.

Chapter 14

Martha stood outside her tipi for a few minutes after
Red Wing left her. The old medicine woman had
sensed Martha's need to talk to someone after the
unexpected meeting with the two white men that afternoon. The encounter had clearly upset her white
friend, so Red Wing made it a point to visit her. Although she had been unable to follow the words spoken between Martha and the one white man, Red
Wing was wise enough to realize the true significance
of the discussion. Six Horses had obviously declined
an opportunity to go with the white men, choosing
instead to remain with the people.

Black Elk would probably not return from the hunt
until sometime the next day, and Six Horses would be
alone, with no sisters or other wives to comfort her.
It was not good for a young woman to be without
family, Red Wing had told her. "Maybe Black Elk will
take another wife, and then you will have someone to
help you," Red Wing had said.

"Black Elk had better not bring another wife into
my lodge," Martha had replied, laughing.

Her reply had puzzled Red Wing. "Ah, young people," she had sighed, shaking her head. "You would

still be the sits-beside-him wife. Another wife would be there to help make your work easier."

Martha just shook her head as she recalled Red Wing's well-meaning words. Many of the men had more than one wife, some several. Usually it was because the first wife had sisters that were taken in by the husband. Black Elk could easily find another wife if he so desired. He was much admired by all in the village. A mighty warrior, he was the leader of the *I-kun-uh'-kah-tsi*—the tribal police force that was called upon whenever discipline or punishment was necessary. There were many young maidens who would be honored to come to Black Elk's lodge. Martha did not deny that she had "gone Injun," as Charley had accused, but there were some customs that she was not ready to accept. Another woman in her lodge was one of them. She was grateful that it was not an issue in her marriage, anyway. Black Elk was not desirous of another wife. Of that, she was certain. She would gladly do without the added help in her chores, knowing that she and her husband were content to be alone.

Red Wing disappeared from her sight as the old medicine woman made her way around the lodges that stood between hers and Martha's. Trying desperately to avoid thinking about Robert and Charley, but unable to keep her mind from returning to the subject, Martha was alone again with her thoughts. Taking one long look at the last rays of light that signaled the end of another day, she sighed and turned to go inside.

One bite of the boiled antelope was all she took before deciding she was not hungry. Pushing the pot aside, she picked up the dress she had been working on and tried to concentrate on her stitching, but she soon found her mind trying to form an image of her late husband. The picture that came to her was vague and confusing. It had been a long time since she had thought about Robert. And now to learn that he was dead . . . Robert, mild-mannered and sometimes meek—so much so that he permitted his younger brother to dominate him . . . It seemed so unlikely that he would meet with violent death. Murdered by outlaws, Charley had said. Her feelings of guilt returned once more. She was sad to hear of Robert's death but not devastated, as one should be to hear of a husband's demise. This was the cause of her remorse, more so than the fact that he was gone.

Feeling a need to pray for forgiveness for her indifference, she closed her eyes and asked God to have mercy on Robert's soul, and to let him know that she was sorry. *I miss Black Elk!* The sudden thought had burst forth in the midst of her reverie, even while she was concentrating so hard on Robert's soul. "I wish he was here," she whispered and laid the antelope skin aside, unable to put her mind on her sewing. Black Elk and the other men had been away for several days now. They should have been back by this time. The hunting was evidently not that good, or they would have returned. She closed her eyes again and asked God to watch over her husband. After thinking about it for a moment, and just to make sure, she also said a little prayer to *Na'pi*. Feeling that she had done the best she could for him spiritually, she tried to sweep the worry from her mind.

It would be chilly again that night, so Martha looked at her stack of firewood. It might be a good idea to bring in a little more, she decided, so she got up from her place by the fire and started toward the entrance of the lodge. Pausing a moment to glance at the pot of boiled meat, she realized that she was not hungry at all. *Might as well throw that out. It won't be any good in the morning.* She picked up the pot and took it outside where she felt sure she would find one of the camp dogs waiting for scraps of meat.

A moonless night had descended upon the little valley, causing the great circle of tipis to glow faintly, like an array of skin-covered lanterns. Martha stood outside the doorway of her lodge, listening to the soft murmur of voices from those lodges closest to hers. It was a peaceful sound, and one that had become one of her favorites because it brought to mind a sound of harmony. She smiled and started toward the stack of firewood beside the lodge, amazed that none of the dogs had sniffed her pot of meat as yet. She whistled softly a couple of times, but there was no response, so she continued to the woodpile.

A figure suddenly stepped from the shadows, and Martha was snatched off her feet. Locked in a steel-like embrace with one dirty hand clamped over her mouth, she was unable to scream for help. "Was you whistling for me?" a coarse voice whispered in her ear, his mouth so close she could feel his breath upon her neck.

Charley! her mind screamed at once as the pot of meat fell from her hand and landed in the dirt, splashing some of its contents on his boots. It seemed to amuse him, and he grunted a soft chuckle and kicked the offending vessel out of his way. Martha struggled furiously, but Charley's hold on her was too much for her to overcome. He carried her down through the shadows until they were deep in the stand of trees by the creek where he had tied his horse.

"Now, Miss Priss, I'm gonna put you down for a second, and I don't wanna hear a sound outta you. If I do, I'm gonna have to hurtcha. You're going with me one way or the other, so you might as well make it the easy way." He lowered her to the ground. While holding onto her arm to keep her from running, he slowly removed his hand from over her mouth. Anticipating her reaction, he immediately dropped his hand

to the handle of his pistol, and as soon as she drew
in her breath to scream, he laid the weapon hard
against the side of her head, knocking her senseless
before she could utter a sound. "Have it your way,
darlin. Suits the hell outta me."

She lost consciousness only for a minute or two, but
it was long enough to be trussed up and gagged. Her
first lucid moment afterward was a sense of extreme
discomfort as her body was being bounced and jostled.
It took a few more moments before she realized what
was happening. As her muddled brain began to clear,
she realized that she was draped across a saddle like
a deer carcass. She tried to move, but discovered her
hands and feet were joined by a rope underneath the
belly of the horse.

"Well, lookee who woke up already," Charley
sneered. "You better hold still if you know what's
good for you. Keep jumping around like that and
you'll wind up under this horse, and most likely get
stomped to death."

She tried to curse him, but could make very little
sound due to the tight gag in her mouth. Knowing
that what he said was true, she stopped struggling, and
tried to let her body ride with the motion of the horse.
Aware then of a throbbing pain beside her right eye,
she remembered the blow that had rendered her helpless. There was a stinging sensation as well, so she
knew that the pistol had broken the skin. Aware now
of another feeling, she forgot the pain in her face.
Charley's hand was resting squarely on her bottom,
groping her as he rode behind the saddle. Furious, she
tried to wriggle away from the offending hand. Her
futile struggles only served to please him more.

Her discomfort lasted for little more than half an
hour before Charley guided the horse down into a
treeless ravine where another horse was tied to the

branches of some low scrubby bushes. Charley took his time dismounting, talking all the while.

"I brought a horse for you to ride if you behave yourself," he said, obviously enjoying the irony of the situation that only he appreciated. "It's Marlowe's horse, but he's just plumb tickled to let you ride him. Marlowe don't do much riding anymore." Still in no hurry, unconcerned with her bruised stomach and ribs from the recent bouncing on his saddle, he untied the rope holding her ankles and hands under the horse's belly. "'Course, if you don't behave, it's all the same to me if you go the rest of the way on your belly again."

Grabbing a handful of her dress, he pulled her off of the horse, standing aside to let her land on the ground. With her hands and feet still bound securely, she could not maintain her balance. As a result, she went down on her back. Almost as soon as she landed, he was on top of her. Straddling her, he held her firmly until she exhausted herself in her attempts to fight him off.

"Damn," he swore, in mock amazement, "you sure are excited to see me, ain'tcha darling?" He lifted her head and untied the bandanna that had gagged her. "There, now you can tell me how much you appreciate me rescuing you from them Injuns. How about a kiss for your dear brother?" Grabbing her face, he tried to kiss her, but she struggled against his efforts, shaking her head from side to side violently. It only served to make him more determined, and he clamped down on her jaw as hard as he could, finally succeeding in overcoming her resistance.

Martha tried not to breathe as he forced his whiskered face down on hers. Her lips pressed as tightly together as she could manage, she tried to draw away but could not. Her mind reeled with the realization that this was actually happening to her. To be attacked in this way by her own brother-in-law was almost enough to send her out of her mind. After what seemed an eternity, Charley sat up, and she could breathe once more.

"Get off me!" she screamed furiously as soon as he ended his loathsome embrace, her voice almost cracking with the anger boiling inside her. Forgetting her fear for the moment, she cursed her former brother-in-law. "You disgust me! Let me go at once!"

Charley's face flushed red with Martha's stinging remarks. "Oh, I disgust you, do I?" he replied heatedly. "I suppose you think I ain't good enough for you. Why, you ain't nothing but a damn whore, sleeping with any dirty Injun that comes along—too good for your own kind."

"I never was your kind," she retorted, struggling again to free herself from his embrace. "I told you before, I don't want to be rescued. I belong with my village now. Why can't you just go away and leave me in peace?"

The lascivious grin returned to his face as he sat astride her, amused by her helpless efforts to free herself. "Go away and leave you in peace," he mocked. "And here I went to so much trouble just to save your hide, too. But I guess I ain't as good as a damn savage Injun, am I?"

"Let me go, Charley," she demanded.

He ignored her, his dark eyes smoldering now with the memory of her earlier rejection. "I wasn't good enough for you back in the cabin, either, was I? All I ever asked for was a little bit of your time. Hell, Robert wasn't taking care of you."

"That's disgusting," she spat. "Robert would be ashamed to hear you talking like that. Now, let me go."

He glared at her for a few moments before replying. "I'll let you go . . . when I'm through with you. I figure you owe me for all the times you wiggled your bottom at me, walking up the hill to the cabin."

"I never—" she started.

"Shut up!" he roared, and slapped her hard across her face. "I'm tired of playing with you." He got off her then, and pulled her up on her feet. "You're gonna pay me what you owe me, all right, but we're a little too close to your Injun friends right now." Holding her under her arms, he dragged her over to the horse tied to the bushes. "Grab onto that saddle horn, and hold still while I untie your ankles." He hooked her bound wrists over the saddle horn while he hurriedly worked the knot loose at her feet. "Get up there," he commanded while he pushed her up on the horse. Once she was seated in the saddle, he pulled the rope under the horse's belly, tying her ankles together. Satisfied that she would either stay on the horse or be trampled trying to escape, he took her reins and climbed up on his horse.

From the lower end of the ravine, Charley led them to the top of a long grass-covered ridge where he paused for a few minutes, listening for any sounds that might indicate Martha's absence had been discovered. There was nothing to disturb the quiet night except the occasional snort from one of the horses, so he started out toward his camp by the river, feeling sure that he was not being followed.

Martha rode silently behind her abductor under the dark starry sky, her feet barely touching the stirrups; Charley did not bother to adjust them for her. As she rode, she contemplated what fate might await her. She had already given up hope of talking Charley out of his evil intentions. He was determined to satisfy his lust for her, a lust that she knew had been nurtured

since they had first set out for the Black Hills. She
was prepared to fight him with every ounce of strength
she possessed. But she knew that, with no weapon,
she had very little chance of preventing him from having his way with her. The thought of it filled her with
a loathing so repugnant that she shivered with dread.
Although she wanted to cry out in her anguish for
someone to help her, she held her tongue, not willing
to give Charley any additional pleasure.

After a ride of a little over an hour, Charley cut
back to the river, and led them into a stand of trees
where she saw the packmules she had seen earlier in
her village. Once inside the trees, she discovered the
faintly glowing embers of a campfire that the two
sleeping men lying nearby had apparently left unattended. From the size of the prone figure closest to
the fire, Martha guessed it was the man called Marlowe. She felt a clammy hand gripping her insides as
she recalled the hairy brute that had accompanied
Charley to Bloody Axe's camp. Would he be next
when Charley was finished with her? The other, a few
yards back from the fire, appeared to be an Indian,
sprawled as in a drunken sleep. She bit her lip, trying
to hold back the tears that threatened to form in the
corners of her eyes.

Charley would have ridden right over the body near
the fire, but his horse balked, refusing to step over it,
and Martha realized then that Marlowe was not sleeping. The knowledge that he was dead made her thankful that she would not have to endure his assault. The
casual indifference displayed by Charley as he dismounted filled Martha's mind with a new fear. He
would not hesitate to kill her when he was done
with her.

"You just set right where you are," Charley commanded sternly while he tied her horse's reins to a

tree. "I wanna build this fire back up so I can see you real good." He reached up and patted her thigh, laughing when she tried to pull it away. "I don't want you to get cold with your clothes off." Leaving her to form that horrifying image in her mind, he picked up some dead limbs and stirred up the coals of the fire. Once the fire had caught up again, he grabbed Marlowe's corpse by the boots and dragged it several yards away in the brush. "Come on, Marlowe, quit hogging the fire." He laughed heartily at his own joke.

Martha was horror-stricken by the scene before her. Charley had always reviled her, but she had no notion of the evil he was capable of until that moment. Even in the dim light of the fire, she could see the dark stain where Marlowe's blood had soaked into the ground. And the way Charley found humor in the grisly corpse made Martha tremble with fear.

Glancing now at the second corpse lying in the darkness just beyond the firelight, she could only see enough to know that it was an Indian. She shivered uncontrollably with the realization that maybe Robert was not murdered by outlaws as Charley had said. He had not seemed to be overly grieved back in the village when he had told her of his brother's death. Martha closed her eyes for a second, praying for God to help her. When she opened them, it was to look directly into Charley's face, grinning up at her.

"It's time for our long-overdue little party," he said. Untying her ankles, he pulled her from the saddle, her hands still tied. "I promised myself a long time ago I was gonna have some of your honey—and then you up and run off with a bunch of Injuns." Standing her on her feet, he took the rope that had tied her ankles together and knotted one end of it around her wrists, holding onto the other end. "Well, it's just you and me now, darlin'." She tried to run, but he immediately jerked her back with the rope. "Now, don't be that way, darlin'," he cooed wickedly. "You're about to get it like you never had it with ol' Robert."

In desperation, she tried to appeal to his sense of conscience. "Please, Charley, don't do this. I'm your sister. It wouldn't be right. Think what your mother and father would say. They'd be so disappointed to know you violated your brother's wife. Please. Just let me go, and we'll forget it ever happened."

Charley fixed her with a long look of amusement. Then he threw his head back and laughed. "I swear, Martha, that's about the most tender story I've ever heard. You keep on and you'll have me in tears."

"You son of a bitch," Martha spat.

Her venom seemed to please him, exciting him even more. "That's more like it," he said, still grinning. "If you do it right, maybe I'll let you live a little longer. But if you don't please me, I'll just slit your throat and leave you to keep company with ol' Marlowe over there."

"You go to hell."

The grin faded from his face, and he suddenly reached out and tried to rip her dress away. But the snow-white antelope skin was too tough and did not tear. She immediately reacted by slapping him hard across his face. Infuriated, he struck her with his fist, knocking her backward. As she struggled to keep her balance, reeling from the force of the blow, he plowed headfirst into her, driving her to the ground. In a flash, he drew his knife and held the point of the blade hard up under her chin, causing her to cry out in pain.

"By God, you're gonna give me what I want, or I'll slice you up right now." He had hoped she would surrender to him out of fear, but he could see that it was going to be a battle. Staring her down for a moment while he considered his next move, he suddenly pulled his knife away and got to his feet. Picking up the loose end of the rope again, he pulled her over to a tree where he looped the rope around it and tied it. On her feet now, her hands still tied securely together, she pulled against the rope with all her strength while she backed around and around the tree, trying to keep him at bay. Her efforts to avoid him became a sadistic game for him, and he laughed at her while stalking her in a circle around the tree. After a few moments, he tired of the game, and lunged forward, knocking her off her feet.

Though struggling desperately, she knew that she could not fend him off. He took her ankles and dragged her away from the tree trunk until her arms were stretched helplessly straight out above her head. With his body pinning her legs to the ground, she was helpless to fight him. Triumphant, his lips parted in a satisfied smile, he slowly pulled her skirt up, revealing the soft white thighs that he had long pictured in his mind. The anticipation of what was to come was enough to cause drool to collect in the corners of his evil grin. She screamed out in horror when she felt his coarse hands groping her inner thighs.

"That's right," he goaded, "yell all you want. I like to hear you holler. It makes it . . ." Suddenly his words were lost in a clap of thunderous hooves and the lightninglike snap of a rawhide whip. It happened so fast that Martha would remember it as only a blur—like an explosion, the horse bursting forth from the darkness outside the campfire—the instant appearance of rawhide coils wrapping around Charley's throat—and then she was free.

The force of Black Elk's attack yanked Charley off Martha and dragged him fully fifty feet before the infuriated warrior brought his charging pony to a stop. At once, Black Elk was on the ground, his war axe in his hand. Rolling over and over in an attempt to scramble to his feet, Charley clawed at the rawhide coils wound tightly around his neck. In his confusion, he was unable to loosen it as he looked around him desperately trying to find his assailant in the flickering light of the fire. Then suddenly he appeared. Like a painted phantom stepping into the circle of light, the warrior stalked his prey, war axe in one hand, a long skinning knife in the other. The shadows from the flames danced across the massive chest and shoulders of the Blackfoot warrior, his face an enraged mask that promised certain death.

Terrified, Charley reached for his pistol, only to realize that he had removed it before his assault upon Martha. In a panic, he made a desperate move toward it. Quicker by far, Black Elk cut him off, standing in his path, quartering him with eyes as black as the dead coals in the fire. Charley froze. His cold fear seeped throughout his entire body, leaving him almost helpless to move. As Black Elk moved slowly toward him, Charley's hands began to tremble. Unable to move seconds before, he now turned and tried to run for his life. With one swift leap, Black Elk planted one foot firmly upon the whip handle trailing in the dust, the other end still knotted around Charley's neck. Yanked off his feet again, Charley landed hard on his back. Grunting with the impact, the frightened man clawed at the rawhide again, his desperation enabling him to loosen the whip this time. Free for the moment, he scrambled to his feet, and ran wildly toward the brush on the riverbank. Right behind him, Black Elk stopped, planted his left foot, took deliberate aim, and hurled his axe end over end, landing it squarely between Charley's shoulder blades.

Charley screamed in pain, and crashed to the ground. He struggled back up on his hands and knees

only to feel the powerful hand that grasped his hair
and jerked his head back. The hellish scream that em-
anated from deep inside him was silenced abruptly
when Black Elk's long skinning knife sliced through
his windpipe. There followed a silence that seemed
almost as loud, as the Blackfoot warrior stood over
his kill.

Martha had been transfixed in a state of shock while
she witnessed Charley's terrifying execution. With her
hands still bound to the tree, she could do nothing
but sit and watch as her husband expunged his wrath
on the hapless white man who had been her brother-
in-law. Such was his fury, that Martha found herself
to be terrified, afraid to speak even after Black Elk
turned to look at her. She had never before witnessed
the full fury of her husband, not even when he had
rescued her from the Crow raiding party. For a long
moment, he stood motionless, staring through her, as
if not really seeing her at all until, gradually, he released his taunt muscles and relaxed his fierce frown.
The flood of his blood lust having finally receded, he
came to her.

Emotionally drained, she fell into his arms as soon
as he had untied her hands. Clinging tightly to him,
she pressed her face against his bare chest, and whispered, "I was afraid I was never going to see you
again."

His tone at once gentle again, he replied, "Did you
think that I would not come for you?" He looked
down at her and smiled. "I will always come for you.
Know that, if you know nothing else."

Exhausted, she lay back while he gently examined
the broken skin beside her eye. Reading the loving
concern in his gaze, she could not help but tremble
when she remembered the intense fury that blazed in
those eyes short moments before. She smiled at him

then, knowing that—as he had said—he would always come for her, no matter what.

When morning came, they rounded up the horses and the pack mules. Out of respect for Charley's father, Martha persuaded Black Elk to leave his scalp, which he did reluctantly. He even helped her dig a shallow grave. Marlowe received no such consideration. After Black Elk scalped him, he left the corpse for the buzzards. They wrapped Wolf Tail's body in a buffalo robe found in one of the packs, and Black Elk lifted it up on one of the mules, to be taken back for a proper burial.

After opening one of the packs to see what manner of trade goods the white men carried, Black Elk decided to carry all the packs back to the village for the people to share. All except the firewater. One by one, he smashed each of them with his axe. When that was done, he looked at Martha and said, "We go now."

Martha never looked back as they led the mules out of the stand of willows by the river, hoping she could somehow erase the horrible memory from her mind. Charley was dead. She would never have to fear him again. Robert was dead, too, in all likelihood murdered by his own brother. She felt compassion for Robert's parents, decent people who would probably never know what had happened to their sons. She shivered involuntarily as the memory of Charley's evil sneer flashed through her mind. She would sleep very close to Black Elk this night.

Chapter 15

"I see 'em," Badger said in response to Clay's out-stretched arm. The old scout had been watching the circle of buzzards for the last two miles. "More'n likely it's just some dead animal, but it wouldn't hurt to take a look."

They cut away from the trail they had been following since sunup that morning and made for the trees bordering the river, both men with a sharp eye out for any sign of danger. It appeared that whatever the buzzards had found was in the stand of willows close beside the riverbank. "I expect it would be best if we duck into the trees below that spot," Clay suggested, "instead of riding right in off the open plain."

"I expect so," Badger agreed. This was dangerous country they were riding through—Blackfoot country—it wouldn't pay to get careless.

When they entered the trees, the two men split up, Clay pulling his horse off to the right of Badger, leaving a space of about twenty yards between them. In this fashion, their two pairs of eyes could take in more of the scrub they were riding into. Walking their horses slowly, they filed through the clumps of goose-berry bushes and junipers, skirting the thickets that

hugged the river's banks, all the while glancing back
and forth, never letting their gaze linger on one spot
for more than an instant. Clay did it without thinking.
After months of riding with Badger, he had acquired
the habit of seeing everything around him, constantly
looking for sign. It was a healthy habit because ambush was the Blackfoot's stock in trade.

It didn't take long to discover what had attracted
the buzzards. There was a small clearing in the midst
of the willows where someone had obviously made a
camp. Near the edge of the clearing, one large buzzard
sat on the chest of a corpse while half a dozen others
flapped about, squawking raucously.

Satisfied that whoever had killed the man was long
gone, Clay and Badger rode on into the clearing and
dismounted. Using their rifles as clubs, they scattered
the cluster of buzzards around the body, backing the
hissing scavengers away long enough to take a look at
the corpse.

"He's a big'un," Badger said as he bent over the
mutilated body. "White man, shot full of holes. Somebody wanted to make sure he was good and dead."
He straightened up again. "Git back!" he yelled at
the emboldened buzzards as they began to crowd in,
reluctant to give up their feast.

Clay moved around to get a better look at the man's
face, what was left of it. The back of the man's head
was shattered, a result of too many bullet holes to
count accurately. "He's been scalped," he observed.
Looking at the congealed blood around the top of his
head, he said, "He ain't been dead more than two or
three days." Clay had seen enough dead men during
his time in the war to make a fair estimate.

"That's about right," Badger agreed, moving
around to have a closer look himself. Then it occurred

to him. "Damn, Clay, ain't he that big ol' feller you whacked on the nose at Fort Union? Marlowe, I believe Pete called him."

Clay took another look and considered. "Hard to tell." He studied the corpse for another few seconds. "I believe you're right, though. I wonder what he was doing way out here. He's a helluva long way from Fort Union."

"No tellin'. That low-down son of a bitch was more'n likely up to no good, I'll bet."

Unwilling to give up what they figured rightfully belonged to them, the ring of buzzards closed in once more on the two men standing over the corpse. Dancing closer and flapping their wings, they issued a loud challenge, retreating only when Clay or Badger would make an aggressive move toward them.

"I wanna take a look around this camp," Badger said. "Let's drag this bastard down in the bushes a'ways, and let the buzzards finish their supper." He and Clay each grabbed a heel, and pulled the heavy corpse down through the brush. The buzzards followed behind them, squawking like chickens waiting to be fed.

There was plenty of sign to tell at least part of the story. The most obvious were the shattered jugs. Badger bent low and sniffed a broken shard. "Whiskey. I thought so. That's what that ol' boy was up to." He stood up again, and looked about him at the ground. "Looks like he tried to sell firewater to the wrong Injun."

"They must have had somebody tied to a tree," Clay observed aloud as he examined the ground around a slim willow. "You can see where the rope burned the bark on this little willow."

Badger nodded his head. "Yeah, looks like ol' Marlowe run into a heap of trouble."

By the trampled bushes and droppings in the trees, they could readily see where Marlowe had hobbled his packhorses. Puzzling were the other bloodstains apart from those where Marlowe's body had lain. "Maybe he got a couple of 'em before they got him," Badger offered as explanation. Then Clay found something outside the clearing, almost hidden by a clump of gooseberry bushes.

"There's a fresh grave over here," Clay called out.

Badger dropped the top half of a jug he had been holding, and came at once to examine the grave. "That sure is peculiar now, ain't it? If it was Injuns what done this, why would they bury one of 'em and leave the other'n for the buzzards?" He looked at Clay, a question on his face. "I think I'll take a look at who's buried in this grave."

"Why?" Clay wondered aloud. He couldn't see that it would help them any to find out.

"Curiosity, I reckon," Badger replied as he started back to his packhorse for a shovel.

The grave was still fresh enough for the dirt to be soft, and after only fifteen minutes' work with the shovel, Badger uncovered the body of a white man. He tossed the shovel aside and pulled the dirt away from the dead man's face with his hands. After another few seconds, he sat back on his heels and said, "Ain't nobody I know."

Clay knelt down on one knee to get a closer look at the corpse. At first, it didn't look like anyone he knew, either. The features were wooden and drawn in death, a ragged slash gaping beneath the scrubby beard. And yet, there was something familiar about that face. He studied it a moment longer before he suddenly realized who he was staring at. "Charley Vinings," he blurted. Then looking back at Badger, he repeated, "Charley Vinings."

"Who's Charley Vinings?" Badger wanted to know. The name meant nothing to him.

Clay explained that Charley was Martha's brother-in-law. "That might explain why Marlowe was in Blackfoot country. Maybe Charley hired him as a guide, and they were trying to find Martha."

"He picked a helluva guide," Badger snorted.

Clay stepped back away from the shallow grave to give himself some room to think. With Charley here, where then was Robert? Maybe some of those other bloodstains in the clearing belonged to Robert. Maybe the murdering Blackfeet took him captive. *Could be that I've misjudged Robert and Charley. They may have been looking for Martha all along.* The cruel image of the savage Black Elk returned to his conscious thoughts, and he could feel his muscles tense as he pictured what had taken place at this lonely campsite.

As if to confirm Clay's thoughts, Badger commented, "That's what it looks like, all right. They was camped here and the Blackfeet jumped 'em." He scratched his head thoughtfully. "What I can't figure out, though, is why they buried this feller, and not the other one. And they scalped Marlowe, but not this one."

Badger dismissed it as just another example of how unpredictable the Blackfeet were. For Clay's part, he wasn't concerned with the why of it. His mind was focused on the murder of Martha's brother-in-law by the Blackfeet, and in his mind, it was by the hand of Black Elk. Who could say what Robert's fate was? The urgency to get underway again was now more crucial than ever. This massacre had occurred no more than a couple of days before. Black Elk could not be far away. Clay only hoped that he would reach Martha and Robert before they were slaughtered, too. He had little hope of being able to help Robert. In all likelihood, the Blackfeet would have already tortured and killed him. But he would not permit himself to think that Martha was dead. The reports they had received from Black Shirt's camp indicated that a white woman was traveling with Bloody Axe's village. *Martha has to be alive. Why would they kill her after all this time?* One fact seemed to be painfully clear, however. There would be no peaceful negotiations with this band of Blackfeet. Probably Robert and Charley had tried that. Charley's battered body attested to the failure of their efforts.

"Well, partner, looks like we'd better decide just what the hell we're gonna do." Badger's comment broke into Clay's thoughts. "I don't think we're far from them Blackfeet you're lookin' for—and there's a plain enough trail they left when they rode outta here. The part I ain't sure about is, what are you plannin' to do when we catch up to 'em?"

Clay was already giving that question plenty of thought. There were only a couple of things he knew for sure. If Martha was in the camp, he was going to get her . . . or die trying. The second thing he was certain of was that he would hunt Black Elk down and kill him. There were other concerns that he had to give serious thought, however. He had no right to jeopardize Badger's life in this personal, and perhaps fatal, quest that now consumed his mind. After a long pause, he finally answered Badger's question. "Nothing's changed. I'm going after Martha." He turned to look the old trapper in the eye. "I don't expect you to risk your neck any further. You've gotten me this far, I reckon I can follow this trail the rest of the way."

Badger studied his friend's face for a moment before replying. He liked this young firebrand, who could smolder so intensely with a fire within, while giving no indication of the burning passion on the outside. "You know it don't look likely this band of Blackfeet is gonna waste time talking. If you try to go in peaceful, you're liable to end up like these fellers."

"I know," Clay replied. "I don't plan to talk to them. I'm gonna tail them until I find where they're keeping Martha. Then I'll wait for a chance to get to her."

Badger continued to study Clay's face, considering his words. "All right, say you do that, and you do get a chance to snatch her. Then what are you gonna do?"

"I don't know," Clay answered truthfully. "Just run for it, I guess. I'll just have to take it as it comes." He shrugged his shoulders, dismissing the concern. "I'll make it somehow. I always have."

"These fellers lying here always made it, too, till they met up with this bunch of Injuns. You ain't got no more chance than a chicken in a den full of foxes. Nah, I reckon I'm gonna have to go with you. You're gonna need my rifle." That said, he turned and gathered up his horse's reins, preparing to mount. As he put a foot in the stirrup, he added, "We're still gonna lose our scalps."

They followed a trail that led north, away from the river and toward Willow Creek, as best Badger could guess. They concluded that it had to have been a small party that jumped Charley and Marlowe because the tracks they followed were left by no more than ten or twelve horses. That conclusion was not one hundred percent accurate, Badger pointed out, because the Blackfeet often went on foot if they were going to steal horses. But he had a feeling that the massacre they had just left was not the result of a horse-stealing party.

The sun had not yet set when Badger reined back hard near the brow of a long ridge. "Hold up," he called back. When Clay caught up to him, he pointed to a fringe of cottonwoods and alders that defined a creek no more than half a mile away. Beyond was a gathering of at least a hundred lodges. "Well, there's your Blackfoot camp."

Clay's heart was pounding with the excitement of knowing that Martha might be less than a mile away. He could feel the blood surging through his veins as he realized that the end of a journey that started nearly a year before had finally been reached. Now he must confirm whether or not Martha was actually here. After looking over the layout of the village from the ridge, they agreed that there was very little concealment nearby. If they were going to scout the camp up close, it was going to have to be at night.

"Best thing we can do right now," Badger advised, "is head for them hills over there." He pointed toward a chain of hills off to the west toward the mountains. "Find us a place to leave these packhorses." He was also thinking of the best possible avenue of escape if indeed they were successful in rescuing Clay's sister. He could already picture a desperate race for their lives with a horde of angry Blackfoot warriors on their tails. They would have a better chance in the hills. Knowing what Badger had in mind, Clay agreed, and they rode westward along the ridge until the hills between them and the village blocked their view.

Crossing the creek well below the Blackfoot camp, they rode up through the tree-covered slopes until they found a narrow gulch running down toward a tiny stream winding its way drunkenly through a tiny meadow. After scouting the meadow for sign, they decided that it was well off the beaten path of the

Blackfoot hunters. In fact, there were no tracks to be found, not even old ones. So they hobbled the horses and waited for darkness.

It was a long wait for Clay Culver. Now that he was so close to Martha, he could not help but worry. He had waited so many long days to find her that he feared something might happen to prevent him from reaching her. What if it was not the right village? But it had to be. The trail from Charley's grave led straight to this camp. It was the right village, and the murdering savage he had built up such a hatred for was in that village. Black Elk. The mere thought of the man caused his muscles to tense, and he unconsciously dropped his hand to the handle of his knife. *I'll open his throat the same way he did for poor Charley.* He glanced over at Badger, his head propped up on his saddle, his hat pulled down over his eyes, sleeping the innocent sleep of the newborn. Clay shook his head, amazed at the man's lack of concern. Then he got to his feet and walked up to the top of the gulch to take a look around.

From where he stood, on the rocky crown of the hill, he could not see the Blackfoot camp some three or four miles distant. But he could see the faint wisps of brown smoke that wafted up from the lodges by the water's edge, and he could imagine his sister working as a slave in one of those lodges. The thought prompted him to turn and cast an accusing glance at the sun. It would still be hours before dark. Other, darker, thoughts crowded his mind. And he wondered if Robert was still alive or if Martha had been forced to witness her husband's slow torture at the hands of Black Elk. "Damn," he swore, his impatience about to get the best of him.

In the Blackfoot camp, the women were preparing meat for the feasts that many of their husbands were calling for. It had been a good day hunting, and there was fresh antelope roasting over the fire. Throughout the camp, men were calling out invitations to their friends to join them in a feast. Martha sat before her fire, watching her supper boil in a new iron pot that had been among the trade goods on Charley's pack-mules. She was preparing food for herself only, since Black Elk had accepted an invitation to feast in Jumping Horse's lodge. As she stared at the shiny black pot, she wondered if the day would ever come when she could look at it and not be reminded of Charley and the violent ending of his life. For that reason, she had been tempted to give the pot to Red Wing, but she could not bring herself to part with it, since her old pot had a crack in the side. Without a good pot, she couldn't cook the meat until it was thoroughly done. Only a few women in the village had no metal containers. For those unfortunate few, meat had to be boiled in a crude stone pot, or a hole in the ground with a green hide for a liner and hot stones to heat the water. As a result, the meat was never cooked thoroughly, usually only long enough to lose the red color.

Ridding her thoughts of Charley, Martha sat back and gazed at the last rays of the setting sun as they streamed through the notches in the mountains to the west, setting a thin layer of clouds ablaze with shades of red and gold. Life was good. She had found a perfect peace here. And while she often had thoughts of her father and mother and her brothers far, far away on the little Rapidan River in Virginia, she would not choose to give up this life she had found here. They would never be able to understand this. In fact, they might be horrified to know that she would choose to live with Black Elk rather than return home to Virginia. For this reason, she knew that she would never see her parents again. The thought always made her feel melancholy, and she would find herself trying to picture each member of her family in her mind, memorizing each face so she would never forget. The one she always saved for last was Clay. Clay was her favorite—tall and strong, always sure of himself. She whispered a little prayer that he would return from the war safely. *The war,* she thought. *I have forgotten about the war.* It had once been the most important event in her young life, now it had not crossed her mind in well over a year. Virginia was so far away, packed away in another lifetime like an old trunk in the attic.

She realized then that the clouds she had been gazing at had lost their gilded edge, and were now only dark blue-gray streaks floating over the distant peaks, as the last rays of the sun faded away. It would be dark soon. *I hope Black Elk does not linger.* The coming darkness did not frighten her; she simply longed for her husband's return.

Lost in her reverie, she had almost forgotten her supper. Turning her attention back to the iron pot, she tested the meat with a wooden spoon to see if it was tender. Satisfied, she dipped it out of the pot into a stone bowl. Placing it before her, she smiled in a brief moment of reflection as she looked at the bowl. She traced the rim of it with her fingertip. Moon Shadow had helped her make the bowl. She had helped her search for the right size rock, a soft rock found along the bluffs of the river. Together, they had pounded it and ground it with a harder stone until it was shaped into a bowl. The memory brought a sad smile to her face. She missed Moon Shadow. She was sure Black Elk missed her, too, but he never spoke of her. It was not polite to speak of the dead.

A soft whisper of buckskin told her that her husband had returned. Without looking behind her, she teased, "I hear my clumsy husband tromping his way home. Or maybe it is one of the horses coming up from the pony herd." She took great delight in their gentle teasing, especially when he attempted to affect his stern expression, pretending he was offended by her playful remarks.

"Maybe I have returned to throw my lazy wife out of my lodge—send you back to your mother." He tapped her playfully on her head. "I think I should get myself a wife like Jumping Horse's, one who really knows how to take care of her husband."

Martha laughed. She knew that Black Elk did not think much of Brown Calf. "How did you enjoy the feast?" she asked, a mischievous gleam in her eye as she turned to look at her husband.

Black Elk crumpled his mouth, making a sour face. "The meat was roasted black. It had the taste of ashes. I don't understand why that woman cannot see when the meat is cooked."

Martha laughed again. "Maybe when you invite them to your lodge, they go back and tell each other that your wife doesn't let the meat get done."

"Maybe," he said, rubbing his stomach as if trying to soothe it. He reached into the bowl beside her and picked up a piece of the boiled meat. She slapped his hand playfully. "Wagh," he blurted, pretending to be enraged. "You are long overdue for a good beating." Then he reached down and snatched her off the ground, lifting her up in his arms as easily as if she were a baby. Laughing delightedly, she threw her arms around his neck as he carried her into the tipi.

Clay made his way slowly through cottonwoods that bordered the wide creek. Moving from tree to tree, he worked his way in close to the outer ring of lodges. Taking cover behind a screen of low bushes, he lay on his belly, watching the Blackfoot camp as the evening approached. His eyes darted from tipi to tipi, searching for the familiar face of his sister among the women tending their cook fires. He started to move on to another vantage point when his eye caught sight of a powerfully built warrior returning to a lodge some twenty yards from his spot. A handsome all-white pony grazed peacefully on the sparse grass by the tipi. Badger had said that it was a common practice among the warriors of many tribes to keep their favorite war pony tied by their lodge. Clay could easily understand why the white horse was a prized possession.

Clay turned his gaze back to the warrior. He lingered a moment to watch as the man stopped to speak to the woman seated before the fire. She was, no doubt, the warrior's wife. It was difficult to see her face clearly in the flickering glow of the campfire, but she looked to be a typical Blackfoot woman. They talked for a few minutes, then Clay could not suppress a smile when the man playfully picked her up and carried her into the lodge.

Moving again, slowly working his way around the perimeter of the camp, Clay cautiously avoided the large pony herd near the bank of the creek for fear they might announce his presence. Crawling on his belly, he made his way up to the rear of a lodge decorated with paintings and buffalo tails. Peering around the edge of the tipi, he could see a great part of the center of the village. So close was he to the back of the lodge that he could hear voices inside, and was even able to catch a few words through the cowskin outer covering.

With evening lengthening, the casual comings and goings in the village began to decrease as the people retired to their lodges for the night. Among all the women busy with their evening chores, there was not a sign of a white woman, and no sign of Robert, either. Maybe, he thought, Badger would have better luck on the opposite side of the village. Disappointed, but not discouraged, Clay remained behind the tipi for almost half an hour, moving only when he heard a man's voice inside announce that he was going outside to relieve himself. Pushing away from the tipi, Clay crawled backward until he felt it safe to get to his feet and make a quick retreat to the safety of the cottonwoods.

By the time a large silver moon emerged from behind the hills, the village was quiet with only an occasional soul venturing out. Clay retraced his path until he came to the edge of the creek, where he found Badger waiting for him.

"See anything?" Clay wanted to know as soon as he glanced around him to make sure no one was in earshot.

"Nary a thing," Badger replied. "Leastways nuthin' that looked like a white woman." Feeling the disappointment his report brought, he added a word of encouragement. "We can't tell much slipping around here at night, anyway. Just 'cause we ain't seen her don't mean she ain't here. Maybe we can find a spot close enough to see in the daylight. If she's here, that's when she'll be out workin' on hides, or diggin' up roots, or whatever they make her do."

It was not possible to move in as close to the village during the day as it had been the night before. So Clay and Badger spent a portion of the morning seeking out a workable vantage point from which they could observe most of the camp's activities. The frustration of their situation began to work on Clay's patience almost from the first hour of watching.

"Damn this waiting," he exclaimed, after lying on

his belly in a stand of young pines for most of the morning. "I've got to get in closer. I can't tell who I'm looking at from this distance, red or white."

The problem was, as Badger pointed out, Bloody Axe had picked a pretty good spot for his campsite: creek on one side and over a hundred yards of open ground between the cottonwoods where his lodges were set up and the low hills where Clay and Badger lay. It made it next to impossible for anyone, enemy or friend, to advance upon the village without being seen. Knowing the anxiety Clay had to be suffering at this point, Badger tried to keep his young friend calm, for fear he might do something rash. Remembering the fight back on the forks of the Milk River when the Blackfeet shot that big sorrel that Clay thought so much of, Badger knew the young man had a temper.

"Everything looks peaceful enough," Badger commented. "If she's in the camp, we're bound to see her sooner or later."

"Maybe they've got her tied up somewhere," Clay replied. He felt certain Martha was in the camp. She had to be. If she weren't with this band of Blackfeet, he didn't know where else to search. Badger was telling him to be patient, but Clay was finding it extremely difficult, knowing that Martha might be suffering at that very moment, no more than a hundred yards or so away. The more he thought about it, the more likely it seemed to him that Martha might indeed be tied up inside one of the lodges. Knowing her determination, it was easy for him to assume that she would have tried to escape at every opportunity. For that reason, it was probably necessary to keep her tied. "This isn't getting us anywhere," he finally blurted. "I've got to come back tonight when I can work my way in close again. I think she's in one of those tipis."

"Maybe so," Badger allowed. "But I doubt it. She's been travelin' with this bunch for a long time—too long for them to be keepin' her tied up. They'da kilt her before now if she kept runnin' away."

Clay cocked his head around to look at Badger. He didn't like to talk about the possibility that Martha was dead. He was about to say as much when Badger suddenly pointed toward the lower end of the camp where a group of women were walking down toward the creek, carrying skin buckets. Instead of stopping at the water's edge to fill their buckets, they turned and followed the bank downstream toward a sand spit covered with low bushes.

"Berry pickin', I'd guess if it wasn't so early in the spring," Badger speculated. "Ain't no berries ripe this early. Probably lookin' for some roots or herbs." He watched the group as they made their way through the trees on the creek bank, then he looked back at Clay. "There's about fifteen or sixteen of 'em. Your sister might be one of 'em."

It took the better part of an hour to retreat from the pines on the hill and work their way around to a point below the camp where they could cross over to the cover of the trees by the creek. Twice they were forced to hide, lying flat, hugging the ground, as a Blackfoot hunting party passed only yards away, talking and laughing among themselves. Thanks to his lessons with Johnny MacGruder's wife during the long winter months just past, Clay could pick up the occasional word that drifted from the hunting parties. After reaching the concealment offered by the cottonwoods and willows, it was a far easier task to make their way upstream until reaching a point just below the sand spit. The women were already busily digging around the roots of the bushes by the time Clay and Badger were in position.

Laughing and chattering lightheartedly, the women worked through the little point of land jutting out into the water. Clay stared hard at each one whenever he could get a clear view through the foliage. His heart was pounding with the anticipation he felt as his gaze went from one woman to another. It would be the best of situations if she were among the women—a real piece of luck. For if she were one of the party, he could snatch her away and be gone before the other women could get back to the village to give the alarm.

Badger peered at the women, trying to discover a white face. Then after a few moments when he was unsuccessful, he turned to watch Clay's face for signs of a spark of recognition. There were none. Instead, he saw his young partner's expression sag with disappointment. "She's not here," Clay said.

"You know, son," Badger began, "I don't wanna discourage you, but maybe she ain't with this band."

"Maybe," was all Clay would concede at the moment. He had been convinced that Martha was still a captive, bound hand and foot in one of the many lodges. But he could not totally dismiss the worrisome feeling that she could be dead. "We'll watch the camp for the rest of the day. Then if I don't see her, I'm going in close tonight. I'll find her if she's here."

"All right," was all Badger said, but he wasn't sure he liked the fatal tone of Clay's voice. He had a pretty strong feeling that, if Clay didn't find his sister, he would be more determined than ever to find Black Elk. And that sounded like a surefire way to commit suicide. He couldn't stop the man if he was bound to go in recklessly looking for revenge against the warrior who abducted his sister, and maybe killed her. Clay was too powerful a man to restrain physically.

But Badger thought he should at least try to talk some sense into his young friend.

"You know, son, you might not wanna throw all your gunpowder into the fire at once. There's a heap of Injuns in this here camp. We ain't hardly give it enough time to see all the women in the whole damn village. Why don't we give it a few more days before you git in too close? She may be here and we just ain't seen her yet." He paused to see if Clay was hearing what he said. "There's another possibility. She might be somewhere else, not in this camp a'tall, and we just have to keep lookin'. Black Elk mighta traded her to somebody else. You don't wanna lose your scalp here if she might be with another band of Injuns."

Clay had considered that possibility, and it gave him pause. Maybe Martha wasn't here, but he knew for sure that this was Black Elk's village, and his hatred for the savage that abducted his sister was smoldering inside him, threatening to explode. His rational mind understood what Badger was trying to impress upon him, and he knew that it would be foolish to get overly reckless in his determination to find out what had happened to his sister. Then, too, there was his responsibility to Badger. He could not take any action that might endanger Badger's life. Still, the longing to avenge Martha was so strong within him that he knew he would not rest until he had settled with Black Elk. As he knelt there in the trees, his mind was in a quandary. He was tempted to go back, get his horse, ride right into the middle of the village, and challenge this Black Elk to face him.

"That would really be suicide," Badger retorted when told of Clay's thinking. "Let's just keep watchin' 'em like I said before."

"All right," Clay replied impatiently. "We'll watch 'em, but I'm going in tonight."

Since they were already on the lower side of the village, near the creek, they decided to work their way up to a cluster of alders across the water from the pony herd. Once they had advanced as close as they dared, Badger made himself comfortable and pulled out a piece of deer jerky to chew on. Offering some to Clay, he joked, "Here, better keep your strength up since you're figurin' on fighting this whole band of Injuns."

Clay declined the offering. "There ain't but one of 'em I'm looking to fight," he stated.

The afternoon wore on. There were a great many people coming and going in the gathering of lodges near the creek. Hunters in twos, threes, and some larger parties returned to the village as the sun settled low in the mountains beyond. The women scurried about busily, taking charge of the day's kill, gathering firewood, and preparing for the evening meal. But amid all the activity, Clay saw no sign of Martha or Robert. By the time the sun began sinking low on the second day of their surveillance, Clay was convinced more than ever that she was dead. He rejected the possibility that she had been traded away. As the shadows lengthened among the alders, he and Badger withdrew from their position near the creek bank. It was time to return to their camp in the hills to take care of their horses.

"Git down!" Badger suddenly whispered, just as they were about to leave the trees below the camp. Both men dived for cover behind a fallen cottonwood only moments before a party of six Blackfoot hunters entered the clearing between the creek and the hills. Their ponies padded softly by, no more than a few yards from where Clay and Badger lay hugging the ground behind the dead tree. So close were the hunters that Clay could plainly hear their conversation.

"The hunting has been good today," one of the hunters said. "There will be many feasts in the village tonight."

Another answered. "It has been good, but I think Bloody Axe is ready to go and find the buffalo that have been reported to the east. At least, that's what Three Bulls told me this morning. What do you think, Black Elk?"

Like a sharp knife, the name Black Elk slashed a jagged scar down the length of Clay's spine, numbing him to his fingertips. As quickly as he could, he crawled over to the end of the dead tree where he could risk taking a look without exposing himself. It was him! The powerfully built warrior he had seen the night before. He scolded himself for not guessing as much when he first saw the young warrior. Now Black Elk was answering the warrior who had asked the question, but the words were lost on Clay. His soul was so filled with the fury that had been building for almost a year that he couldn't even hear Badger's whispered warnings. "Easy, son, easy." His concentration centered on one thing, Clay began to slowly rise up from the ground until he felt the steel grip of Badger's hand on his arm, holding him back.

He was about to wrench his arm free of Badger's grip when he looked back into the old trapper's face. Badger slowly shook his head, then motioned over his shoulder. When Clay looked in the direction indicated, he saw why Badger was trying to hold him. A second party of hunters was following Black Elk's party, and was only a dozen or so yards behind. Clay hesitated, stone still for a long moment, as if deciding what to do. Finally, seeing the folly of what he was about to do, and realizing there was also Badger's neck to consider, he sank back to the ground and waited. He felt Badger's hand relax as the old trapper sighed in relief.

They remained flat on the ground behind the fallen tree until all the hunters had passed and were out of sight. When the way was clear, Badger scurried up from behind the log and headed for the tiny meadow in the hills where the horses were tied. Clay was close behind him. Once they had gained the cover of the hills, Badger spoke.

"For a minute back there, I thought you was gonna cook our bacon for sure."

Clay didn't answer. His mind was still locked on the image of the fierce Blackfoot warrior, and his body was still tense from the closeness of the encounter. Badger, fully realizing just how close they had come to losing their scalps, kept up an almost constant stream of conversation all the way back to their camp, hoping to cool Clay's temper. It seemed to work, for Clay appeared to be calm once again as the two of them took care of their horses.

"I'm going in after that son of a bitch," Clay suddenly blurted.

"What?" Badger replied, surprised by his young friend's outburst. Clay had been sitting silently for a long time, staring into the fire, apparently submerged deep in thought.

As if just coming out of a trance, Clay turned toward him. "I said I'm going in that village after the son of a bitch that killed Martha." The steady blue eyes firmly fixed upon Badger told of the sincerity of his statement. "I know which lodge is his. I saw it last night when we went down to their camp. I'm not making that decision for both of us, mind you. I don't want to put you in any danger, so it might be a good idea if you packed up and put a little more distance between you and this place." When Badger was obviously too dumbfounded to reply right away, Clay continued. "Badger, I'm much obliged for taking me this far, but I'm not gonna risk your neck any further."

"Well, if that ain't somethin'," Badger finally found his voice. "That's about the dumbest thing I've heard in a while. Is livin' that damn unpleasant to you?"

"I know, I know," Clay said impatiently in an attempt to cut the lecture short. "You might as well save your breath. It's just something I have to do. But I ain't asking you to help me."

"What if your sister ain't dead? Maybe she's just with another band of Injuns."

"She's dead," Clay pronounced solemnly. "We know for sure she was with Bloody Axe's band, and she's not here now. That murdering devil Black Elk killed her. I know my sister. She wouldn't give in to them, so he killed her."

"Clay, what you're thinkin' about doin' don't make a lick of sense. There's maybe a hundred Blackfoot warriors in that camp. Even if you git in there and kill Black Elk, you're gonna have the whole blame bunch of 'em on your tail."

Clay was unmoved. "That's why you better make some distance between you and them while you've got the chance," he said calmly.

Badger was about to protest further, but decided it would be wasted effort. "Damn, Clay . . ." was all he offered.

"I know," Clay said softly. He understood Badger's concern, and he appreciated it. "I'm much obliged for all you've done for me, but I reckon this is where we part company. I don't aim to commit suicide any more than the next man, but that damn Indian is gonna have to pay for stealing my sister, whether he murdered her or not. I didn't come all this way to just turn around and go home when I didn't find her."

There was little more to talk about after that. Badger could do no more than shrug his shoulders and wonder at the impetuousness of youth. Clay was a grown man, and if he wanted to risk his neck . . . well, it was his neck. Out in this country, a man did pretty much what he wanted to—if he had the iron to back it up. And Clay Culver had more than his share.

A half-moon hung low over the ridge far to the east of the little valley Clay had just crossed. It provided just enough light to cast faint shadows from the silent cottonwoods along the creek bank as Clay made his way through the trees looking for a good spot to tie his two horses. It was important to pick a spot that he could easily find again in the dark because, if things went the way he hoped, he'd be in one helluva hurry when he came back. Contrary to Badger's thinking, Clay was not intent upon committing suicide, but he was determined to settle the score with Black Elk. He owed Martha that much—somebody owed her; Robert and Charley had failed her. So it was up to him.

Ahead of him, he could now see the glow from the cook fires through the trees. Most of the women were cooking outside this time of year, and all but a few had already finished, leaving the flames to die. He decided to wait to make sure the camp had settled in for the night before advancing to the lodge where he had first noticed the young warrior on the night before. As he sat waiting, he remembered how impressed he had been when seeing the powerful warrior. He should have guessed then that the man he was watching was none other than Black Elk, if only by his physical appearance. He stood out among all other

Blackfoot men Clay had seen. Under different circumstances, he might have thought it a shame to kill such a specimen, but Clay could not rid his mind of the terrible abuse Martha must have suffered at the hands of one so powerful.

At last it was time. Clay felt the excitement of this long-awaited confrontation. It would have to be done with his knife; a rifle shot would bring the whole village down on him in an instant. He would need to find a convenient place to leave his rifle so he would be able to get to it in a hurry if he had to.

Thoughts of Martha ran through his head as he checked to make sure his rifle had a full magazine. He wished he could apologize to her for taking so long to find Black Elk, but it couldn't be helped. Once his rifle was ready, he removed his cartridge belt and hooked it over his saddle horn, ridding his body of anything that might be cumbersome. He hoped it wouldn't be necessary to use his rifle, but it might be the only thing that would permit him to escape after he had done what he came to do. One last look at his horses and he turned to make his way silently through the trees.

Working his way slowly and cautiously forward, he moved to the same point from which he had first seen Black Elk. Kneeling low to the ground, he waited there for a while, watching and listening, staring at the cowskin lodge. As before, the white pony was tied close by. He looked away toward the other lodges. All seemed quiet in the Blackfoot camp. While he scanned the sleeping village for any sign of sentries, he thought about the look of sheer power in the warrior's shoulders and arms. A man of lesser courage might have thought twice about engaging such a physical specimen in hand-to-hand combat. Clay never questioned his resolve to conquer the Blackfoot warrior.

Then another image invaded his thoughts. On that first night, he had watched while the warrior playfully picked his wife up in his arms and carried her into the lodge. Clay snorted silently like a mountain lion trying to rid its nostrils of an offending odor, and shook his head in an effort to clear away thoughts of his prey as a loving husband. His was a mission of vengeance. He could not think of the effect Black Elk's death would have on his widow. To remind himself of the cruel nature of the man he stalked, Clay forced his mind to picture Martha, beaten and starved, tortured and raped. Once again his anger flamed up in his soul, and he rose to his feet. Knife in hand, he advanced toward the Blackfoot lodge.

Sensing her husband's eyes upon her, Martha turned to smile at him. Black Elk found it fascinating to watch her brush her hair. Her soft dark tresses seemed to reflect the firelight so that there was a mystical sheen about it. And the way she pulled the brush slowly through them caused the long gentle locks to float about her shoulders with the softness of a cloud. It pleased him that she had found the brush in the packs he had taken from the two evil white men. She brushed her hair with it every night, and he never tired of watching her. He didn't say anything when she smiled at him. She knew his heart. Words weren't necessary.

Finished with the brushing, she began to braid her hair again in the style worn by the other women in the village. He continued to watch for a while before returning his attention to the bowl of boiled meat before him.

"Red Wing says that we will soon pack up our things and follow the buffalo," Martha said as she tied a braid with a rawhide strip.

Black Elk nodded, and then said, "In two days. I talked to Bloody Axe and some of the others. The ponies have eaten most of the grass here. It's time to leave."

He sat quietly watching while she finished braiding her hair, and then she came to sit beside him while he ate. Pushing the bowl aside, he put his arm around her and pulled her close to him. She smiled contentedly as he stroked her hair softly. It pleased her that he was fascinated with the fiery softness of her hair.

"You pet me like you would pet one of the dogs that follow the camp," she teased.

He smiled. "Maybe, but I don't share my bed with the dogs."

She laughed and playfully slapped his hand. "You may not want to sleep with me when winter comes again, and my belly is this big," she said, holding her hands out before her.

Laughing at her exaggeration, he replied, "If your belly gets that big, my son may come out fully grown—or maybe you are going to have a buffalo."

She started to say something else, but he held a finger to his lips in a gesture to silence her. Then he cocked his head to one side, listening. Then she heard it, too. His horse was whinnying and pawing the ground outside as if a wolf or coyote was near.

"War Cloud is nervous tonight," Martha said.

"It's probably nothing," Black Elk said, still listening. When the pony continued to fidget, he sighed and said, "I'd better see what's bothering him."

Black Elk pushed the skin flap aside and stepped out into the chilly night air. He stood for a brief moment, letting his eyes adjust to the darkness before he turned to look at his favorite war pony. Seeing nothing out of the ordinary, he walked over and took the pony's head in his arms, stroking its forelock to calm it. Suddenly sensing a presence, he turned his head quickly toward the rear of the tipi where he discovered a figure standing in the shadows watching him. More curious than alarmed, Black Elk stepped away from the pony to get a better look at the figure now walking slowly toward him. Thinking it to be one of the men of the village—for he was dressed in clothes made of animal hides—he stood waiting for the man to identify himself.

Clay spoke not a word as he slowly approached the Blackfoot warrior. He continued to advance until he reached the edge of the firelight. As the mysterious figure emerged from the deep shadows, Black Elk suddenly realized that it was a white man. Startled by the discovery, he quickly looked beyond the lone figure, expecting to see others following, but there appeared to be no one. Now, confounded by the mysterious appearance of a white man in the heart of Blackfoot country, Black Elk could only stand mystified.

Both men stood completely motionless for a long moment—Black Elk not knowing what to make of it; Clay silently measuring the powerful warrior before him. Then Clay spoke. "Are you called Black Elk?"

"I am Black Elk."

"Prepare to die, Black Elk."

Clay's charge was so sudden, and so quick, that Black Elk was barely able to escape the long knife that searched for his ribs. Moving with the nimbleness of a puma, the Blackfoot warrior just managed to evade the upward thrust of the gleaming blade as it slashed the air inches from his side. In the wink of an eye, Black Elk was on the counterattack, rushing to meet his assailant. The two men met, their bodies colliding heavily while they strained to gain control of the knife. Locked in powerful conflict, each man sought to overpower the other, like two great beasts, knowing that to yield would mean certain death. Each man now fully realized the power of the other. They were both equal in strength.

Clay could feel the muscles in his back rippling like steel bands as he fought against Black Elk's efforts to bend him backward. Calling on every ounce of strength he possessed, he strained against the relentless pressure from the powerful arms until gradually Black Elk was slowly forced back. Then suddenly his feet went out from under him as Black Elk hooked his leg around him. Both men went down, landing heavily on the ground. Over and over they went, each man desperately struggling to gain the advantage as they rolled beneath the startled white pony, causing it to squeal and try to jump out of the way. Out of a tangle of straining bodies and stamping hooves, Clay managed to end up on his feet, his knife still in his hand. Scrambling from under the nervous hooves of his horse, Black Elk hurried to his feet, only to bear the full force of Clay's flying body. Crashing against the side of the tipi, Black Elk's wind was knocked from his lungs when Clay's shoulder drove deep in the Indian's midsection. Straining for breath, Black Elk tried to roll away from the tipi, but Clay quickly jumped on his back, locking an arm around the warrior's neck. In that instant, both men knew the Blackfoot was doomed. Though fighting with all his strength to break Clay's choke hold on his neck while gasping to regain his breath, Black Elk could not grasp the hand that held the knife. Clay pulled back on the warrior's neck with all his might while he held the knife poised to strike deep into Black Elk's stomach. The moment of vengence he had waited for over so many months had finally come.

"Stop!" The words rang out from behind him moments before he felt two hands lock onto his wrist, straining to stay his arm from delivering the fatal thrust. Perplexed, but still enmeshed in the fury of mortal combat, Clay fought to overcome this new adversary even as his brain registered the familiar sound of the woman's voice. "Stop!" Martha screamed again, fighting with all the strength she could summon, determined to save her husband's life.

Equally determined to accomplish the execution of the hated Blackfoot warrior, Clay fought to free his wrist from the desperate woman's grip, finally managing to fling her against the stack of firewood beside the tipi. The effort caused him to loosen his grip on Black Elk's windpipe momentarily, enabling the powerful Blackfoot to wrench himself free, quickly rolling over on his back. With one solid kick to the kneecap, he sent Clay reeling backward a couple of steps before he could regain his balance. By the time he did, Black Elk was on his feet and poised to attack.

"Stop!" Martha sobbed, as she scrambled to her hands and knees in her panic to rejoin the fight. Suddenly finding a heavy piece of firewood in her hand, she charged the dark assassin, her weapon ready to strike.

Seeing that he now faced two adversaries, Clay stepped back into the firelight and prepared to meet the attack from both quarters. He welcomed the challenge. So intense was his lust for revenge, that there was no concern for his personal safety. His blood was hot, scalding his veins as he threw his foxskin cap aside in order to see his enemies clearly. "Come on, you murdering bastard," he growled, beckoning with one hand, his knife in the other.

Martha was stunned, unable to believe her eyes. She was stopped in her tracks by the unexpected image of her brother as the light from the fire revealed his familiar features. "Clay," she gasped, then screamed,

"Clay!" Both men were stopped by her outburst, but for only a moment before slowly advancing toward each other.

The horrible realization of what was happening suddenly struck Martha with such force that she felt her heart stop. Frozen for a moment, she then thrust her body between the two combatants. "Clay! Stop! I love him! He's my husband."

Her words reverberated through Clay's brain like echoes in a canyon, and he realized then that it was Martha standing before him and not a vision sent to befuddle him. Dazed, he suddenly relaxed, releasing the fury that had driven him, as he stared at his sister. Hair braided and dressed in antelope hides, looking very much like an Indian . . . still it was his sister. "Martha?" he asked, "is that really you?" She smiled then, and nodded yes. Scarcely able to believe his eyes, he stepped back, almost stumbling. "Well, I'll be . . ." That was as far as he got before she rushed to embrace him. He picked her up and whirled her around, forgetting the perilous situation he had been faced with moments before, and the dangerous adversary still poised to attack him. "I thought you were dead. I swear . . ." He put her down. Then he grasped her by the shoulders and held her at arm's length while he looked at her. Realizing then that she was the woman he had mistaken for a Blackfoot on the first night he had scouted the camp, he shook his head, amazed.

Greatly confused by this astonishing turn of events, Black Elk did not understand why the white man had ceased to fight. Close to death only moments before, and angry over the unprovoked attack by this mysterious stranger, he started to push Martha out of the way so he could settle with this crazy man. Martha quickly stepped in front of Clay again to protect him while she frantically explained to her husband. "This is my brother. He doesn't know how it is with us. He came to rescue me."

Suddenly, several people from the nearby lodges appeared, attracted by the noise of the fight. In a few minutes, several more appeared, and Clay began to wish he was closer to the spot where he had left his rifle. Martha was almost hysterical in her effort to quickly explain to Black Elk that it had all been a tragic mistake, that Clay was not an enemy. But Clay didn't like the looks of some of the warriors who were now crowding around, a few of them making threatening gestures. Much to his relief, Black Elk understood what Martha was trying to explain. The powerful warrior relaxed his stance, and held up his hand to quiet the angry voices in the crowd. "It's all right. The white man means no harm. He is Six Horses's brother. He thought she was in danger."

Immediately the crowd calmed, and Clay drew a long breath in relief. In the silent void that followed, his ears caught the unmistakeable sound of a Henry rifle cocking. It came from the darkness behind Black Elk's lodge. Clay tensed at first, then smiled. "Is that you, Badger?"

"Reckon so," the familiar voice came back. "I figured you'd have yourself in trouble the minute I left you alone."

"Well, you might as well come on in and join the family reunion," Clay said, then turned to explain Badger's sudden appearance to Martha and Black Elk.

There was another swell of murmuring among the gathering of people around Black Elk's lodge when the grizzled old mountain man walked into the firelight, carrying a rifle in each hand. "Here's that Winchester of your'n," he said, handing the rifle to Clay. "I was kinda hopin' this big ol' buck here had already

scalped you so's I could keep it." He looked Black
Elk up and down, then turned his attention to Martha.
"Evenin', ma'am. From what I heard back yonder,
looks like me and Clay wasted a heap of time and
effort trying to rescue you."

Before long, the entire village had turned out to
meet Six Horses's brother and his friend. Noticing that
Clay and Black Elk were still eyeing each other warily,
Martha pulled the two aside. These were the two men
she loved most in the whole world, and it was important to her that there must be a truce between them.
Clay had been so surprised to discover Martha alive,
and overwhelmed by the news that she was married
to a Blackfoot warrior, that he had forgotten another
concern. Suddenly he remembered. "Robert," he
blurted. "Where's Robert? We found Charley back
there by the river, and I thought maybe Robert had
been captured."

"You didn't know about Robert?" she asked, then
went on to explain that Robert had been killed.

When told of Charley's probable role in the treachery, Clay couldn't say that he was surprised to hear
it. "I never did have much use for Charley Vinings,"
he said. After hearing all the facts, Clay's disposition
toward his new brother-in-law took on a much warmer
tone. Speaking in the Blackfoot tongue, he apologized
to Black Elk for attacking him.

"I understand," Black Elk replied. "I might have
done the same if I thought as you did." He smiled at
Martha, then said, "We must find something to eat
for your brother and his friend. It is late now, but
tomorrow we must have a proper feast for them."
Turning back to Clay, he said, "You and your friend
will sleep in my lodge tonight."

Clay and Badger graciously accepted the invitation,
and after retrieving their horses, unrolled their blan-

kets inside Black Elk's tipi. It was an odd experience for Clay, looking around him at the typical Blackfoot lodge and the simple homemaking utensils that were now his sister's. The furnishings of her home in Virginia, hardly elegant at the time, seemed luxurious compared to her present cowhide dwelling and the few simple tools she used to cook and sew. He found he could not keep himself from staring at Martha, still finding it hard to believe how she seemed so at home in these surroundings. Her movements were silent and efficient as she busied herself around the fire. Every few minutes she would pause and smile at him as she prepared food for her guests. *Like an Indian,* he thought. *Martha married to a Blackfoot warrior—it's gonna take some getting used to.* Glancing back at his host, the quiet Blackfoot warrior, he marveled, *Sure is a helluva difference from Robert Vinings.* He was also quite different from the savage image Clay had carried in his mind for so long.

The food prepared, Martha sat down across from her brother, and watched him while he ate. She could well imagine how different she must seem to Clay as she sat next to her Blackfoot husband. But he had changed as well. All traces of the impetuous young man were gone from his handsome face. She supposed the war had been responsible for that. In its place, there was a quiet confidence that no doubt sprang from the strength that had come within a hair of killing someone as powerful as Black Elk. She could not help but tremble when she recalled that frightening moment. Clay, always her favorite, before her now, every bit as much a mountain man as the grizzled old scout seated at his right hand. *We have come a long way from Fredericksburg, Clay and I,* she thought.

After Clay and Badger had their fill, they sat before the fire and told Martha and Black Elk of their jour-

ney to find Clay's lost sister. Martha, in turn, told of
her capture by Black Elk's warriors, and the events
that ultimately led her to adopt her new way of life.
In an earlier time in his life, Clay might have found
it incredible that Martha would be drawn to such a
wild and primitive existence. But in this time and
place, it seemed not the least bit unusual, for he realized that he was also drawn to the wild mysteries of
the high mountains.

When it was finally time for sleeping, Clay experienced some slight discomfort at seeing his little sister
snuggle under a buffalo robe with a Blackfoot warrior.
After he thought about it for a minute, however, he
realized that he was probably seeing Martha as con-
tented as he could ever remember. Nodding his head
as he made his final judgment of the union, he decided
that she was where she wanted to be, so he was content as well. That done, he turned his back to them
and went to sleep to the low drone of Badger's
snoring.

The next morning Clay and Badger visited with the
people of Martha's village. Clay couldn't help but be
amused by Badger's enthusiastic conversations with
the "treacherous Blackfeet"—as Badger had always
referred to them. The village certainly seemed peaceful enough at present. They talked at great length with
Bloody Axe and Black Elk, answering the questions
the Blackfoot chief asked about the soldiers that were
rumored to soon be taking over the old trading posts
on the Missouri. Badger assured the chief that his
band of Blackfeet were too far away from the forts to
be concerned. It was their enemies, the Sioux and the
Cheyenne, who had to be concerned with the army's
intentions.

"This has been my thinking," Bloody Axe said.

"There is no reason for the white man to come to this country. It will always be the land of the Blackfeet."

Listening to the conversation, Clay had to agree with Badger. This wild, open country was so far removed from the rest of the world that there seemed little chance settlers would ever push this far north. Who but an Indian could live here?

The remainder of that day was spent with Martha and her husband, and before the day was over, Clay decided that there was much to be admired in his sister's choice for a mate. Black Elk was very much interested to know about the war between the white men in which Clay had fought. It was difficult for him to understand what the two sides were fighting over, however. Clay tried to explain, but when it got right down to it, he wasn't certain himself.

After the evening meal, Martha and Clay sat by the fire and talked late into the night. They talked about home, and she wanted to hear all the news about her mother and father and her brothers. Black Elk and Badger had long since drifted off into deep slumber when Martha wrote a short letter to her parents on a square piece of deer hide, written in black paint made from charcoal. Clay promised to see that the letter reached their parents, and he took the rolled piece of hide and packed it carefully in his parfleche.

"Clay, Mama and Papa are going to find it hard to understand why I don't want to come back with you." Her voice softened as a tiny tear caught by the firelight glistened in the corner of her eye. "Try to make them understand that I'm happy where I am."

"I will," Clay promised. "Don't worry your mind over it. Just be happy. That's all the whole family wants for you."

*   *   *

The following morning was a day of parting. The village was busy as the women took down the lodges and packed them on travois and ponies, along with all their belongings, in preparation to move to buffalo country. Clay and Badger prepared to start back toward the Yellowstone where Badger was anxious to find his wife's people. It had been a long time since he had left Gray Bird back on the Belle Fourche, and he complained that he had an itch that only she could scratch.

"What will you do now, Clay?" Martha asked as she and Black Elk stood by while her brother and his partner secured their packs on the horses. "Will you go back to Virginia right away?"

Clay hesitated before answering. "I don't know," he finally admitted. "I haven't made up my mind yet. "This country kinda grows on you." Ignoring the knowing grin on Badger's face, he went on. "I'm sure of one thing, I wasn't cut out to work a farm, so I'm not planning to go back to Virginia to stay. Pa and the boys don't need me, anyway. I expect I'll go back for a while, though, just so I can let everybody know that you're all right—and tell Robert's folks what happened to him and Charley." He shook his head thoughtfully. "I guess I'll have to put a coat of paint on Charley's story so it'll look a little better to his folks. No sense in telling them what a bastard he turned out to be."

"You could come back here," Martha suggested.

Black Elk nodded and said, "My wife's brother would be welcome in our village. Come back and we will hunt together."

"You never can tell, I might," Clay said to Martha, smiling as he gave her a quick hug. Turning to Black

Elk, he replied, "I thank you for the invitation, but for now I have to see that this old scout gets back home to his wife." He looked at Badger and grinned.

Badger snorted indignantly. "If you're goin' with me, you'd best mount up. We're burning daylight."

With a quick wink for his sister, Clay Culver stepped up into the saddle. With a smile on his face, he drew gently on the reins, turning his horse toward the rolling prairie to the east, knowing that Martha was where she belonged. He had a feeling deep inside that this wild country had already claimed his soul as well.

Completely at peace now that all the pieces of her life had seemingly found their proper places, Martha stood by her husband's side, her hand gently resting upon his arm. She had traveled a long and difficult path, but she was content knowing that she, Six Horses, was where she was meant to be. *You're where you belong, too,* she thought as she watched her brother wheel his pony with only a slight movement of his hand. There was no resemblance to the boy she had watched as he marched off to join the army. Tall and confident, it was obvious to her eye that Clay Culver was now as much a part of this wild country as the solemn mountains behind her.

Ralph
Cotton

**"Gun-smoked, blood-stained, gritty believability...
Ralph Cotton writes the sort of story we all hope
to find within us."**—Terry Johnston

"Authentic Old West detail."—*Wild West Magazine*

JURISDICTION   20547-2
Young Arizona Ranger Sam Burrack has vowed to bring
down a posse of murderous outlaws-and save the impres-
sionable young boy they've befriended.

DEVIL'S DUE   20394-1
The second book in Cotton's "Dead or Alive" series. The
Los Pistoleros gang were the most vicious outlaws
around—but Hart and Roth thought they had them under
control...Until the jailbreak.

Also Available:
BORDER DOGS   19815-8
BLOOD MONEY   20676-2
BLOOD ROCK   20256-2

Penguin Putnam Inc.
Online

Your Internet gateway to a virtual environment with
hundreds of entertaining and enlightening books
from Penguin Putnam Inc.

*While you're there, get the latest buzz on
the best authors and books around—*

Tom Clancy, Patricia Cornwell, W.E.B. Griffin,
Nora Roberts, William Gibson, Robin Cook,
Brian Jacques, Catherine Coulter, Stephen King,
Ken Follett, Terry McMillan, and many more!

**Penguin Putnam Online is located at
http://www.penguinputnam.com**

PENGUIN PUTNAM NEWS

Every month you'll get an inside look at our upcom-
ing books and new features on our site. This is an
ongoing effort to provide you with the most
up-to-date information about
our books and authors.

Subscribe to Penguin Putnam News at
http://www.penguinputnam.com/newsletters